JUSTIFIED

Also by De'nesha Diamond

The Parker Crime Chronicles

Conspiracy
Collusion
Collateral

The Diva Series

Hustlin' Divas
Street Divas
Gangsta Divas
Boss Divas
King Divas
Queen Divas

Anthologies

Heartbreaker (with Eric S. Gray and Nichelle Walker)
Heist and *Heist 2* (with Kiki Swinson)
A Gangster and a Gentleman (with Kiki Swinson)
Fistful of Benjamins (with Kiki Swinson)
No Loyalty (with A'zayler)

Also by Briana Cole

The Marriage Pass
The Wives We Play
The Vows We Break
The Hearts We Burn

JUSTIFIED

DE'NESHA
DIAMOND

BRIANA
COLE

www.kensingtonbooks.com

To the extent that the image or images on the cover of this book depict a person or persons, such person or persons are merely models, and are not intended to portray any character or characters featured in the book.

This book is a work of fiction. Names, characters, businesses, organizations, places, events, and incidents either are the product of the author's imagination or are used fictitiously. Any resemblance to actual persons, living or dead, events, or locales is entirely coincidental.

DAFINA BOOKS are published by

Kensington Publishing Corp.
119 West 40th Street
New York, NY 10018

Compilation copyright © 2021 by Kensington Publishing Corp.
Black and Blue copyright © 2021 by De'nesha Diamond
Pseudo copyright © 2021 by Briana Cole

All rights reserved. No part of this book may be reproduced in any form or by any means without the prior written consent of the Publisher, excepting brief quotes used in reviews.

All Kensington titles, imprints, and distributed lines are available at special quantity discounts for bulk purchases for sales promotion, premiums, fund-raising, and educational or institutional use.

Special book excerpts or customized printings can also be created to fit specific needs. For details, write or phone the office of the Kensington Sales Manager: Kensington Publishing Corp., 119 West 40th Street, New York, NY 10018. Attn. Sales Department. Phone: 1-800-221-2647.

The Dafina logo is a trademark of Kensington Publishing Corp.

ISBN: 978-1-4967-1149-6
First Trade Paperback Printing: October 2021

ISBN: 978-1-4967-1151-9 (e-book)
First Electronic Edition: October 2021

10 9 8 7 6 5 4 3 2 1

Printed in the United States of America

R0460778358

In loving memory of De'nesha Diamond

CONTENTS

Black and Blue
by De'nesha Diamond
1

Pseudo
by Briana Cole
193

BLACK AND BLUE

De'nesha Diamond

CHAPTER 1

The Moonlight Club

Charlie Jean Warren stared at the four-carat diamond ring nestled in a black velveteen box with her heart lodged in her throat while her vision blurred behind a pool of tears. A large crowd of family and friends waited in silence while her handsome, six-foot-three fiancé, Hennessey Rawlins, held his pose on bended knee.

Worry worked its way into Hennessey's dark eyes. "Are you going to keep me down here all night?" he joked.

Charlie swiped tears from her eyes. "Yes, of course, I'll marry you."

A cheer rippled through the crowd.

Hennessey climbed back to his feet. His Texas-sized grin showed rows of perfect, pearl-white teeth. He removed the ring from the box and tried to hide his trembling fingers. "Thank you, baby. You've made me the happiest man in the world tonight." He slid the platinum band onto Charlie's finger.

"Not as happy as you've made me." Charlie threw her arms around his neck and kissed him with every ounce of passion she had in her five-foot-eight body. *Engaged.* They were going to do this thing.

The crowd closed in and pulled them apart. The women

encircled Charlie, wanting a better view of the large rock Henny placed on her finger. The men seized Henny and pounded his back in congratulations. Everyone had waited for this day to come. Henny and Charlie had been an official couple since junior high school. Before then, they had been frenemies in denial. In high school, they were king and queen of prom three years out of four. Hennessey was the captain of the football team and Charlie the head cheerleader. It couldn't have been more textbook-perfect.

After high school, all the problems came.

Hennessey went to Howard University while Charlie, like most of her sisters, joined the military. It was a shocking move to most of her counselors, more so than to the people who knew her. Her father, a strict disciplinarian, was a military man through and through. Since he had never had the boy he wanted, he drilled the military life into his five daughters: Billie, Teddy, Michael, Charlie, and her twin, Johnnie.

College could wait.

And it did.

After three tours in Afghanistan and Iraq, Charlie returned home, went to college, and received her nursing degree. Marriage was the next natural step. Hennessey had waited for her for ten years.

"It's about time you put that man out of his misery." Johnnie used her enormous pregnant belly to clear space next to her baby sister. "Henny would've gone postal if you had said no."

Charlie's circle of girlfriends laughed.

Johnnie added, "Don't think every single woman in Chicago hasn't tried to move in on your man while you were out there playing *Where in the World Is Carmen Sandiego*, either."

"Oh, please." Charlie laughed. "Don't try to sell me Hennessey had been a monk out here in these streets. I know better."

"Nah, he sowed his wild oats. I'm saying none of these desperate heifers could get him to forget your ass."

"Damn right." Charlie winked.

Laughter encircled the women.

From across the room, Hennessey tracked his fiancée as she worked the crowd and showed off her new ring.

Henny's best friend, Ramsey Holt, pounded him on the back. "Don't worry, man. She's not going anywhere."

"You never know with her," Henny joked.

His boys laughed. His clique had been road dawgs–slash–homies since Ms. Rachel Pendleton from the old neighborhood ran a daycare center out of her home back in the nineties. It was a joke since she used the money to buy crack. Ms. Rachel spent most of her time on the couch, nodding, drooling, and mumbling shit. The kids had the run of the place. More than a few times, Ms. Rachel and her boyfriend would disappear into her bedroom and make animal noises, which the kids would mimic when they returned home. Despite the outbreak of diaper rashes and mysterious bruises on the kids from time to time, most of Ms. Rachel's clients loved her because she was the cheapest babysitter they could find while they went out and worked at minimum-wage jobs. Eventually, the DEA raided Rachel's home and shut her down. However, Hennessey and his boys reconnected in kindergarten and had stayed friends ever since.

"Do you know when you two are going to do this thing?" Ramsey grinned.

"Soon," Henny assured him. "Hell, I'd do it tonight if we had a license."

"Damn, it's like that, huh?" Ramsey laughed. "Home girl got you wide open."

"Look, you can spend half your life chasing hoodrats if you want to. I already found my diamond in the coal mine, and I intend to keep her."

"All right, I hear ya."

Dominic laughed. "Spoken like a true pussy-whipped man."

Trudy, the youngest member of their crew, wormed his way over to Hennessey. "Yo, man, Henny. We have a situation."

"Aw, man. No bad news tonight." Hennessey draped his arm around Trudy. "I won't have it."

Trudy leaned into Henny's ear and whispered.

Hennessey sighed. "Gentlemen, hold my champagne. I'll be right back."

Charlie tracked Hennessey as he, Ramsey, and Trudy strolled toward the back of the club. She nibbled the bottom of her lip as she watched him maneuver through the crowd. She wasn't the only one watching. Hennessey had a way of drawing women's eyes. Tall, broad-shouldered, and with skin the color of rich, dark chocolate, Hennessey could send a diabetic into shock by looking at them. Hennessey in a dark-navy Armani suit with a Colgate smile slayed the game.

In high school, the kids used to call them Twix. Hennessey's chocolate mixed with her caramel skin. Soon they would have candy-coated children. She smiled. She still needed to tell him they had a little one on the way.

Alexis Glover slinked next to Charlie and confessed, "I wish I could get a man like Hennessey. He's fine as hell, stacking real paper, and making boss moves in these streets. First, his independent recording label artists are jumping all over the charts and now this club? You two are going after the Carters or what?"

"Sure. As soon as I learn how to carry a note." Charlie rolled her eyes. "Nah, we're going to do *us* until the wheels fall off this bitch."

Her girls laughed.

"You're not going to make him wait another ten years before you walk down the aisle, are you?" Johnnie asked.

"No. I would marry Hennessey tonight if we had a license," she admitted and meant it.

Eventually, everyone coupled back up and returned to the dance floor or bar.

Charlie waited for Hennessey to return from whatever was keeping him. The ring was beautiful, but she preferred to have her fiancé back by her side. *Fiancé.* It was going to take a while to get used to saying that.

An hour later, Henny returned, and Charlie struggled to hide her annoyance.

"Miss me, babe?" Hennessey kissed her cheek, but she pulled back and looked him over.

"You're sweating."

"Manual labor will do it to you." He smiled, but it didn't erase Charlie's frown. "I'm sorry. Something came up."

On the cuff of his shirt, she noticed something else. "Is that blood?"

"What?" He glanced at his jacket's sleeve and tugged it down. "Aw, it's nothing. Don't worry your pretty head about it."

"But how—"

"I said let it go," he insisted.

"Is this going to be a habit? You disappearing on me at inopportune times and reappearing with mysterious bruises?"

"Not if I can help it." He pulled her flush against his body, and her defenses crumbled. "If I had my way, we would never leave each other's side. But since I plan on being a good provider for you and our future children"—he placed a hand on her belly—"I have to work from time to time."

Charlie blinked. "You know?"

Hennessey's grin expanded. "Are you kidding me? I know your body like the back of my hand."

Charlie's smile beamed. "I was going to tell you tonight."

"Do you want to make another announcement?"

Charlie scanned the dancing crowd. "Nah, I don't want them saying I'm only marrying you because I'm knocked up."

"Whatever it takes to change your last name." He kissed her.

Charlie cocked her head. "You're crazy about me, aren't you?"

"I've been telling you that for almost twenty years." He tipped his head forward and kissed her ruby-red lips.

At 2 a.m., Hennessey and Charlie were ready to call it a night. Their friends continued to congratulate them as they headed out of the Moonlight. It was dark, and a fog thickened around them. Once settled into the seats of Henny's Range Rover, Charlie peppered the side of Henny's face with kisses.

"Wait until I get you home," Charlie teased.

"All right now. I'm going to have to keep my eye on the road."

"Who's stopping you?" She made a trail of kisses along the column of his neck. "We're actually going to do this," Charlie giggled, hugging Hennessey's right arm.

"You're damn right." He planted another kiss. "How about this summer?"

"This summer?" She blinked. "That's in three months."

"Problem?"

Charlie's mind raced through all the things she needed to do and panicked.

Hennessey lifted a brow as he backed out of his parking space.

"No," she lied. "No problem at all.

Hennessey braided his free hand with Charlie's and kissed the back of it. "Get your sisters to help. I'm sure they're dying to jump in anyway."

"You know my family so well." Charlie kicked off her pumps and tucked her feet underneath her. She leaned against his broad shoulder while their hands remained entwined. Her heavy eyelids closed while Hennessey hummed notes from their favorite song. It had been their love song since high school. It always took Charlie back to them sidestepping in the center of the school's gymnasium—it was like a lifetime ago.

Hennessey brushed a kiss on her forehead and returned his attention to the road. "So, how far along are we?"

She smiled. "Eight weeks. We have to wait another month before we make the announcement."

"Why?"

"Because it's considered bad luck to announce before completing your first term."

Hennessey laughed. "Let me guess, some old wives' tale?"

"No." She made a face. "Maybe. I don't know. Does it matter?"

He snuggled closer and inhaled her signature perfume. "Mm. You smell wonderful."

"You always say that."

"Because it's true." Charlie smiled and opened her eyes. Her gaze zeroed in on the specks of blood on the cuffs of his sleeve and the other bruises on his knuckles.

"So . . . are you going to tell me what happened here—or am I supposed to act like I don't notice all your mysterious bruises?"

"What?"

"You know every inch of my body, and I know every inch of yours. So, come on. What gives? Someone is going to think I'm abusing you."

"Ha. That will be the day."

"Come on, what gives?" Charlie pried.

"I had some business to take care of."

Charlie pulled back from him. "You said that already."

"The truth doesn't change because you want it to."

"And what's the truth?"

"What's this?" Hennessey slowed the car.

"Detour," Charlie read the traffic signs. "Looks like they're doing construction or some shit."

"Fuck." Hennessey followed the alternate route signs. "Where the fuck is this shit taking us?"

"I don't know. I've never been this way before." Charlie turned on the car's heat. She could already tell they were headed through a bad section of town, judging by the few streetlights on the dark road.

The night was pitch-black. Their headlights barely penetrated the fog, and according to their lying-piece-of-shit GPS, the road they traveled on didn't exist.

Hennessey turned the radio down as if it was going to help him see the street signs better.

It didn't.

"Where the fuck are we?"

Blue and white lights flashed behind them.

"Shit," Hennessey swore, releasing Charlie's hand.

Charlie twisted in her seat and squinted back at the strobe of lights. "What the hell? Were we speeding?"

"No." Hennessey pulled over and grabbed his wallet tucked in his back pocket.

Charlie settled all the way back into her seat and cast a nervous glance into her side-view mirror.

After a full minute, she questioned, "What's the holdup?"

Hennessey sighed. "Who knows?"

A second police vehicle parked behind the first. Charlie's heart sank to the pit of her stomach. No matter how many times she told herself to remain calm, she couldn't get the nerves in her gut to stop looping into knots.

Hennessey covered her hand. "It's okay."

She glanced around. "Are the windows soundproof?"

"Aw, shit." Hennessey powered down the windows in time to hear the officer's words.

"Again: Place your hands visible on the steering wheel!"

Charlie's heart shot back into her chest.

Hennessey sighed.

"Do it," Charlie ordered, elbowing him. "No need to get into a pissing contest."

Hennessey sighed and placed his hands at ten and two. "I'm tired of dealing with these muthafuckas."

"I know, baby." Charlie heaved in frustration and twisted around in her seat.

The patrol car's door popped open. She couldn't see the officer's approach from her side mirror, but she heard the crunch of gravel beneath the officer's feet as he took his sweet-ass time approaching the car.

CHAPTER 2

Charlie groaned as she came into consciousness. Pain greeted her and almost made her pass out again.

"We got a pulse," a voice boomed.

Charlie winced and shrank from the sudden cacophony around her. Seconds later, the scent of grass faded as several pairs of hands lifted her from the shrubbery on the side of the road.

"Careful, careful," another voice ordered.

Pain ricocheted throughout her body as they jostled and strapped her to a gurney.

"Don't worry. We're going to get you some help," a woman told her.

Charlie parted her bruised and cut lips to ask, "Henny?"

"What was that? I think she said something," the woman informed her team.

Charlie attempted to speak again, but her dry throat sent her into a coughing frenzy, which detonated more misery and suffering in her broken body.

"It's okay. Try to relax." The woman placed her hand on Charlie's shoulder. "We're taking you to Provident Hospital. They are going to patch you up in no time."

Where is Hennessey? Charlie turned her head from the woman and struggled to open her eyes, but they seemed glued shut.

They lifted her again.

Despite her closed eyes, the bright light inside the ambulance stabbed her irises and caused pain to explode in her temples. There was a lot of bustling and shuffling around her before there was a prick in her arm and something cold rushed into her veins. She must have passed out because the next thing she knew, she was jostled again. Struggling for strength, Charlie opened her eyes. Her gurney wheeled at a maddening clip through a long hallway. Men and women in white coats ran alongside her, gripping the side railing. They talked over each other, making it difficult to make out what they were saying.

At last, they plowed through two sets of swinging doors and wheeled her to a stop beneath an enormous circular beam of light. Charlie slammed her eyes closed and squirreled away from the pain, but it was everywhere. Again, they injected something cold into her veins and the world dissolved, and she was back on the side of the road with Hennessey . . .

Apprehension tied every muscle in Charlie's body into knots while her mind went through every fatal traffic stop scenario she'd seen on the Internet for years. Would their black lives matter tonight?

When the big Robocop-looking muthafucka arrived at Hennessey's left side with his hand near his holster, Charlie wondered how the hell this muthafucka was already on ten.

"Keep your hands where I can see them!"

"They're up," Hennessey huffed, keeping his hands at ten and two on the wheel.

Instinct told Charlie to look back into the car's right-side mirror. Sure enough, another cop was doing a slow creep to-

ward her. Lord knew she had performed the same tactic in Kabul plenty of times. Stay calm. Breathe. Play it cool.

However, Charlie's head and her heart weren't in agreement at the moment.

"License and registration," Robocop ordered.

With his wallet already in hand, Hennessey removed the requested cards and handed them to the officer. Only the officer was too busy flashing a light into the car.

When the beam hit Charlie, she frowned and twisted away.

"Where are you two coming from tonight?" the officer asked. The light traveled from Charlie's face and down her body. Despite the open window, tension thickened the air.

Hennessey spoke through gritted teeth, "Just heading home, Officer."

"That's not what I asked you, boy," the cop growled.

Aw. This is about to be some shit. *Charlie grabbed Hennessey's hand again.*

"We were at the Moonlight Club," Charlie answered for Hennessey.

"Is that right?" the cop questioned, taking the cards from Hennessey. "Are there any weapons in the vehicle?"

Fuck.

"I'm going to ask you two again. Are there any weapons in the car?"

Hennessey sighed. "I have a legally registered handgun underneath my seat, Officer."

"Step out of the vehicle."

"What?" Hennessey barked.

"STEP OUT OF THE VEHICLE."

Charlie woke again to the sound of someone crying and hushed voices buzzing. Faintly, she wondered what the crying was about, but she lacked the energy to ask. Instead, she attempted to block it and the buzzing out. However, it soon sounded like a million bees were trapped inside of her head and drove her mad. She twisted away from the noise, but her head weighed a ton, and her neck muscles were about to snap from the effort.

"Look. She's awake," Johnnie gasped.

Charlie heard an army of feet rush around the bed.

"Charlie? Can you hear us?" Michael asked. "We're right here, sweetheart."

Someone took hold of her hand. Their trembling transferred to Charlie, and she attempted to pry her eyes open to see what was happening. She sacrificed a few lashes in the process but managed to get her eyes open about a quarter of an inch. None of the images made any sense. It was as if she was underwater. The world was one big blur; there was no real shape to anything. She blinked, but it was harder the second time around to open her eyes. When she managed it, her vision didn't improve much.

"We're all right here, sweetheart," Johnnie assured her. "We're not going anywhere."

Where is here? Charlie ran her thick tongue over cracked lips. "Henny?"

The room fell silent.

Didn't they hear me? There was a good chance she'd only thought the question. Charlie licked her lips and tried again. "Where is Henny?"

Everyone's gazes shifted around.

Charlie's heart pounded in her ears. *"Get off of him! Get off."*

Pop! Pop! Pop!

Charlie jerked as if the gunfire had sounded in the room.

"Calm down, Charlie. Everything is going to be all right."

Charlie pushed her sister's hand away. They were hiding something from her—something bad. "Where?"

Teddy got to the point. "I'm sorry, Charlie. But . . . Hennessey is gone."

The oxygen sucked out the room as Charlie twisted her

head towards Teddy's blurry image, but because of the pounding in her ears, she hadn't heard her sister correctly. She couldn't have.

Pop! Pop! Pop!

But her heart had heard and understood.

"No." She shook her head.

"I am sorry." Teddy clutched Charlie's other hand.

Charlie snatched it free as if Teddy's touch scalded her. "No," she repeated as tears rushed to the surface. Her vision submerged deeper underwater. A round of empty promises flowed from her sisters' lips while pain seized every inch of her body, especially between her legs.

A new fear rippled through her. She inched her bruised hand over to her flat belly. "No."

When her sisters turned away, the truth chiseled its way into her head. "Nooo." Her tears were hot as they slid down her face, and she choked on the sob lodged in her throat. Hennessey was gone. The love of her life—dead. And the child she'd been carrying had gone with him.

Charlie sank into despair—sure she would never recover.

CHAPTER 3

Vic Caruso jumped when the phone rang and knocked a half a dozen beer bottles off the coffee table in the process with his foot. During the second ring, clouds parted in his head. He'd passed out on the couch again.

Grumbling, Vic snatched the phone from its cradle and answered the call before it went to voice mail.

"Yeah."

"Are you fucking catching the news?" Crews snapped a couple of octaves above his normal register.

"What is it?" Vic dismissed the near hysterics in his partner's voice—mainly because Crews stayed in a state of panic over one thing or another.

"Shit is about to hit the fucking fan," Crews whined.

"Can you be more specific?" Vic's eyes drifted closed again, while the alcohol sloshing through his veins was already spinning his thoughts away from this phone call.

"The bitch is still alive."

"Mmm," Vic moaned, not hearing a word.

"Vic! Are you listening to me, man?" Crews snapped.

Annoyed, Vic snatched his eyes open again. "What the fuck are you going on about, Chris? It's too fucking early for this shit." *Ain't it?* Vic pried one eye open and looked around for the time. *Why isn't there a clock in this room?*

"Turn the fucking television on, Vic. That muthafucka's bitch we capped last night is plastered all over the news. The shit is even on CNN."

"What?" Vic opened his second eyeball and patted the sofa's cushions around him in search of the TV remote.

"I got a bad feeling about this," Crews whined. "If the bitch starts talking—"

"Shut the fuck up," Vic ordered as he powered on the television. "Ain't shit going to happen to nobody. We're cool."

"I believed you last night when you told me the bitch was ghost."

"She *was* dead." Vic struggled to follow what the journalist and Crews were saying, but the segment ended, and he had to switch channels.

"She must've risen from the dead then."

That's impossible. Vic remembered checking the chick's pulse himself. He didn't make those types of mistakes.

"We're gonna have to get Jace and Thomas and make sure our stories are straight on this before we talk to our union rep. I got ten years on the force without a single scratch on my record. I can't lose it along with my benefits over some bitch."

Vic rolled his eyes. "Calm the fuck down. Nobody is going to lose shit. Let the chick hurl her accusations. They aren't going to stick to shit. We were off duty, and no electronic eyeballs were watching a muthafuckin' thing. If it gets down to it, it's our word against hers. There's not a grand jury in this country who is going to take a nigga's word over ours."

Crews remained silent.

"Exactly."

Crews sighed. "But we still need to get our story straight, right? I mean, in case she can identify one of us."

Unimpressed with the news reports, Vic shut off the television. "Fine, whatever." He lumbered to his feet and shuffled toward the kitchen with the phone tucked under his ear. "You and the guys can come over here to make sure we're all on the same page."

Crews sighed again. "Yeah, see? That's all I'm saying. We need to get our stories straight. Just in case."

Vic grabbed the last Heineken from the refrigerator. "Fine. Be here in an hour."

"You got it."

Vic disconnected the call and popped the top off of his beer. A second later, the phone rang again. He took one look at the caller ID screen and groaned.

He answered the call on the second ring. "Yeah."

The caller's voice rumbled over the line. "You left a witness?"

"We fucked up," Vic admitted. "But don't worry. We'll clean it up."

"You're damn right. I paid you good money to take care of *both* of them."

Vic's grip on the phone tightened. "I *said* we'd clean it up."

"I'll be watching." The caller hung up.

Stunned, Vic pulled the phone from his ear and looked at the screen again. *Fuck you, too.*

Provident Hospital

"Look straight into the camera," a female officer said.

Battered and broken, Charlie opened her swollen eyes the best she could, but when the camera flashed, the bright light stabbed her irises, and she had to slam them closed again.

"One more," the woman said.

Charlie pried her eyes open again; this time, tears streamed and matted her mascara-coated lashes together. Blood rushed into her head, sounding like a rolling storm, crashing inside against broken veins and vessels.

Another camera flash blinded her and sent pain shooting into the center of her brain. "*I'll teach you, you fucking bitch,*" a voice echoed in her head.

"Turn to the right," came the next order.

Charlie shuffled her feet and turned on her stilt-like legs. Hours ago, they had been snapped apart by animals in blue. "*Say something slick now, bitch!*"

The camera flashed.

"Turn to your left." Charlie's earlier screams of outrage rang in her ears. Her hands balled at her sides.

"Ma'am? To your left."

Charlie closed her eyes and turned, but her left foot dragged. She stumbled, sharpening her pain as it ricocheted. Still, this was easier than enduring the rape kit. And the rape kit was nothing compared to the rape.

If she could survive that, she could survive anything.

"Open your hospital gown," the officer said.

Charlie hesitated.

"Ms. Warren?"

Charlie pressed her lips together and chanted in her head, *You can do it.*

The officer's voice softened. "Take your time."

Charlie's scarred hands fumbled with the gown's strings, and after taking a deep breath, she opened it. The flashes came in quick sessions, burning her irises. *It's almost over.*

She needed it to be over.

"Okay, ma'am. You can get dressed now."

Charlie closed her gown and shuffled toward her hospital bed. The pain intensified with each step. Once in the bed, she rushed to press the button for the nurse.

The cop packed her gear and exited the room.

Alone, Charlie's composure slipped, and tears flowed. *"Fuckin' uppity bitch thinks she's too good for this dick!"* She pulled the covers over her body while tears soaked her pillow. *"Henny!"*

"Scream all you want to," the cop growled. "That dead nigga can't help you."

A nurse's voice came over the intercom. "Can I help you?"

"Pain."

"Yes, ma'am. Someone will be there in a second."

A hospital second meant anything from five minutes to an hour. Charlie didn't want to wait. She wanted everything numbed. It made it easier for her to check out of reality and quiet the voices echoing inside her head.

Ramsey rushed into the hospital like a hurricane. Rashid and Dominic flanked his sides while Trudy pulled up the rear. His long strides stormed across the hospital. People rushed to get out of the way. When he spotted Charlie's sisters in the waiting area, he made a direct beeline.

"How is she doing?" he asked them as a group.

Their father, William, unbraided his hands and then used his cane to stand up. "There is no way to answer that, son. She's still with us, but . . . I don't imagine she's going to be the same Charlie we all know and love. Those bastards have stolen everything from her."

Ramsey digested the information.

Teddy noted Ramsey's veins bulging along his temples and his nostrils flaring. Hennessey's oldest friend was having a hard time controlling the rage boiling inside of him.

"Is she talking?" Ramsey asked. "Is she, at least, saying what happened?"

The Warrens shifted looks among each other.

Ramsey didn't miss it. "What? She told you what happened?" He stepped forward. "What did she say? Who did this shit?"

They shared another look.

"It was Kong, wasn't it?" Ramsey guessed. His hands

balled into boulders at his side. "I know that nigga did it. Tell me, and we'll go over there right now and handle this shit."

Kong's name was short for King Kong on the street. He'd been called that for as far back as anyone could remember. Muthafucka had been slinging dope since he was in diapers. No lie. Kong's daddy used to stash dope in his son's diapers. It was no surprise Kong followed in the family business. Somewhere in junior high, guns replaced drugs. Kong was better than the muthafuckin' military when it came to getting his hands on weapons.

Kong bumped heads with Hennessey and Ramsey when they started making names for themselves in the music industry. Suddenly, Kong wanted to spit bars on their label. However, Hennessey and Ramsey didn't want anything to with Kong. Besides, gangster rap died out in the nineties. Kong didn't want to hear that shit and started his own label. The beef between them turned out to be great for business. The rivalry made both labels famous.

But the bad blood remained real.

"Say the word," Ramsey said, hyped up. "I'll go over there and squash this beef right now!"

"Calm down." Michael approached. "It wasn't Kong or any label beef."

Ramsey frowned. Michael's words didn't compute.

She lowered her voice. "They were cops."

Ramsey cocked his head like a confused puppy. "Cops?"

Everyone in the group nodded.

"The cops did this shit?"

William attempted to assist. "It was a fucking traffic stop."

"You're shitting me."

"Afraid not. Charlie is in there right now filing the report and documenting the abuse."

The moment Teddy finished informing Ramsey, the family saw an officer leave Charlie's room. "I'm going to go and check on her."

"I'm coming with you," Johnnie volunteered.

"Wait. I want to come," Teddy and Billie chimed together.

Michael shook her head. "We don't want to crowd her. You two stay out here with Dad and Ramsey. We'll be right back."

Teddy and Billie twisted their lips, but they agreed to Michael's directive.

Charlie heard a knock at the door before Michael poked her head around the corner of her hospital room. "Mind if I come in?"

Charlie minded, but her family was worried sick.

"Sure. C'mon in." Charlie swiped her eyes with the back of her hand and pushed the button on the hospital bed to raise her head up.

Michael entered and waved Johnnie to follow in behind her. "How are you feeling?"

"Worse," Charlie answered, ignoring the throb of her busted lip. "How else am I supposed to feel?" She lowered her gaze to her toes. Better to focus there than to see their pity. She'd had enough already.

"We got you some clothes." Michael held up a duffel bag. "Has the doctor been in to discharge you yet?"

"Not yet." Charlie took the bag and started getting dressed. She was more than ready to leave.

"Do you need any help?" Johnnie asked.

Charlie jammed her head through the neck of her turtleneck and spread her thick hair out across her shoulders. "Nah, I got it." Charlie slid one foot into a boot but hissed when she had to bend over and zip it up.

Johnnie rushed forward. "I can do that for you."

"No!"

Johnnie froze.

"I'm sorry." Charlie shook her head. "I didn't mean to snap."

"It's all right. I understand." The corners of Johnnie's lips curled, but it didn't look like a smile. "Everyone is on edge." She jutted a thumb over her shoulder. "You should see Ramsey out there. He and his boys are ready to go to war with the police."

Charlie hung her head.

"He's been asking to come in and see you."

"Oh God."

"You don't have to deal with him right now," Michael assured. "I'll go get rid of him. Wait here."

"Thanks." She squeezed Michael's hand.

"Hey. This is what family is for. Give me five minutes, and I'll come back and get you two when the coast is clear." Michael rushed out the door.

"Here, sit back down. It's going to take Mike more than five minutes to clear the coast."

Charlie sighed. She could only imagine the type of hell Ramsey was raising. He and Hennessey were tighter than blood brothers. They came up and built everything together. Hennessey was the brains, and Ramsey the muscle. They could've used more muscles that night on the side of the road.

Another knock sounded at the door before a doctor and a nurse breezed into the room.

"I see you're all set to go," the doctor said, avoiding Charlie's eyes. "Everything has been sent off to the lab. Here is a prescription. You'll experience some discomfort, but it will fade with time. I'll need to see you back in six weeks to check on those stitches." The doctor crossed his arms and chiseled on a fake smile. "Do you have any questions?"

Charlie shook her head. "I'm ready to go home."

"I bet you are." He pushed his glasses up the bridge of his nose. "You're cleared to go. I hope to see you in a few weeks.

Take care of yourself." He turned and strolled out with his nurse following behind.

Michael sighed. "Bedside manners are a lost art."

"Let's go home."

"You got it." Michael looped her arm around Charlie.

Before they took a step toward the door, three officers strolled through the door without knocking.

"Are you Charlie Warren?" The shortest of the men thrust out his barrel-sized chest, establishing himself as the leader of the three stooges.

Charlie thrust up her chin and met his stare head-on. "I am."

Shorty hitched up a half smile and looked at his sidekicks before he stepped forward. "And you are?" he asked Michael.

"Her sister." Michael placed her hand on Charlie's shoulder.

The short cop moved farther into the room, his two amigos pulling up the rear.

"What can I do for you, Officer?"

"It's more like what we can do for you." His smile morphed into a smirk. "Like, help you correct the police report before it's filed. It looked like there was a lot of misleading statements in it."

Charlie's hands balled at her sides. "Every word is true."

The short cop cocked his head, but his smile remained in place. "It's not uncommon for women who have been through this sort of thing to make mistakes."

"You mean being raped and almost beaten to death by four cops? *That* sort of thing?"

The smirk transformed into a full-on smile. "The kind of mistakes you're alleging in the report are reckless and can cause serious consequences and repercussion. A lot of them I'm sure you haven't considered."

"What's that supposed to mean?"

"It means you should rethink filing that report before you set off a chain reaction."

Charlie buttoned her lips but made sure she held the cop's silver gaze. "I'm not changing a single word in that report. I was raped and beaten within an inch of my life."

"I'm looking at you, sweetheart. I don't doubt that."

"My name isn't 'sweetheart'."

The officer's smile flatlined. "I'm trying to give you some helpful advice."

"Funny. It sounds more like you're making a threat."

Michael pulled Charlie to her side.

"Threat?" He chuckled and looked at his partners again. "Who's threatening you? I said *advice*. See? This is the kind of thing I'm talking about: misunderstandings. Sort of like how I believe there's a misunderstanding on who attacked you tonight."

"Is this what you people do now, patrol hospitals and intimidate your victims?"

The officer's smirk returned. "Threats and now intimidation? Ms. Warren, you have an active imagination."

"It's not going to work," Charlie warned him. "I'm not changing one word in that report."

"Look, lady"—a six-foot-four cop stepped forward—"we're trying to be nice. If you file that report, we'll bring down so much heat on you, your parents will regret the day you were born. You and *anyone* who has ever given a damn about you." He dragged his gaze over to Michael. "Are you catching my drift?"

Charlie opened her mouth to respond, but Michael placed a hand on her shoulder.

O'Connor, according to his name tag, smiled. "At least your sister has some common sense. You should be more like your sister."

Charlie had had enough. "And you and your *friends* in the department should go to hell. My report stands. I was pulled over and raped and beaten by *four* police officers. I don't care how many assholes you send down here or how many threats you make. You assholes messed with the wrong bitch."

"I hate to do this," Banner said, shaking his head.

Banner slapped a pair handcuffs on her wrists. "Charlie Jean Warren, you're under arrest."

CHAPTER 4

Cook County Department of Corrections

"These fuckin' charges are bullshit," Charlie hissed into the phone behind the Plexiglas. "Drug possession with an attempt to distribute? It's bullshit. It's so obvious they're setting me up." She hopped and twisted in her seat. The injustice made her anxious. She wanted to scream, yell, or hit something.

Charlie's father hung his head. "I can't believe they got one of my babies. I can't believe you're in here."

"You're blaming *me*, Daddy?" Shocked, she wheeled back.

William shook his head. However, he had trouble meeting Charlie's stare.

Michael took the phone from her father. "No one is blaming you for anything, Charlie."

It wasn't true. The clouds in her father's face refused to evaporate. They hung over his brows like a gathering storm.

"We're going to get you out of here," Billie said.

"I did the right thing by filing that report," Charlie persisted, pressing her hand against the glass to get her father's attention. "You believe that, don't you, Dad?"

"Of course I do." He shifted uncomfortably. "It's the fucking drugs I have a problem with. I *always* believed Hennessey and his boys weren't slinging poison. How many times did I warn you? Didn't I say he was trouble?"

Hurt, Charlie slid her hand away from the glass. "Daddy, don't tell me you believe these assholes. *If* those bricks were in the car, it's because they *planted* them there. They are fuckin' infamous for pulling this type of shit."

Her father shook her head and mumbled something.

Charlie's body imploded. "You're going to believe them over me?"

Her father looked torn.

"Of course not," Billie and her other sisters insisted.

"I want to hear *him* say it." Charlie nodded toward her father.

William snatched the phone back from Michael. "You charged into a war blind. No plan. No backup plan." His grip on the phone tightened. "Have you paid attention to *nothing* I've taught you?"

Charlie's face twisted in confusion.

"Hennessey was not my choice for you, but you loved him, and therefore he became like a son to me."

Charlie relaxed.

Her father wasn't finished. "It doesn't mean I turned a blind eye to things. I saw and know things you refuse to accept. Just like I see things you girls think you're hiding from me." He swallowed. "No, I don't expect you to turn the other cheek after what happened, but there are different ways to engage the enemy. In this life, in this skin, we're walking targets. But one by one, we march to their tune, we fall into their traps. I raised you to be smarter—better than them. Now *I* got to get involved."

"You?" She thought about the cache of weapons he kept stored in a basement bunker at the house.

His grip tightened on the phone. Next to the clouds above his brow, veins bulged along his temples. "I've devoted my life and my legs to my country only to watch it renege on every promise it's ever made. Now they've attacked my own." He shook his head. "It can't stand. It can't—"

"Daddy?"

Their father grunted and pitched forward.

The Warren girls gasped in alarm. "Daddy!"

"Daddy!" Charlie pounded on the Plexiglas. "Guards!"

"Back in your seat, inmate."

Charlie ignored the order. "Somebody help him!" She watched as her sisters pried the phone out of their father's hand while screaming for help.

Guards rushed forward on both sides of the glass. A few men helped her father, and a few assholes dragged Charlie away from the scene.

"No! Let me go," Charlie yelled. "He needs help." However, Charlie's pleas fell on deaf ears. "Daddy!" She squirmed and wrestled to break free of the guards—to no avail. It was the last time she saw her father alive.

Forty-eight hours later, Charlie's sisters posted her ridiculously high bail. By then, her father was on a cold slab in a morgue. Dead from a heart attack. It was one more person the system had taken away from her. Only this time, Charlie believed she'd also played a part in his death. He'd been disappointed in her. That hurt more than anyone would ever know.

"Where's my ring?" Charlie demanded after the cop handed over her personal effects.

The bored cop held up a piece of paper. "There's no ring listed on here."

"It was a four-carat engagement ring!"

"Sorry, honey. I don't know what to tell you. If it's not on the list, it doesn't exist."

"I don't fucking believe this," Charlie grumbled. The Chicago Police Department added robbery to their long list of crimes committed against her.

"I'm sorry. What was that?" The cop dropped the fake smile.

Charlie clamped her mouth shut and grabbed the rest of her things. When she marched out of jail, there was a horde of news cameras shoved in her face. She couldn't make out anything anyone said because they all shouted at the same time.

In the center of the sidewalk, Charlie stopped and looked into one camera. "I want to make one thing clear," she said. "Hennessey and I are *not* guilty of these trumped-up charges the city and the federal government has leveled against us. I look forward to clearing our name and putting the four criminals, hiding behind their badges, in jail where they belong."

The media frenzy escalated as microphones were shoved closer to her face. Charlie pushed them out of the way and pressed forward. She didn't have shit else to say.

Once she climbed into the back of Teddy's car, she sat in a tomb of silence as they pulled away from the curb. Charlie's tears fell in earnest. At the morgue, Charlie said her good-byes to her father's cold body. His disappointment was still frozen on his face. That look haunted her long after the morgue turned his body into ashes.

After he caught the local news over the bar at Dugan's in Greektown, Vic Caruso lowered his frosted mug of beer and seethed. "The bitch is going to be a problem."

Detective Thomas Graham growled, "You should have snapped her neck when you had the chance. She was a mouthy bitch from the get-go." He glanced over his shoulder to ensure no one listened in on the conversation.

Detective Jace Wallace chuckled. "Her mouth could do more than just talk. I've had nothing but wet dreams ever since that night. I wouldn't mind having another go." He adjusted his crotch under the table.

The men snickered. Despite the bruises and busted lip, she was still beautiful. The cameras loved her.

"You've been in to talk to the union rep?" Crews asked.

"What for?" Caruso sneered. "She hasn't dropped any names yet."

"No, but they are going to bring her in and maybe sit her down with a sketch artist."

Jace jumped in. "And don't forget the evidence from the lab." He gestured to his covered chest. "The bitch scraped me up good. I would say my cat did it, but . . ."

"Fuck." Vic shook his head.

The guys all shared a look before Thomas asked, "Is there any way Joanne can help out down at the lab?"

Vic grunted. "We're not exactly on good terms at the moment."

Jace leaned forward. "Any way you can get on good terms? She has done this shit for us before."

The table went silent as the men stared at Caruso while he sipped his beer.

Crews pushed. "Whatever is going on between you two, you need to squash the shit and call in a favor."

Caruso nodded while he prepared himself to eat crow with Joanne. "Fine. I'll see what I can do. Meanwhile, nobody says shit to the reps until we have to. We stick to the plan."

"Got it," they all echoed and returned their attention to the news.

CHAPTER 5

On a gray, cold, and wet spring day, Hennessey Rawlins was laid to rest. While the preacher rambled on about how great a man, son, and brother Henny was to all who knew him, the funeral attendees packed in as tight as they could to stay warm. Only, it wasn't working. The icy wind sliced everyone to the bone. The local weatherman had forecast cloudy and light showers. At noon, the sky turned dark, and the rain made it impossible to see.

Numb, Charlie stared at the silver casket, wishing she could crawl inside and lie there with Henny through all eternity. What was she going to do now? For the last three days, it had been damn near impossible to breathe—and it had nothing to do with her cracked ribs and everything to do with her heavy heart. This was what she had to look forward to for the rest of her life?

Tears broke through her iron will and warped her vision. Everything looked like it was happening at the bottom of the sea. That, too, was fine by her. Henny's mother, Betty, leaned over and wrapped her small arms around Charlie. When she didn't react, the older woman squeezed. Charlie closed her eyes, causing more tears to fall. She was supposed to be comforting Henny's mother, not the other way around. Despite that knowledge, Charlie couldn't pull herself out of her grief.

At long last, the preacher thumped his Bible closed.

Everyone murmured, "Amen" before the casket was lowered into the ground. As the crowd thinned, Charlie remained rooted in place while screaming inside. The loss was one thing; the injustice was another. There would be no justice. She knew it. The family knew it. Half of America who'd read about the case knew it, too. And more important, those assholes who had pulled them over also knew it.

When Betty Rawlins couldn't get Charlie to move, her sister Michael helped by also wrapping an arm around her and dragging her forward. "C'mon, Charlie. It's time to go."

The child in Charlie wanted to throw a hissy fit and scream at the top of her lungs, *"It isn't fair!"* But the adult Charlie had to tame those childish impulses.

At Hennessey's reception, Charlie wasn't any better. She moved from one huddle of mourners to another; each one expressed their condolences and assured her Henny was in a better place. After an hour of listening to their bullshit, Charlie was ready to take an AK-47 and level the place—including Henny's mom, who was already talking about forgiving the monsters who took her baby from her.

Charlie wasn't willing to turn the other cheek.

"Sharpton called," Mrs. Rawlins told her friends. "He said he'd like to put a march together."

"Oh, that would be lovely," Ethel, Betty's white cotton–haired friend, said.

Charlie rolled her eyes. Marching was something else black folks always did. Pray and march. This wasn't the sixties. Nobody cared whether they wore the hell out of the soles of their shoes anymore. People changed the channel or clicked on the next article on Facebook.

Charlie wanted to *do* something.

She wanted revenge.

She wanted those dirty cops to pay for what they did to her and Henny. Charlie wanted their deaths to be slow and painful. She wanted them to beg her for mercy.

Images of her giving each of their throats a bloody necktie while they screamed in agony played in her head and carved a genuine smile on her lips for the first time in three days. It was no less than what those pigs deserved. Charlie drifted away from the crowd and stood by the window so she could enjoy the revenge film playing in her head.

Her sanctuary didn't last long.

Teddy, her baby sister, weaved her way behind Charlie. "Are you all right?"

"Does it matter?" she countered without looking over at her sister.

"Of course it matters."

Her laugh got stuck behind the lump in her throat.

"Henny wouldn't want you to mope around like this."

How the fuck would you know?

"He would want you to remember the good times. Like when you guys were eight, and you beat him up for calling you a bitch on the playground."

A corner of Charlie's lips hitched up at the memory. "He had me fucked up."

"Yeah, he did. And you made sure he knew it, too."

"And don't forget how he beat up Akeim Moses for kissing you in the school play."

"We were playing Romeo and Juliet," she remembered.

"It still didn't go over too well with Henny."

"True."

"And there was prom." Teddy wound her arm around Charlie's hip.

"We were king and queen."

"Because you guys were the hottest couple at the school. His boys were jealous he had you on his arm."

"And half the senior class hated me for dating him."

"*I* hated you for dating him."

Charlie scrunched up her nose. "But you're gay."

"I can still appreciate a strong, handsome brother." Teddy winked.

Charlie shook her head. "I can't keep up with you and your fluidity issues."

"Nobody can. I like to keep people on their toes."

They chuckled.

"By the way, I brought you something to eat." Teddy held up a thick paper plate.

Charlie glanced at it and then at her sister.

"All right," Teddy lowered her voice. "I know you don't eat everybody's cooking, but you need to eat something. You've been eating like a bird the last three days."

"I'm not hungry."

"You can't plot revenge on an empty stomach." Teddy winked.

Charlie took the plate. "Who said anything about revenge?"

Teddy laughed before Charlie even finished asking the question. "My last name is Warren, too, you know. We think alike."

"Great. Any idea how we can accomplish going against the fucking blue wall? The whole damn country is one big-ass police state."

"Don't look at the whole pie, concentrate on only the slices you're going to eat," Teddy said.

Charlie reflected. "I hate it when you make sense."

"I know you do."

Michael, Billie, and Johnnie joined them by the window with plates in hand.

"What are you two over here gossiping about?" Michael asked.

"We're not gossiping." Charlie took a bite of a Swedish meatball.

"No, we're plotting," Teddy corrected.

Johnnie huddled closer. "Again?"

Teddy cut Johnnie a sharp look. "Don't you come over here with your Debbie Downer bullshit. Nobody wants to hear it."

"It's Debbie Downer bullshit to point out that you can't go up against the police?" Johnnie hissed. "Damn! Here I thought I was making a public service announcement."

Charlie rolled her eyes, tuned out her hissing sisters, and stared out the window. *Why is that man pacing outside of the house?* The six-foot, beer-gut Italian paced and glared at the house. Charlie picked off the man's partner on the other side of the street. Of course, they pretended like they didn't know each other, but there were enough covert looks and hand signals between them. *Something is up.*

"Do you see those guys over there?" Charlie asked her crowding sisters.

"What guys?" Johnnie inquired.

"The big Italian guy in front of the house and the Fat Albert lookalike across the street."

"What about them?"

"Cops," Teddy and Michael said.

Johnnie appeared lost. "How do you know?"

"Because they have to be."

"But what are they doing here?"

"Whatever it is, it can't be good," Charlie said.

"You girls okay over here?" Ramsey asked.

The Warren sisters pulled their gazes from the window, all except Charlie. "Everything is fine," Teddy assured him.

Ramsey's gaze centered on Charlie. "How about you, Charlie?"

Charlie ticked off a third cop parked two houses down.

"Charlie?" Ramsey touched her elbow.

She nearly leaped out of her skin before spinning around to hiss, "Don't touch me."

Ramsey's hands went up like he was in the middle of a stickup. "I'm sorry. My bad."

An awkward moment of silence drifted between them.

Charlie had everyone's attention. "Sorry," she told the whole room. "I guess . . . I'm a bit jumpy."

Ramsey smiled. "It's okay."

Betty approached. "It's understandable, my dear." She draped a supportive arm around Charlie. "Especially after all you've been through." Betty pulled Charlie toward the buffet table and ladled her out some punch.

Charlie didn't want it or the Swedish meatballs. But she nibbled and sipped so people would shut the hell up.

When she least expected it, Betty's grip on her hand tightened, and her gaze grew pointed. "My boy loved you. I hope you know that."

The meatball lodged in Charlie's throat. "I do."

"He was looking forward to making you his wife. The last few times I saw him, he talked of nothing else." Betty leaned close. "I even helped him pick out the ring."

Charlie's gaze fell to her bare finger. Her tears started up again.

Betty gripped her hand. "I'll always think of you as a daughter—as Hennessey's beautiful wife. You two may have never said *'I Do'* in front of a preacher, but your souls have belonged to one another for years. You two shared a love like his daddy and I had. It's the kind of love that will stay with you forever."

Charlie leaned over and kissed the woman's weathered cheek. "Thank you."

Charlie stayed at the reception another twenty minutes before she was ready to go home and crawl into bed. She might have portrayed an avenging angel in front of the media cameras the other day, but inside she was lost, heartbroken, and exhausted.

"Let me help you." Ramsey assisted in easing her good arm into the sleeve of her coat.

"Thanks." She flashed him a smile.

"My pleasure." Afterward, he shuffled his feet. "I'll walk you to your car."

"That's not necessary."

"I don't mind." She didn't know if she could handle one more conversation about how great Hennessey was or how much someone was going to miss him. It was too much.

Charlie allowed Ramsey to escort her out of Mrs. Rawlins's home.

"I guess a whole lot of shit is gonna change now, huh?"

"That's one way of putting it."

"That didn't come out right," Ramsey acknowledged. "I mean—hell. Look, we all have lost a lot of cats from back in the day. The streets body-bag niggas on the regular—most of the time over some bullshit."

Charlie couldn't see where he was going with this. "What's your point?"

Ramsey rolled his shoulders. "You declared war on the Chicago Police Department?"

"So?"

"So? They are coming after you with everything they got, guns blazing. And not only you, but my man, Henny, too."

"They've already done everything they could do to him. He's dead—in case you missed the point of a funeral."

"Sometimes death is the beginning. Those muthafuckas go poking around, and they will kick a hornets' nest. There's a lot about our boy he kept hidden from you."

"Like what?"

Ramsey smiled. "Trust me. It's best it's laid to rest in that casket with him and not on the front page of the *Chicago Tribune*."

Charlie spun around. "I don't believe this."

"What? You find it hard to believe that Hennessey kept shit from you? He had skeletons. Shit, we all do."

"Ah." She nodded. "I see."

"Do you?"

"This isn't about Hennessey. This is about *you*."

"It's about *all* of us," he hissed, dropping the smile.

"Un-fucking-believable." Charlie spun away and marched off.

Ramsey cut off her path. "All right. All right. I'm not saying this shit right."

"No. You made your point loud and clear. You want me to shut the fuck up because getting justice for what those sick fucks did to me, to Hennessey, and to our *child* is going to fuck up whatever bullshit hustle you got going. Does that sound about right?"

"Charlie—"

"Go fuck yourself, Ramsey." She raced off toward her car, her tears blending with the rain.

CHAPTER 6

Cook County Criminal Court

Officer Caruso paid a visit to Joanne Lloyd, who worked at the Illinois State Police Forensic Center, and pled for a favor dealing with Charlie Warren's rape kit. It cost him a weekend of lovemaking with the beautiful, plus-sized single mother, but he didn't mind. Joanne's more-bounce-to-the-ounce performance left him spent and satisfied—she also fed him well.

However, when it came to Charlie Warren's case, he took one step forward in covering his and his crew's tracks, only to fall two steps back. Not only did Ms. Warren have a great memory, but she was an artist and had made dead-on sketches of all four officers involved in the traffic stop. Within an hour of her turning those pictures over to the police, copies were broadcasted over both local and national news outlets. An hour later, Vic and his crew dialed their union reps and gave identical statements to their police chief.

"Charlie! Charlie," Billie called out from their father's living room. "Quick! Come and see this!"

Charlie stopped packing the books from the office's bookshelf. "What is it?"

"Hurry! Hurry!"

"I'm coming." Charlie rushed out of the office.

"They got them." Billie pointed at the television screen.

"Got who?" Johnnie inquired. She and Teddy rushed up from the basement.

Charlie took one look at the screen and froze. *Robocop.* "Gotcha, you assholes."

"It's them?" Teddy flanked Charlie's side.

She nodded, refusing to take her eyes off the news broadcast. The four officers who had been haunting her nights stood in their uniform in a semicircle behind the mayor, the chief of police, and the police superintendent. *Police chief warns about a rush to judgment* was printed on the screen next to *Breaking News.*

"Turn it up," Charlie instructed Billie.

She obliged, and they listened to the police chief.

"So far all we have to corroborate Ms. Warren's harrowing story are four sketches. Each of these officers has served more than fifteen years on the force and has an impeccable record. We can also go on to say that none of these officers were on duty on the night Ms. Warren was attacked. Also, it is important to know that Officer Victor Caruso had a history with Mr. Hennessey Rawlins. Caruso had arrested Mr. Rawlins twice in the past in drug-related matters."

Billie shook her head, confused. "What is he saying?"

"He's calling me a liar and saying I have a motive for coming after them." Charlie ran her good hand through her hair. "Shit."

Johnnie wrapped her arms around Charlie. "Don't worry about it. The truth is on our side."

Is it?

One year to the day after Hennessey Rawlins's death, Charlie placed her hand on the Bible and swore to tell the truth. The prosecutor approached with a benign smile and instructed Charlie to tell the court her version of what had happened that fateful night on the side of the road.

Charlie had prepared, but now that the moment had arrived, her stomach looped into knots. She looked at the bored-looking grand jury and began to tell them what had happened after she and Henny were pulled over on the side of the road . . .

"STEP OUT OF THE VEHICLE!"

"Okay, okay." Hennessey sighed and then informed the officer, "I'm reaching for the door." He was halfway out of the vehicle when Caruso grabbed him, dragged him out, and slammed him against the Range Rover. "What the fuck, man?"

For his outburst, Caruso slammed Henny's head against the roof of the vehicle.

"Hey!" I unbuckled my seat belt.

"Calm down, ma'am," Officer Crews warned.

Hennessey and Caruso scuffled.

"Muthafucka, what is your goddamn problem?" Henny barked.

Officer Graham and Officer Wallace joined the brawl.

"Hands on the vehicle," they shouted.

I twisted around in my seat to get a better view of what was going on, but Henny's chest obscured what was happening.

Belatedly, I went for my purse on the floorboard.

"Ma'am, keep your hands where I can see them," Officer Crews shouted outside my door.

I ignored the order and scooped out my cell phone. However, before I could punch in my security code, my door flew open, and the cop snatched the phone out of my hands. "What the fuck?"

The cop jerked me out of my seat and slammed me against the side of the vehicle.

"Hands behind your head!"

"What?"

"Hands behind your fuckin' head," Crews ordered while damn near wrenching my arm out of its socket.

"Ow!"

Crews must have holstered his weapon because suddenly his hands were everywhere, patting me down. Nothing was off-limits: my breasts, my ass—everything. I attempted to move away from the officer's rough violation. But there was nowhere to go.

"What the fuck is your problem?" I demanded.

"Hey! Get your hands off of her!" Henny attempted to break away from the officers' wrestling.

Wallace kneed Henny in the groin for his efforts, and then the batons came out.

"Henny!" I freaked at the sound of metal hitting bone.

"Get off of him!" It was three on one.

"Ow! Watch it, asshole." No matter how many times I told myself this couldn't be happening, reality confirmed the nightmare was real.

"Stop resisting," Crews seethed in my ear.

I closed my eyes and willed myself to be still. It was impossible while listening to the merciless beating Hennessey endured. He was down, but none of the cops appeared interested in arresting him—only committed to beating him to death.

With no other option, I screamed for help, but there was no one else around. Not a single car had driven by since we had been pulled over to the side of the road.

"Please! Stop! Get off of him!"

"Shut that bitch up," Caruso yelled.

"I'm trying," Crews shouted.

Caruso left Hennessey to Graham and Wallace and marched toward me.

I screamed, "Let him go, you fuckin' asshole!"

Officer Caruso reared back, and I ducked. Sensing what was coming, I snatched my hands from Crews. From my mil-

itary training, I went on autopilot and double-punched Caruso in his solar plexus—that's in his midsection. It stunned him for a second, but he recovered fast and hit me like a man, square across the jaw.

I cried as stars exploded in my head while my knees buckled. When I hit the ground, gravel scratched away flesh from the side of my face.

Roaring, Hennessey launched to his feet and raced toward us.

Pow! Pow! Pow!

At the series of gunshots, the stars circling my head disappeared as horror rushed over me in waves. "NOOOOOOO!"

Everything moved in slow motion as I watched Hennessey fall forward. Pain and shock covered his chiseled features before he hit the ground a few feet from me.

Both Officer Wallace and Officer Graham had shot him.

I scrambled over the sharp gravel to reach Henny. However, I was jerked back by my hair, and as I turned to demand release, a second punch whipped my head in the opposite direction. Pain now ruled my world on a level I had never experienced before. The fact my head was still attached to my body was a complete shock.

I didn't see stars.

I saw color. One color.

Red.

Enraged, I bucked, squirmed, and almost broke my wrists trying to break free. However, my screams and wails had stopped. It was much too painful to open my jaw. It had to be broken.

I kept bucking and fighting, even though my cocktail dress was around my waist and my panties had been snatched off. Crews's fingers penetrated me. I was dragged over into the grass.

Caruso hovered above me and said, "No sense of letting a fine piece of ass go." He unzipped his pants, exposing himself for a brief moment.

I jammed my knee up, smashing his nuts.

He tumbled over. "Fuck!"

I scrambled away, even managed to get to my feet.

Crews yelled, "Freeze!"

I had no time to react before volts of electricity shut down my nervous system, and I dropped like a stone. Mercifully, I hit grass instead of gravel. Even after I was on the ground, Crews shot the second voltage into my back. I seized up, teeth clenched.

"Get her in the van," Caruso ordered.

The cops wrenched me off the ground and carried me to the back of a van, where they hurled me in like garbagemen tossing in the trash.

I heard a loud crack *when I landed—and then came the pain.*

Caruso and Crews climbed in and shut the door. My nightmare was far from over. They raped me and strangled me until I passed out. When I woke, the paramedics were putting me in the back of an ambulance . . .

When Charlie finished her story, no one on the grand jury met her gaze. Only the special prosecutor gave her a thin smile and thanked her for her courage to testify before she was ushered out of the room.

"How did it go?" Johnnie inquired as she and the other sisters clustered around her.

Charlie bunched her shoulders and shook her head. "I'm not sure. But we'll know soon enough."

Charlie was right. Seven months later, Officers Victor Caruso, Christopher Crews, Jace Wallace, and Thomas Graham stood before a packed courtroom as nine jurors filed back into the room and took their seats. The Warren and Rawlins families sat rigid behind the prosecution team.

Or, in this case, the *reluctant* prosecution team.

Charlie sat ramrod-straight and studied each juror's face. They confirmed what she already knew before the trial had started.

Judge Bailey addressed the jury, "Have you reached a verdict?"

The foreman stood. "We have, Your Honor." A slip of paper was handed over to the bailiff, who carried it over to the judge to read.

The judge made a big production of putting on his glasses and reading the verdict before handing it back to the bailiff.

"What is your verdict?" the judge asked.

"We, the jury, find Officer Victor Henry Caruso on the charge of murder in the second degree . . . *not guilty*."

Charlie's blood boiled as she listened to the foreman read the charges one by one, repeating the same outrageous verdict of *not guilty*. This was the American justice system. Charlie's gaze sliced toward the defendants' table. The four towering officers smiled and pounded each other on the back.

The state prosecutors turned toward the Warrens and the Rawlins and mumbled a load of bullshit about how sorry they were for losing the case.

Charlie ignored them. After all, she was next in the hot seat, where the same prosecutor's office would be gunning for her on trumped-up drug charges.

"Let's go." Charlie slid on her sunglasses and led her sisters out of the courtroom.

Once again, a horde of cameras raced toward her. Each reporter was shouting one question: "What do you think of today's verdict, Ms. Warren?"

"The justice system is a fucking joke," Charlie growled into a microphone thrust underneath her mouth.

"You're not happy with today's verdict?"

"What do you think?"

Michael injected herself between Charlie and the microphone. "No comment."

An hour later, Charlie watched her response play on a loop on CNN. Their paid pundits were divided between left and right politics.

Charlie listened for ten minutes and then muted the television.

"You sounded like the stereotypical, angry black woman," Teddy commented, handing Charlie a large glass of wine.

"We have a right to be angry. Everyone always has their foot on our necks."

Johnnie fretted. "I'm worried."

"About what?" Charlie sipped her wine.

"Your case. If the system plays true to form, they're going to put you away. We're talking five to ten years mandatory, at a minimum."

Charlie smiled at her twin. "Don't worry about me. They've already done their worst. When this is all over with, they are the ones who need to worry about me."

CHAPTER 7

Five years later, West Side Chicago

Big Red, the last of King Kong's street captains, dipped out of a black Trailblazer, carrying two bulging black bags of cash. He waited half a minute for his driver and two flunkies to flank his side before he strolled toward the back of Lenny's Pawn Shop. Four sets of eyes watched one of Red's men jab the buzzer and then repeat the password into the speaker. Seconds later, the metal door swung open, and the men disappeared inside.

Like clockwork.

"Let's move," came the rough order.

Black ski masks covered four faces in the back of a nondescript black van. The armed robbers burst out of its back doors and hustled to the same metal door. They placed two C4 prop bombs on the door and took cover.

BOOM!

"Move it. Move it. Move it," came the shouted order over the men's ringing ears.

The moment they poured in through the back door, the four men were met with a hail of gunfire. But having watched where everyone was through hidden surveillance, the robbers were more than equipped to match the heavy artillery and pick everyone off with ease.

The gunplay lasted less than a solid minute, and it took even less time for the robbers to grab all the duffel bags of cash brought in from the hoods and the suburbia of Chicago. After another minute, the men were back in their black van and jetting off into the night.

Miss Alice's Soul Food was open well past closing and serving only one customer: King Kong. He chomped on his plate of fried chicken, collard greens, yams, and corn bread while making small talk with the restaurant's chef. In the middle of their conversation, Kong's cell phone buzzed. Groaning, he wiped his fingers and scooped the phone from his pocket. Just once, he'd like to get through a meal without muthafuckas blowing him up.

"Yeah." He grabbed his sweet tea and listened to the caller on the other end. "Say what?"

"They're dead," Birdie repeated. "They're all dead, and the money is gone, too."

"What the fuck are you talking about?" Kong unfurled his mountainous frame from his chair and shoved the table back a good foot.

His four bodyguards snapped to attention.

"Who?" Kong demanded, marching toward the door.

Birdie stammered. "I-I have no idea. Whoever it was, the muthafuckas pulled a clean hit."

"Bullshit," Kong growled. "Did you pull the surveillance cameras?" he asked, climbing into the back of his whip.

"The cops got here too fast. Muthafuckas used explosives and woke two neighborhoods. But we got digital playback servers at your office. We can still see everything the cops have as soon as you get here."

"Are the cops still there?"

"The cops, the media, and I'm betting pretty soon the

mayor. I'm telling you. These muthafuckas caused one hell of a ruckus and left too many dead bodies."

"Ramsey." Kong swore.

"No offense, boss. But that nigga ain't this muthafuckin' bold."

Kong shook his head. "Get the breast milk outcha mouth, nephew. I done told you too many times not to put no shit past no muthafucka. Where that nigga at?"

"At the Emperor's Club. It's his birthday."

The Emperor's Club

The Moonlight Club was long gone—renamed and rebranded under its sole owner's image. It was still the hottest place to be, with famous artists sliding through to show Ramsey Holt some love. Tonight, in particular, the crowd had gathered to ring in his thirty-first birthday. Drinks were on the house—except for the expensive shit. He wasn't fuckin' crazy.

The place was packed wall to wall with the hottest people the city had to offer. The music's bass thumped to the rhythm of everyone's heartbeat. The hard, pulsing beats flowed through him like a conduit as he stood above the crowd and took it all in.

"My man, the world is yours," Dominic cheered and held up his bourbon.

Ramsey lifted his glass. "Started from the bottom and now we're here," he joked before tapping the glasses of his closest friends.

Trudy, now wearing an eye patch and walking with a slight limp, sidled up beside his boss. "I bet Henny is looking down on you right now and is proud as fuck."

Ramsey bobbed his head. "True. I wouldn't be where I am if it wasn't for that real nigga. For real." He tapped Trudy's glass a second time before tossing back the rest of his drink. He didn't need it since he was already floating higher than a

747 after a couple lines of coke. It was all right for one night. After all, it was a special occasion.

"Yeah," Dominic chimed. "Hennessey was a real straight-up nigga."

Feeling nostalgic, Ramsey nodded. Had it not been for Hennessey's clear vision, Ramsey would have never gotten into the music scene. He was too much of a street nigga. He and Kong were cut from the same cloth on that account. Hustling and slinging dope were a part of their DNA. It was a good thing, too. No dream gets off the ground without cold, hard cash.

If there were a heaven for a G, Ramsey hoped Hennessey was seeing this shit right now.

Alexis took to the main stage, forcing the deejay to lower the music. "If I can have everyone's attention for a minute. Everyone?"

A few disappointed moans and groans rumbled through the otherwise hushed crowd, but Alexis, with her coke-bottle curves, managed to gain most of the crowd's attention.

"Thank you." She beamed while the spotlight centered on her. "First, I want to thank everyone for coming tonight. You guys look wonderful—but tonight is a special night, as you all are aware. Tonight, we're celebrating an extraordinary man—an icon in the music industry, a trailblazer: Ramsey Holt." She gestured up toward the club's top floor, where Ramsey stood.

Everyone cheered and applauded him.

Like a king, Ramsey waved at the people. His gaze scanned the crowd, but he had to do a double take when he saw a familiar face. However, when he searched among the people again, the face was gone.

Alexis blew him a kiss and waved, too. Her enormous engagement ring sparkled under the spotlight. "Baby, we are all here to celebrate your first thirty-one years of life. We love you and cherish you. We can't wait to see what you do in the next thirty-one years. Cheers! I love you, baby!"

Another round of applause rose to the top floor while three waitresses in skimpy, two-piece uniforms walked toward Ramsey, holding a three-tier birthday cake with sparkling birthday candles.

He chuckled because the damn thing looked like the cake was getting ready to explode in the women's face. Living in the moment, he went ahead and tried to blow the candles out. The waitresses helped, and a final cheer resounded before the deejay turned the music back up.

"Y'all niggas dig in," Ramsey told his boys after directing the girls to set the cake at his reserved table.

His men swarmed the cake like locusts, giving him another big laugh.

When Alexis made it to the VIP area, she slinked into his arms and shared a kiss. "Are you happy, baby?"

"I am now." He winked and grabbed her ass.

When Alexis giggled like a prepubescent girl, Ramsey's left eye ticked. Despite the grating sound, he pressed on a smile and pulled her closer. Alexis had a few annoying quirks, but it was no reason to toss her fine ass away. Since Charlie Warren had been locked up, Alexis was the best dime in the city—and a king always had to have a queen.

"Happy birthday, baby," Alexis whispered.

"Thanks, babe." He squeezed her ass again.

Alexis's best girl, Sheila, stood inches away from them, rolling her eyes. "When are you two going to settle on a date?"

Judging by the way Alexis pressed her lips, Ramsey realized his new fiancée had instigated the question.

"Soon enough," he answered with a wink and this time a *slap* on Alexis's ass.

"Uh-huh." Sheila rolled her eyes again.

Ramsey ignored their games and glanced back at the crowd. He saw the face again and whispered, "Charlie."

CHAPTER 8

From the moment Charlie entered the Emperor's Club with her sisters, she was transported back in time. The place had the same vibe and was still filled with beautiful and sexy people having a great time. Of course, the music was banging and had her itching to get on the dance floor, but instead, she leaned against the bar and watched the crowd. Pride swelled in her chest as tears brimmed her eyes. Hennessey would be pleased. Ramsey had kept his promise and kept his and Hennessey's dream alive. Charlie smiled. At least something of Hennessey's would live on.

"It's weird, huh?" Michael shouted to Charlie above the music. "The more things change, the more they stay the same."

"Yep," Charlie agreed, still soaking it all in.

Billie shouted, "What do you say we get a couple of drinks before we face the birthday boy?"

"I'm down." Charlie spun toward the bartender. "I'll have a Sidecar." She ordered.

"Make that two," Michael amended.

Billie and Johnnie ordered their usual White Russians.

Once the drinks arrived, Charlie lifted her glass. "What should we drink to?"

"To Charlie," her sisters declared, clinking her glass.

Michael added, "It's so great to have you back home again."

Charlie's eyes misted. "It's great to be home. You have no idea how much I missed you girls—even your bad cooking, Billie."

"All right. Watch it, heifer. Don't have *me* catching a case out here."

Michael rolled her eyes, laughing. "Girl, you know your ass can't cook."

"Amen," Teddy put in before the sisters laughed.

A man thundered from behind them, "Whatever you do, please don't tell me my eyes are deceiving me."

At the familiar voice, Charlie turned around. "Ramsey."

"My God. It *is* you."

"The one and only."

"For a brief second, I thought maybe you were Johnnie trying to fool me."

"Nope. It's me. We couldn't pull Johnnie away from the kids tonight."

"I'll be damned," Ramsey marveled. He stared at her for another minute before he wrapped his arms around her. "Come here, you. When did you get out?"

Charlie stiffened and remained as straight as an ironing board until he let her go. "Today. It's my first night of freedom."

"I can't believe you're here. Tonight, of all nights." Ramsey's white-picket-fence smile stretched from ear to ear. "It's a sign or something."

"Of what? That you're getting old?"

"Age is a state of mind."

"Sure, it is." She rolled her eyes. "Happy birthday, anyway."

"Ah, you know how it is. After your twenty-first, the

damn things don't mean shit. It's an excuse to throw a big-ass party."

Charlie offered a half smile. "You have a point there."

"Charlie, Charlie, Charlie." He shook his head. "It's so good to see you again. Why don't you come on up to VIP and say hi to the old gang? I know they'd love to see you—all of you." He acknowledged her sisters.

Charlie glanced toward the second level and hesitated. "I don't know."

"What's with you? You're shy all of a sudden?" Ramsey held out his arm. "Come on. You know you want to."

She did want to—out of morbid curiosity. Plenty of her old friends had written to her while she was behind bars—letters she had never bothered to read or reply to. It was too hard. If life was going to go on without her, she preferred not to read about it.

"All right. We'll come up." She signaled for her sisters to follow them.

"Trudy and I were just talking about Hennessey," Ramsey said as he navigated through the crowd and led her up the glass and steel staircase.

"Oh?"

"We were patting ourselves on the back, bragging about how proud Henny would be about this place. It was his vision, after all—this and the RawDawgs music label. We've turned his vision into a real dream factory."

Charlie's eyes misted. Ramsey was right. Henny would have been proud.

"Look who I found downstairs," Ramsey boasted, reentering the VIP.

When heads turned, eyes widened, and audible gasps echoed around them. Then, everyone lurched toward Charlie in a giant wave.

Charlie stepped back but was still pulled in several directions almost at the same time.

"I can't believe it."

"When did you get out?"

"Why didn't you call me?"

"Why have you never responded to my letters?"

Charlie couldn't keep up with the questions hurled at her, so her nerves made her laugh instead. "One at a time, please."

"Okay. Me first." Alexis settled her hands on her hips. "Why didn't you ever respond to my letters, *and* why didn't you call me when you got out?"

"Got out?" Sheila echoed. "I thought you died behind bars, bitch."

Charlie laughed again. "I'm not dead. Thank God."

"Then answer my question, bitch," Alexis demanded with a smile. "Why did you cut us off? We wanted to support you."

Uncomfortable with the captive audience, Charlie had to give them something. "It was too hard," she admitted. "I'd lost too much, and it hurt too much."

"Aww." Alexis cocked her head. "Come here, you." She wrapped her thin arms around Charlie and squeezed.

Again, Charlie tensed. Being in Alexis's arms was like being ensnared in a black widow's web; it was futile to do anything other than to submit to her fate.

Charlie forced a smile as family and friends she'd known more than half her life beamed back at her and welcomed her home. As each one pulled her into an embrace, she read the same question on their faces: *What was she going to do now?* More than half of them appeared satisfied that she had been brought low within their clique, perhaps even thought she'd gotten what she deserved.

Ramsey dragged her into another unwanted hug. "Time off for good behavior." He laughed. "I didn't think you knew how to behave for any extended amount of time."

"Is that a joke, or are you being an asshole?"

"Can it be both?" He grinned.

Alexis approached and laid a hand on Ramsey's chest. "Stop teasing her, sweetheart. It isn't nice."

At the sparkling rock on Alexis's hand, Charlie's smile vanished. "That looks like . . ."

"It does, doesn't it?" Alexis chuckled. "Ramsey remembered how much I liked the ring Hennessey gave you and allowed me to have a similar one made."

"It's not similar. It's an exact copy," Charlie hissed.

"Is it?" Alexis took another long look at the ring on her finger and pretended to be ignorant. "No, I'm sure yours didn't have the small baguettes on the side. Let me see yours."

"You know damn well I lost it."

"Did you?" She clutched at her imaginary pearls. "No, I didn't know. What a shame."

Charlie took a step back. It was either that or catch a case on her first day out of jail. She counted to ten before she asked, "So, you two are engaged now?"

"Yep." Alexis laughed. "It's funny. It's like we've switched lives. I'm engaged to a successful mogul with a baby on the way, and you're . . . well, I'm sure the next chapter in your life will no doubt be as interesting as all the others."

"Damn. You've been practicing that bullshit for five years, haven't you?"

A few inches shaved off Alexis's smile. "Don't be bitter. It's not a good look."

Michael rode to the rescue. "Ramsey, control your pet or take her out to get neutered."

He chuckled and wrapped an arm around Alexis's waist. "Sorry. I was turned on."

Charlie rolled her eyes. "You would be."

"Nothing like a good catfight to get a man's blood pumping." Ramsey leered at Charlie.

Charlie rolled her eyes and waltzed over to the next group of friends with her sisters.

For the next hour, Ramsey kept track of her as she moved around the VIP, reacquainting herself with old friends.

Charlie had always known that Ramsey felt some kind of way about her, but he had always respected Hennessey enough never to make a move. But now, with Henny being dead and buried, Ramsey didn't hide his open interest—not even for his annoyed fiancée.

At some point, Charlie and her sisters made their way back downstairs and on to the dance floor. Charlie had forgotten how invigorating and therapeutic music could be, and she ended up staying on the floor longer than any of her sisters. When she hustled off the floor, it was to quench her thirst. Exhaustion was still a long way off.

"If it isn't the dancing machine," Billie joked when Charlie joined them back in VIP.

"I hope you're saving a dance for me," Ramsey injected as he Bogarted into the sisters' circle like an unwanted stalker.

"Won't your girl get jealous?" Charlie asked.

"Let me worry about that."

"Jealous girlfriends usually take out their revenge on the other *woman*, not the low-count, two-timing dog who caused the drama in the first place."

Ramsey slapped a hand over his heart. "You wound me. Deeply."

"Uh-huh." Charlie laughed and turned her attention to the dancing crowd below. Her heart stopped as she froze and stared at the man leaning against one of the downstairs bars. From this distance and under the circular emerald lights, the man bore a striking resemblance to Hennessey. To make sure she wasn't imagining things, Charlie tapped Teddy on the arm and pointed toward him. "Who does he look like to you?" she asked.

"Who?" Teddy searched in the general direction Charlie pointed.

"The guy at the right end of the bar. In the purple shirt."

"Holy shit." Teddy leaned over the steel railing. "He looks like . . ." She turned to look at her sister, but Charlie was already on the move.

"Hey, Charlie. Where are you going?" Ramsey blocked off her path. "Surely you're not going home. It's early."

She pushed up a smile. "Nah. I'll be right back." Charlie maneuvered around him. However, the weight of his stare followed her as she made her way downstairs. Nearing the bar, she kept waiting for her vision to adjust and reveal the Hennessey lookalike to be a trick of the light or a figment of her imagination.

It didn't happen.

Okay, maybe he was a couple of inches shorter, but the profile remained the same. He had the same rich, chocolaty complexion, the same low haircut, and the same fit physique.

Charlie found a spot about a foot away from the stranger and willed the man to look in her direction.

A few seconds later, Hennessey's twin pulled his contemplative gaze from his drink and surveyed his surroundings. A smile touched his lips as he rocked his head to the club's music.

Charlie waited.

Near the end of the song, the stranger's gaze swept across the bar and landed on Charlie. Surprise and interest shone in his black gaze while Charlie's heart raced. Belatedly, she remembered to smile. The stranger accepted the open invitation it was meant to be and headed toward her.

"May I buy you a drink?" His voice was deeper than Hennessey's—almost Barry White deep.

"The drinks are free."

"Oh yeah. I forgot." He grinned.

"But I am thirsty," she admitted.

"I got you." He winked. "Bartender, a drink for the lady."

"And what will the lady have?" The bartender smiled.

"A whiskey sour."

"Coming right up."

"Make that two," her admirer added before glancing her over again. "I didn't have you pegged for a whiskey kind of girl."

"No?"

"Nah, I figured you for one of those froufrou drinks that ladies love to order because they're sweet."

"Ha." Charlie laughed. "I'm afraid there's nothing sweet about me."

He looked her over. "I find that hard to believe. You have the face of an angel."

"Lucifer was an angel." She inched closer.

The handsome stranger arched a brow. "That deep, huh?"

"You have no idea."

"Two whiskey sours," the bartender announced, setting down their drinks. He tossed a wink at Charlie before being called to the other end of the bar.

"Thanks." Charlie assessed the smiling stranger. She wanted to touch his face and verify the image before her was real. He even had Hennessey's cocky confidence dancing in his eyes.

She pulled the corners of her lips upward while she sipped her drink. Her body tingled all over. It had been a long time since she'd been with a man. Too long.

He inched closer. "Not to sound corny, but do you come here often?"

"You can't help but sound corny with that line."

"True." He chuckled.

"But to answer your question, no. I haven't been here in a long time."

"Ah, then it's my lucky night. My first time here, and our paths cross. It must be destiny."

"Destiny?" She tossed her head back with a laugh. "You're corny."

He shrugged. "Our little secret?"

"My lips are sealed." She zipped her lips and took another

scan around the club. The music and the energy made it impossible to stand still.

"Care to dance?" her admirer asked.

She shook her head, but her hips kept moving.

He cocked his head. "Are you sure?"

Charlie bit her bottom lip and reconsidered.

He took her by the hand. "C'mon. You know you want to."

After a deep gulp of alcohol, she abandoned her drink on the bar and allowed him to pull her toward the dance floor. Once there, she lost herself in the music. For the first time in years, Charlie wasn't obsessed with Vic Caruso or her plans for revenge. She lived in the moment.

Her dance partner showed her a few new moves and impressed her with his endurance. By the time they took a break, they were out of breath and sweaty. They returned to the bar and ordered more drinks.

"So, what does a guy have to do to get your name?"

"He has to ask."

"Now, why didn't I think of that?"

She shook her head. "Good question." She shook her head. "But at least you have some nice moves."

"You noticed, huh?" He leaned into her personal space. "I still have a few moves you haven't seen yet." He winced. "Did that come out as corny as I think it did?"

Charlie nodded. "Uh-huh."

He laughed. "My name is Karl, by the way."

"Nice to meet you, Karl. I'm Charlie."

"Charlie?" He nodded, drinking her in again. "It suits you."

"I'm glad you approve." She touched his hand. "But what do you say to us getting out of here?"

His eyebrows lifted in surprise. "I say I like the way you think." He pushed away from the bar. "Where would you like to go?"

"Having a good time?" Ramsey unmistakable voice sliced through the music.

She turned with an uneven smile. "As a matter of fact, I am."

Ramsey's dark gaze swept over her before shifting to the man standing next to her. "Aren't you going to introduce me to your friend?"

"That's not necessary." She leaned against her handsome stranger. "We're leaving." She pulled out her cell phone and texted her sisters in a group text.

Ramsey's gaze hardened. "Oh?"

"Uh-huh. Now, why don't you find that delightful fiancée of yours and tell her it was nice seeing her again? Who knows, maybe we'll play catch-up again in another five years." She turned toward Karl. "Are you ready?"

Karl shoved on another smile. "Whenever you are."

Charlie attempted to move around Ramsey, but he blocked her path.

"I'm not trying to get into your business." Ramsey chuckled.

"Could have fooled me." She laughed.

"Still—" He pulled her aside. "You've been tossing back a few, and maybe you're not in the right frame of mind."

Charlie laughed. "Are you cockblocking me right now?"

"I'm looking out for you." Ramsey looked over at Karl.

She followed his gaze.

"Are you sure you're leaving with this guy for the right reasons?" he asked.

"Believe me. It's for *all* the right reasons." She winked and marched off with Mr. Right Now out of the club.

CHAPTER 9

"Whoo-hoo, boys! Three million," Vic Caruso declared, pulling the last stack of hundred-dollar bills from the money counter. "I told you we could pull this shit off." He high-fived Jace and Thomas and then looked at a stunned Chris. "C'mon, buddy. You should be happy. We did it!" Vic hooked an arm around Crews's neck and pulled him close to ruffle the top of his head. "We're rich, man!"

A smile crept onto Crews's face. "This is more money than I've made in my entire life. It more than my parents and I made combined."

Vic nodded. "And it's a muthafuckin' shame. It's way past time the universe evened shit out. We'll do far more good with this money than those cockroaches killing their own kind. This right here"—he gestured to the cash on the table—"will put your three kids through college and get Bernice off your back."

Crews and the rest of Chicago's Special Task Force nodded and rubbed their hands together.

"But what about King Kong?" Jace asked. "He ain't going to take this hit lying down."

"Nah, and I pity the muthafuckas he's gonna pin this hit

on, too. As long as everyone in this room keeps their fuckin' mouth shut, there's no way Kong will be able to trace this shit back to us. Right?"

Everyone continued nodding, never pulling their gazes from the tall piles of cash stacked in front of them.

"We're not going to do anything stupid. That means no big, fancy houses, midlife-crisis luxury cars, or flashing cash around. Don't put this shit in a bank, triggering suspicious activity reports. Get a shovel and dig a hole if you have to, but none of this money better come up on anybody's radar. You feel me?"

Again, they all nodded.

Satisfied they were all on the same page, Vic plopped his cigar back in his mouth and returned to the table. "Good. Now, let's divvy this money up and get the hell out of here."

The rest of the team grabbed duffel bags and returned to the table.

However, Worrywart Crews still had another question. "So, who do you think Kong will try to pin this hit on?"

Vic chuckled around his cigar before pulling it from his thin lips. "If I was a betting man, and I am, I'd put my million on Ramsey Holt."

The rest of the team shared amused looks while Vic's rumbling laughter grew louder. "I wouldn't want to be that shiny nigga for nothing in the world right now."

Charlie and Karl stumbled through his front door with their hands tearing at each other's clothes and their mouths fused together. Animal lust raged through their veins, dissolving the reality that the two were complete strangers.

For Charlie, she was making love to a ghost. It was Hennessey's lips she tasted. It was Hennessey's heart, pulsing beneath her hand. *Sorry, baby. I didn't do more to protect you,* she repeated in her head. She was unaware she was crying until Karl pulled back.

"Am I hurting you?" he asked.

At the withdrawal of his sweet mouth, Charlie emerged from their lustful haze to notice she was in the center of a stranger's bed. "What?"

"Am I hurting you?" he asked again. "You're crying."

Charlie touched her face and verified it was true. "No." She hooked her arm around his head and pulled him close. "Now, shut up." In an instant, their lips sealed together again, and she tumbled back into the past.

In her mind, it was Hennessey who pulled her red panties over her hips, down her long legs, and tossed them over his shoulder. When he parted her knees east and west, Charlie guided his head to her body's flower. She came undone at the flick of his tongue. It had been a long time.

Despite her coming within minutes, Hennessey locked her legs apart and kept sapping up her body's honey. Her orgasms slammed into her, one right after another, until she squirmed to get away. She needed a break. She needed to catch her breath.

Chuckling, Hennessey came up for air. But it was only to share the taste of her essence while his hard cock rubbed against her wetness. Her body's tart honey was more potent than any aphrodisiac she had ever had. Her mind spun into a zone it had never been before.

It might have been because of the long dry spell, but by the time he entered her, she was having something akin to a spiritual awakening.

Karl was in the same zone. He'd never had such a responsive partner before. It amazed him how the woman's body was as snug as a glove over his cock. The heat they generated had to be fogging the windows. No matter what he wanted, this Charlie was down for it. Her body was a wonderland, and he was determined to experience every ride.

* * *

The birthday party at the Emperor's Club was still in full swing, but the birthday boy looked ready to chew on a box of nails. Nothing Alexis or his boys did or said cheered him up. He'd also been taken aback by how much the dude Charlie had bounced out of the club with had looked like his old boy Hennessey. Desperate for information, Ramsey sent Trudy out in time to catch the nigga's license plate. Now he had to wait until morning to get in contact with a connect down at the DMV to get some answers. But Ramsey didn't have to wait to deduce what Charlie was doing at this moment. He saw the look in her eyes—and he was jealous.

"C'mon. Don't you want to dance?" Alexis whined.

"Later." He waved her off.

Alexis slapped her hands on her hips and opened her mouth to give him a piece of her mind, but she was interrupted by a smattering of gunfire blasting in the club.

A cacophony of screams and shouts followed as mayhem broke out.

Ramsey slung Alexis toward Trudy as he barked, "Get her out of here."

The rest of the crew drew their weapons and rushed toward the danger, but the club's stampede made it nearly impossible to thread their way too far.

"Where's that muthafucka at?" Kong thundered with the voice of Zeus.

Rashid grabbed Ramsey and tugged him back. "We're outnumbered," he shouted.

Another spray of gunfire went straight into the ceiling.

"RAMSEY!"

"Nigga, I know you're in here. I want my stacks, muthafucka."

Rat-at-tat-tat-tat.

"We'd better head out back," Rashid shouted.

Ramsey jerked free from Rashid's grip on his shoulder and

for a split second had a clear shot at one of Kong's men, and he took it. One tap on the trigger nailed Kong's henchman's shoulder and spun him around. In doing so, the henchman's fire went wild and sprayed into the crowd. The screams changed—from fright to horror.

Ramsey also gave away his position.

In the blink of an eye, a cache of weapons aimed in his general direction. Ramsey reconsidered Rashid's suggestion and turned on his heel and dove as more gunfire went off.

Bullets whizzed by his head, but one in particular hit him in the ass.

"Fuck!" He hit the floor. Some bitch even kicked him in the head. But at least his boys, Rashid and Dominic, grabbed him, and half-dragged his body to the hidden escalator in VIP. The small cabin took them straight to the club's basement.

There, Ramsey crammed into the back of his custom-made Range Rover. He howled in pain. Dominic started the vehicle the exact moment another spray of bullets pinged and ricocheted off the bulletproof glass, but a few punctured the vehicle's body.

"Get us the fuck out of here," Ramsey demanded.

Dominic jammed the accelerator and rocketed toward the three shooting men. A short game of chicken ensued, until the last second, when two of the shooters dove out of the way. The third kept firing until he was mowed down and dragged underneath the SUV a few feet.

Once the coast was clear, Dominic asked, "Where to, boss?"

"Somewhere I can get this fuckin' bullet out of my ass!"

The phone jarred Karl out of dreamland. He groaned as he untangled his limbs from his Egyptian-cotton sheets. He patted down the nightstand, but his cell phone wasn't there.

It trilled again.

Desperate to shut it off before the call woke Charlie, Karl

pried open his eyes and followed the sound to his clothes piled on the floor. "Yeah," he croaked.

"Oh, thank God," Kacie sighed. "I was afraid you were down at the Emperor's Club."

"What?" He glanced around the dark bedroom. Something was wrong.

"It's all over the news. There was a shooting."

"A shooting?" He returned to the nightstand to find the television remote. He powered on the TV and hit the mute button so he wouldn't wake Charlie. But when the blue-gray light from the television washed over the bedroom, Karl's bed was empty.

"What the hell?"

"Are you seeing it?" Kacie asked. "They said it might be part of a gang war. I'm glad you didn't go down there."

"I *was* there." Karl stared at the empty bed.

"Yeah? You must have gotten out of there before the shit hit the fan."

Karl nodded, still ignoring the news report on the television screen. *When did she leave?*

"I'm glad you're all right. I can go back to sleep now."

Sighing, he shut off the television. "Thanks for checking in on me. Makes me feel like somebody cares."

"Hey, I will always care. Fuck that bitch Ellen. She doesn't know a good thing when she sees it."

"Yeah, she's not the only one."

"What?"

"Nothing." Karl sighed and swallowed the knot in his throat. "I'm going to go back to sleep, too."

Kacie's keen hearing kicked in. "Are you all right?"

"I'm . . . fine."

"You don't sound fine. Tell me. What is it?"

"Don't do this, Kacie. I'm not your responsibility. And you can't keep worrying about me. I'm a cop, for Christ's sake."

"It's because you're a cop I worry about you," she said. "And now, with that stunt Ellen pulled—"

"Kacie—"

"I'll never forgive her for breaking your heart. *Our* hearts. Fuck. I loved her like a sister."

Karl sighed. "Let it go. And please, don't waste your time hating Ellen. It hurts right now, but she saved us from making a big mistake."

"I hate her because she hurt you."

"It's love, Kacie. It's supposed to hurt."

CHAPTER 10

Breakfast was well past noon at Billie's place. The girls stayed up recapping the night while Billie burned bacon on the stove. Charlie's sisters managed to get out of the club unscathed, but still marveled over the wildness of the night.

"So, are you going to see that guy again?" Billie asked, handing Charlie her morning coffee.

"What guy?"

Charlie's sisters stopped eating to stare at her.

"Oh, *that* guy."

"Yeah, *that* guy." Billie shook her head. "It's creepy how much he looked like Hennessey though, right?"

Charlie shrugged one shoulder while she risked burning her tongue on her first sip of caffeine.

The sisters squirreled secreted looks before crossing their arms and waiting Charlie out.

"What?"

"What do you mean, 'what'?" Michael chuckled, smacking her sister on the arm. "First time you get laid in five years, and it's with a man who could pass for your old fiancé's twin. You think we're going to let that shit go? You must have forgotten how we roll."

"He was . . . something I needed." Charlie shrugged again. "An itch I needed to scratch."

Her sisters stared at her.

"What? Is that a problem?"

"Did you at least exchange numbers?"

"Nope." Charlie sipped her coffee. "Any more questions?"

"How about a name?"

Charlie raised an eyebrow.

"Charlie!"

"I don't remember." She rolled her eyes. "Kevin or Karl. Something like that."

"Please tell us you at least used a condom."

"Of course, we did. I'm not crazy."

"That's good to know." Teddy bit into her burnt bacon and watched it crumble onto her plate.

Charlie chuckled, then lifted the spoon from her soupy grits and shook her head.

Michael pressed. "Kevin *or* Karl?"

Sighing, Charlie pushed her food away and turned to her sisters. "Look, I got what I needed and left. End of story. I don't know why you guys are making a big deal out of this. You have had a few one-night stands in the past."

Four sets of hands went up, surrendering before an unnecessary war was declared.

"Okay, new subject." Michael clapped her hands together. "Now that you're back home, what's next?"

"What else?" Charlie shrugged. "Find a job, an apartment—get on with life."

Her sisters again shared dubious looks.

Charlie sighed and set down her coffee. "What?"

"Nothing," Billie placed a plate of burnt bacon and runny eggs in front of Charlie. "We're surprised. That's all. We thought you'd pick up your crusade against the Chicago PD."

"Surprised about what?" Charlie's eyes narrowed.

Billie cocked her head. "What about Caruso and his gang?"

The kitchen fell silent while all eyes centered on Charlie.

She made a quick calculation. "What about them? They got away with it—and nobody cares." She shrugged. "I have to get on with my life—and stay the hell away from cops."

Officer Karl Nelson and his partner, Elliot Massey, arrived at Mrs. Berry's brick ranch house for the fifth disturbing-the-peace call that week. After pulling up in the driveway, Nelson parked the patrol car and looked over at his partner.

"It's your turn."

"How the fuck do you figure? I went to the door the last time."

Karl sighed and dropped his head back against the headrest. "All right. How about I flip you for it?"

Elliot laughed. "Now, why would I flip when it isn't my turn?"

"You're a real asshole."

"That's what the old lady keeps telling me."

Karl flipped his partner off and climbed out of the car.

The kids tossing the football in the streets yelled at him, "Hello, Officer Nelson!"

"Hey, boys," Karl shouted back with a wave. He spotted Li'l Jimmy leaping and catching a ball that should've sailed over his head. "Way to go, Jimmy!"

Jimmy beamed back and pumped out his chest.

"You've been practicing, huh?" Karl asked as he knocked on Mrs. Berry's front door.

Jimmy nodded. "Just like you taught me."

Mrs. Henrietta Berry snatched open the door with her left hand already settled on her hip. Dressed in her usual bright, floral housedress and with her hair wrapped and held down with a black satin head scarf, Mrs. Berry looked as if she was born in a bad mood. "You took your sweet-ass time getting here, didn't you?"

Karl plastered on a smile. "We got here as soon as we could, ma'am," he lied.

"Uh-huh." She cocked her head. "What's it gonna take for you and your partner to do your jobs and lock those trifling-ass kids up? Every day, they keep up all that damn racket out in front of *my* house. I can't hear my TV shows. And when *I tell* them to keep it down, those bastards got the nerve to curse *me* the fuck out."

"Yes, ma'am."

"One of these damn days, their mouths are going to write checks their asses can't cash, and then you'd be up in here hauling *my* ass off to jail."

"Yes, ma'am. We don't recommend you lay hands on the children."

"Then do your goddamn job!"

"Ma'am, like we've told you before, they're kids. They aren't breaking any laws."

"Bullshit. You mean to tell me there are no laws against children playing in the streets? There is a law for every mutha-fuckin' thing in this city. Don't fix your face to tell me otherwise."

The children's peals of laughter rang out.

Karl sighed, but maintained his smile. "I'll talk to them."

"Lock. Them. Up," she hissed. "I don't see what the big damn deal is. They're going to be behind bars in a couple of years anyway. You'd just be giving them a head start. Might even be saving a few lives."

Karl's jaw tightened. "I don't know. My brother and I used to play football in the street all the time when we were growing up—and we turned out all right."

"That's debatable." The old bat slammed the door in his face.

Karl dropped the smile and turned from the door in a huff. When he stepped off the porch, he saw his partner was no longer in the patrol car but was holding court with the kids at the street curb. He strolled over and joined them.

"How did it go?" Elliot asked.

"The usual."

"Officer Nelson, do you guys only shoot black people?" eight-year-old Patrick Dawson asked with open curiosity.

"No. That's *not* true." Karl rubbed the top of his coiled hair.

"Have you ever shot a white guy before?" Patrick grilled.

"That's not the point. We—"

"But you've shot a black person before, right?"

"It isn't about the color of people's skin. Our jobs are to protect and serve the community. We only go after *bad* guys."

"And only black people are bad?"

"I didn't say that."

"Then how come you haven't shot any white people?"

Elliot laughed. "He's got you there."

"Me? That uniform you have on isn't a costume, you know?"

"Yeah, but I've never shot *anybody*." He grinned.

Karl grabbed the football from Marcus. "Who wants to toss this baby around?"

"I do! I do!" The kids bounced on their toes.

"All right. You guys are going to have to promise to keep the noise down for Mrs. Berry. She doesn't like it when you guys get too loud out here."

The kids booed and hissed.

Elliot chuckled. "I take it you guys don't care for Mrs. Berry too much?"

"She's mean," Debbie, the lone girl in the group, said, frowning. "She's always out here yelling and calling us names. We don't like her."

"You might not like her, but she has the right to have some peace and quiet."

"Then she should stop yelling so much."

"Yeah." The boys nodded.

Emboldened, Debbie continued, "My momma said she's evil because her husband left her and married her sister."

Karl laughed before he could stop himself. "Is that right?"

Debbie nodded. "It's because her sister is skinnier than she is."

"That'll do it." Elliot laughed.

Karl elbowed his partner.

"What? What did I say?"

"Enough about Mrs. Berry. Just keep it down." He winked at the kids. "Now, let's toss this baby around."

CHAPTER 11

From his penthouse in Chicago's Gold Coast, Ramsey watched the news broadcast while lying on his belly—off of his bandaged ass. The reporter repeated gossip and rumors about gang violence run amok that extended to the label's beef between his RawDawgs and Kong's Gorilla Beats. Immediately, Ramsey's blood pressure escalated.

A few of the eyewitnesses placed a single fist over their hearts, a RawDawgs symbol of solidarity. A few club witnesses, still in last night's clothes, relayed their horrible experience with comical exaggeration for the cameras.

"Man, it was wild. Everybody was partying and having a good time, celebrating my man Ramsey's big day and—Bam! *Muthafuckas—oops. Can I say 'muthafuckas' on television?"*

"We prefer if you didn't."

"Anyway, as I said, these . . . guys . . . burst through the door. There must have been like twenty of them. They came in blasting and demanding to see the big man, you know? It was wild. Niggas scattered like cockroaches." The man laughed. "My old lady made me eat her dust. She beat me home."

"Lunch time," Alexis sang, entering the bedroom, carrying

a tray of food. She wore a red kimono that barely stretched past her ass and captured Ramsey's attention for a hot second.

"Later," he said.

"I made you a homemade cheesesteak club, just the way you like it," she teased, setting the tray in front of him. She grabbed the remote from his hand. "Enough of this."

Ramsey snatched it back. "I'm watching the news."

"Why? It's only upsetting you."

"Those bastards shot up my fuckin' club *and* left a bullet in my ass!"

"I know, sweetheart," she cooed, climbing onto the bed. She straddled him above his waist to avoid his wounded butt and so she could rub the tension out of his shoulders. "C'mon, baby. Relax. You're tense."

Ramsey rolled his eyes. "Of course I'm fuckin' tense. That muthafucka sent an army to take me out last night."

"We don't know if it was Kong yet," Alexis insisted.

"Who else would it fuckin' be? That nigga is out of control. This shit is war!" He grabbed his cheesesteak and chomped down.

Alexis sighed.

The doorbell rang.

"Fuck!" Ramsey slapped the sub on the tray, bucked Alexis off him, and snatched the TEC-9 from the compartment at the foot of the bed. However, getting off the bed was another subject. His ass ached like a muthafucka.

Dominic's voice boomed through the bedroom's speaker. "Ramsey, man. It's the police."

Relieved, Ramsey ejected the cartridge and placed the TEC-9 back in its hiding place before his bedroom door opened. Trudy entered first, before three cops in casual street wear strolled inside and looked around.

"Ah, this must be where the magic happens," Detective Vic Caruso joked, entering the palatial bedroom. "Nice."

Detective Christopher Crews bobbed his head. "This room is about as big as my first apartment."

Caruso chuckled and gestured toward Ramsey's bandaged ass. "Please, please. Don't get up."

Alexis covered her man's naked ass before scrambling to the corner of the bed.

Ramsey rolled his eyes after watching the cops' weak comedy act. "What can I do for you, gentlemen?"

Dominic entered the room last and posted next to Trudy with his arms crossed.

Vic hooked his thumbs into the front belt loops of his jeans. "It's more like what *we* can do for you. Your club took a lot of heat last night."

"So what? Are you here to harass me instead of the muthafuckas who blazed my shit up?"

Officer Graham laughed. "You know how these investigations go when nobody saw shit, heard shit, and ain't saying shit."

Ramsey's lips curled. "Oh, we're playing this game, huh?" He shook his head. "You know who pulled this hit. Everybody knows who did this shit."

Caruso's shit-eating grin matched Ramsey's. "Knowing a thing and proving a thing are two *different* things. But you know, we'll check into it."

"As a tax-paying citizen, I'd appreciate that," Ramsey sneered.

Caruso's smile tightened before he launched into the real reason for his visit. "Under the circumstances, it appears you may be in the market for some real protection."

"Ah, here comes the marketing speech. What? *You're* selling me protection now?"

"Looks to me like your *homies* aren't up for the job. You had to know Kong was going to extract revenge for the hit job on the west side."

Ramsey frowned. "What the fuck are you talking about?"

"C'mon now. You ain't heard? Your place isn't the only one that made the news last night." Caruso nodded toward the television.

Another reporter clutched a microphone in front of Lenny's Pawn Shop. The news crawl reported fifteen people dead.

"What the fuck is this shit?" Ramsey punched up the volume.

Caruso's grin stretched. "Lenny's is Kong's property, isn't it?"

"That crazy muthafucka thinks *I* pulled that hit?"

"Didn't you?" Crews challenged. "Makes sense why you were hit a few hours after the job."

Ramsey winced and grunted as he climbed out of bed. Once he was up with his cock swinging between his legs, he grabbed the top sheet and wrapped it around his waist. "What else happened?"

What do you mean?" Caruso asked.

"I mean, what are they not saying in the news reports?"

Caruso and Ramsey locked gazes for a drawn-out minute before Caruso answered, "The streets are saying an awful lot of money was jacked."

"How much we talking?"

"Enough to piss him off."

"How much?"

"Somewhere in the neighborhood of three million—according to the streets."

"Three *million*?"

Caruso shrugged. "Give or take."

"The streets are full of shit."

Ramsey's cell phone rang from the nightstand.

Alexis picked it up, glanced at the screen. "Unknown." She handed it over to Ramsey.

Ramsey looked at the screen.

"Aren't you going to answer it?" Caruso dared him.

Annoyed, Ramsey answered the call. "Yeah."

Kong's unmistakable voice rumbled over the line. "I want my muthafuckin' money."

"As much as I'd like some *chump* change, you got the wrong muthafucka on this one."

"Nah, nigga. I got the right one. And you got forty-eight hours to make this shit right—or I guarantee you've seen your last fuckin' birthday."

Click.

"Kong?" Ramsey pulled the phone from his face and saw on the screen the call had ended. "Fuck!" He tossed the phone onto the bed and ran his hand through his hair. "That nigga is trippin' if he thinks I'm about to un-ass three million dollars."

"He's likely to declare war," Caruso warned.

"Then it's fuckin' war."

"So, you *won't* be needing some protection insurance?"

Ramsey groaned.

"C'mon." Caruso opened his arms. "It'll be like old times."

Twelfth District Chicago Police Department

Commander Robinson stood at his office door when Karl and Elliot returned to the department. "Ah, Officer Nelson. Come in here."

A dozen pairs of eyes swiveled in Karl's direction. "It looks like *somebody* is in trouble."

"Cut it out." Karl shoved his partner before switching directions to head toward the commander's office. As he sliced across the department, some of the guys made childish remarks, like he was a wayward kid headed off to the principal.

When he arrived at Robinson's office, Karl saw the commander wasn't alone. Superintendent Whitehead stood next to Robinson looking like white sculpted marble. If it weren't for the occasional eye blink, Karl wouldn't have believed he was real.

"Come on in and shut the door," Robinson ordered.

"Yes, sir." Karl followed the commander's instruction while his stomach looped into knots. *What did I do?* Had Mrs. Berry called and filed a complaint against him?

"Have a seat," was the next order.

"Yes, sir." Karl made it to the chair in front of the commander's desk. When he sank into the seat, he was an ant staring up at two giants. Was he going to get suspended? Fired? He prepared for the worst, but the knots in his stomach made it impossible.

"Congratulations." Robinson broke into a smile. "I'm pleased to see you taking the initiative to move your career in the right direction."

The unexpected praise gave Karl mental whiplash. "I'm sorry. What?"

"You've made detective, son." Whitehead's voice was as hard as his facial features. "Impressive work on both your oral and written exams. I have no doubt you'll make one hell of a detective for the department." He stepped forward and offered his hand.

Karl sprang from his seat and accepted the handshake. "Thank you, sir. I-I hope to make you proud." He told himself to release the superintendent's hand, but he couldn't get himself to stop pumping it. He'd never been this excited.

"Yes, I'm sure you will." The superintendent snatched his hand free and shook it at his side to get the blood flowing again.

"There's more news." Robinson moved toward his chair behind the desk.

"Sir?" *Get ready for the other shoe to drop.*

"We're putting you with the Special Task Force," Robinson announced, dropping into his chair. "The anti-gang division, headed by Detective Caruso."

"Vice?" Karl needed to sit, but he remained standing. "I see."

"Detective Caruso and his men are doing a hell of a job out there. On paper, they are pulling some impressive numbers, making record numbers of busts, closing cases . . ."

Karl cocked his head and swung his gaze between the two men. "But?"

"There's no 'but,'" Robinson lied. "Only, we want to make sure everything is running as smoothly as it appears on paper."

"There have been a *few* complaints," Whitehead corrected. "Some questionable tactics and offenses used by the division, including unprovoked shootings, beatings, planting false evidence, dealing in narcotics, and perjury to cover up these . . . offenses."

Karl's gaze swung between the men again. "I see."

"Do you?" Robinson bridged his hands together.

"I think so. You're asking me to spy on Caruso and his men. To be a blue snitch."

"We're asking you to make sure this department doesn't have a Rampart scandal brewing under our noses. The city is already battling bankruptcy with a record number of civil cases in the last five years alone. If we have corrupt cops in our midst, it's up to us to root them out."

"Yeah . . ." Karl frowned.

"But?" Robinson asked.

"*But* you know what happens to cops who cross the blue line for Internal Affairs. I'm no kamikaze pilot."

"All we're asking you to do is to keep your eyes and ears open. That's it. No one will ever know."

Karl didn't believe them.

Robinson tried again. "I understand your concerns. This is a big risk, and we're more than prepared to reward you for—how should I say it?"

"Risking my neck?"

Robinson and Whitehead nodded together.

"Yes, you will be putting your neck out on the line," Robinson added. "But one hand washes the other. I can see you moving up the ranks in this department."

"The sky is the limit," Whitehead agreed.

"Yeah?"

They nodded again.

Still, Karl hesitated.

Whitehead slapped a hand on his shoulder. "Why don't we give you, say—the night to think it over? Whatever you decide to do, we'll respect your decision. But we're hoping you'll come on board."

Charlie headed out to Lake Shore Drive to see Ramsey. No better way to prove you're a mogul on the rise than living in the Chicago Gold Coast neighborhood. It was a long way from where he and Hennessey had grown up. With last night's shooting all over the news, she wanted to make sure Ramsey also had made it out of the Emperor's Club all right before heading out for her first job interview.

Arriving at the address Billie had given her, Charlie couldn't help but be impressed. The only eyesore, at the moment, were the two news media vans parked out front of the penthouse building. *What if they recognize me?*

She dismissed the thought. It had been more than five years. Her fifteen minutes of fame had long expired.

Not wanting to deal with valet, Charlie parked against the curb across from the high-rise. As she killed the engine, her gaze swept toward two cars behind the news vans in front of the penthouse. A driver chilled out behind the wheel. Her hackles rose after her first casual glance at the man. She removed her shades and leaned over her wheel to get a better look. The distance made it difficult. With an empty car parked between them, Charlie relied on the man's side-view mirror. She had a view of his beard and full lips, but his eyes remained hidden behind a pair of mirrored sunglasses. Unable to place the face, she shook off the bad feeling and grabbed her purse.

Ramsey's penthouse building's front door opened, and Officers Vic Caruso, Chris Crews, and Thomas Graham strolled out like there was a red carpet underneath their feet.

Charlie froze as oxygen evaporated out of the car. Her eyes had to be playing tricks on her. But it wasn't a trick.

"Fuckin' uppity bitch thinks she's too good for this dick!" Caruso's large hand locked around her neck again.

Charlie's heart pounded in her ears. She was in the back of the van again. With them clawing at her underwear. *"Henny!"*

"Scream all you want to," the cop growled. "That dead nigga can't help you."

Charlie's hands clenched on the steering wheel as she watched the news reporters flock to the cops, who warded off their questions. Caruso and Crews hopped into one car while Thomas slid in next to a maple-colored man with a discolored birthmark stretched across the left side of his face . . .

Jace Wallace. She blinked. The old gang was still thick as thieves.

Her brain struggled to process this while Caruso and his team pulled away from the curb. Charlie had only a second to think before she started her car again and followed.

CHAPTER 12

"A new team member?" Caruso repeated, swinging his sharp gaze between his commander and the superintendent. "Aren't me and my guys posting good numbers?" Robinson's plastic smile extended. "The task force's numbers are impressive. I'm sure you know that, which is why you've earned yourself another member on the team. We want to put our resources behind what's working."

Caruso nodded as his smile tightened. "My team . . . we run a tight unit."

"I'm sure you'll find Detective Nelson to be a good team player."

"Detective Nelson?" Caruso ran the name through his memory Rolodex and drew a blank.

"Karl Nelson. He made detective today."

"So, me and my guys will be training him also?"

"He's an open book. I have complete confidence in your team showing him the ropes."

Caruso had no choice in the matter and kept smiling. "I'm sure this Nelson guy will be a great addition to the team."

"Excellent." Robinson buoyed out of his chair and waltzed around his desk to shake Caruso's hand. "Nelson's paperwork is still being processed, but he'll be transferred over to your division before the end of the week."

"Looking forward to it." Caruso gave an extra pump to the handshake before turning toward Whitehead and shaking his clammy hand as well.

"Good to see you again, Caruso." Whitehead flashed his blinding white veneers.

"You, too, sir." After a final head nod, Caruso spun toward the door and marched out. An hour later, he and his team met up at Dugan's and hunched over four frosted beer glasses.

"How is this going to work with another member on the team?" Crews asked nervously. "Are we going to have to watch everything we do and every word we say around this guy?" He inched across the table toward Caruso. "It's going to make collecting street taxes difficult, don't you think?"

Caruso nodded and backhanded the beer foam from his upper lip. "Difficult, but not impossible."

Thomas shook his head. "I don't like it."

"I don't, either," Jace agreed. "Especially after pulling the last job. The streets are hot. We're already watching our backs like a muthafucka, and now we have to watch our fronts, too?"

"Are you guys finished bitching?" Caruso caught the bartender's attention and signaled for another round of drinks.

Crews's face twisted. "You mean, this shit is cool with you?"

"No," Caruso snapped. "But I fail to see what bitching about it is going to do. It's not like I could tell Robinson we didn't need another member on the team. He shoved the guy down my throat."

"Whoa." Jace leaned forward. "Shoved how? What did he say?"

"Nothing—other than they wanted to put their resources behind what's working." Caruso shrugged. "They complimented our bust numbers and then said Detective Nelson is a *good* team player."

Thomas frowned. "What the hell is that supposed to mean?"

"Shit." Jace shook his head. "Do you think Robinson is planting an inside guy?"

Their drinks arrived by way of a perky crème au lait–skinned black chick with a giant golden-blond Afro. "Here you go, boys." She plunked down their frosty mugs and removed their empty ones. "Enjoy."

"Will do." Jace followed the sway of her hips as she walked away. When he faced the guys again, he wore a big Kool-Aid smile. "What?"

"Why don't you put yourself out of your misery and ask the girl for her phone number already?"

"Don't worry. I'm going to make my move."

Thomas laughed. "When?"

"Don't worry about it."

"Can you two knuckleheads focus?" Crews barked before returning his attention to Caruso. "How about it? Do you think this Nelson guy is a plant for Robinson?"

Caruso wanted to reassure his guys, but the question had been running through his mind since he'd walked out of Robinson's office, too.

"Vic?" Crews needled.

"I don't fuckin' know, a'ight? He *could* be. So, until we can figure this Detective Nelson out, we're going to have to be careful. Cross every T and dot every I."

"And if he *is* a plant?" Crews pressed.

Caruso didn't want his thoughts to go down that road, but with three sets of eyes leveled on him, he considered the worst-case scenario. "If Detective Nelson is a plant, we'll take care of him."

"Wait. What does that mean?" Jace asked, shifting his gaze around the table. "Are we talking about"—he glanced around and lowered his voice—"killing a cop? Are you fuckin' serious?"

"Nothing is concrete," Caruso hissed, leaning into Jace's

face. "But if the situation ever calls for it, are you telling me you would have a problem with it?"

Jace blinked. "Nah, nah. I want to make sure I understand what we're talking about. That's all."

The table went silent.

Jace stressed, "I'm down for whatever needs to be done."

"Yeah?" Caruso challenged.

"Yeah." Jace forced a smile. "You know me. I've always got your back. Always."

Caruso's gaze shifted to the other guys. "What about the rest of you? Any questions about what we might be up against? What we might have to do?"

Crews and Graham looked at each other and shook their heads.

"Good." Caruso grinned. "We're all on the same page."

At the opposite end of the pub, Charlie sat hunched in a corner booth hiding her face behind her hair and large sunglasses. For over an hour, she nursed a glass of bourbon on the rocks while she remained laser-focused on the four cops who'd ruined her life. The grinning and laughing boiled her blood. Buried terror from the back of that van roared to the surface.

Over and over.

She was a soldier—but it was four against one. She couldn't take them. After all her military training, she couldn't take them on. Tears seeped from beneath her sunglasses. Charlie made a quick swipe at them as the blond-Afro waitress made it to her table.

"Is there anything else I can get you?"

Charlie shook her head. "No, I'm good."

"Are you sure? We serve hot wings, nachos, and some mean burgers." She smiled. "The jalapeño bacon double cheeseburger is my favorite."

"Sure, fine. Whatever. I'll have that."

The waitress's smile widened with a wink. "You'll thank me later." She sauntered off with an extra bounce in her step, and Charlie wondered whether the Afro-punk waitress was flirting with her. She shook her head and refocused her attention on Caruso and his gang. By the time she'd drained her bourbon, her burger had arrived.

However, she only took one bite before Jace Wallace stood from his booth alone, tossed some money down on the table, and saluted his boys a good night.

"How is the burger?" the waitress asked, springing up from nowhere.

"It's great. Thanks." Charlie grabbed her purse, also tossed down a few twenties, and scooched her way out of the booth.

"You're leaving?" the waitress asked.

"Yeah, sorry. But the burger was great." She flashed a smile and maneuvered around the stunned waitress to follow Wallace out of Dugan's.

Outside, Wallace was already pulling out of the parking lot, and Charlie had to rush to her car. It took her no time to find him on the road. She hung back a couple of car lengths and followed him across town.

Charlie glanced at herself in the rearview mirror. "What are you doing, Charlie?" She had no idea. Wallace pulled up to a ranch-style home around the corner from Evergreen Park. When he parked in the driveway, it was the only car. *Does he live alone?*

Charlie stopped at a curb two houses down and across from Wallace's place, and killed the lights. *Now what?*

Wallace's car keys jingled as he jogged up to his front door, grabbed the mail out of a box, and let himself inside. If he'd turned on a light, it wasn't visible to the front of the house. Charlie scanned the quiet neighborhood twice before going for her door handle. After silently climbing out of the car, Charlie crept toward Wallace's place and cased the house, peeking through windows and checking to make sure there wasn't a dog around, waiting to snatch a bite out of her ass if she broke in.

If?

When.

It was happening. It had to happen. All the windows were locked—except for the kitchen. And when it moved, Charlie's heart almost stopped. She hesitated for a second and then used a lawn chair to hoist herself inside.

Once in, Charlie closed the window and struggled to climb out of the sink. A black cat meowed from the kitchen counter. Startled, Charlie hit the faucet's lever and turned on the water.

"Shit." She scrambled to shut it off and froze. No fucking way Wallace hadn't heard her. Sitting in the sink in wet clothes, Charlie waited for the cop to charge in, shooting.

But it didn't happen.

The cat jumped off the counter and dashed out of the kitchen.

Relieved, Charlie resumed climbing out of the sink. From the corner of her eye, she spotted a butcher block filled with knives. It wasn't a .45, but it could work. She gripped one handle and pulled out a 12-inch blade. The steel gleamed from the moonlight behind her. Charlie crept out of the kitchen on her tiptoes, relieved to find both the dining room and the living room cloaked in darkness. However, she was still able to make out the cat's yellow eyes as she moved past it, hissing from the back of a La-Z-Boy.

In the hallway, Charlie heard the steady water flow from a showerhead. She relaxed, but her hackles stood, and her heart enlarged in her throat. She didn't think; she relied on her instincts.

The last time she'd inched toward danger, she was a soldier in Jalalabad, Afghanistan, weighed down with seventy pounds of gear and armed with an M4 rifle.

Now this was a different kind of combat.

The deep piled carpet swallowed the sound of Charlie's footsteps as she moved down the long hallway. She passed a closet and an empty bathroom. The first bedroom she came across was apparently a home office. The second bedroom was a kid's bedroom—a girl's, judging by the pink walls and boy-band posters. It was also empty.

Something in the air shifted, and her gut instinct told her to duck. A muffled gunshot fired. A bullet whizzed by Charlie's head. When she glanced over her left shoulder, Wallace stepped out from the corner of the last bedroom with his weapon leveled on her.

"Who the fuck are you?" he barked.

Charlie straightened but kept a firm grip on the knife at her side.

"Wait." Wallace's face twisted as recognition settled in. "I know you." He took another step into the hallway. "What the fuck are you doing in my house?"

Charlie glared and willed him to move closer.

"When did you get out of jail?"

She didn't answer.

Wallace glanced down the hallway. "Who else is in the house with you?"

Silence.

He adjusted his grip on the weapon. "Answer me."

Charlie smiled.

"What the fuck is wrong with you?" Wallace took a half step forward and another nervous glance down the hall.

It was all Charlie needed to drop low and launch forward.

Startled, Wallace delayed his tap on the trigger and missed.

Charlie didn't.

The butcher knife pierced below the left side of his rib cage and sank deep.

Stunned, Wallace dropped his gun and slumped against Charlie. His eyes were as wide as silver dollars.

"Scream all you want to," he'd growled once. *"That dead nigga can't help you."*

Charlie never stopped smiling. "Fuck you, you sick son of a bitch. Who is going to help you now?" She stepped back, pulling the knife out with her.

Wallace dropped to the floor like a stone. He wheezed and gurgled blood while he attempted to plug the hole in his gut with his hands. Four large house cats crept down the hallway toward their owner. They meowed and rubbed their bodies against him as they licked the blood seeping between his fingers and staining the carpet.

The smile melted off Charlie's face as she squatted across from him and watched as death drained the color from his face and the light from his eyes. Satisfied, Charlie stood. "One down. Three to go."

CHAPTER 13

"Where the hell have you been?" Billie snapped. "It's almost midnight. We've been looking all over the place for you."

Charlie looked up, unprepared for the interrogation.

Billie relaxed. "Yes. She's here now," she said into the phone tucked under her chin. "Yes, she is in one piece. Let me talk to her and call you back later." She nodded. "I promise. All right. 'Bye."

Charlie headed toward the guest room, hoping her sister would get the picture that she wasn't in the mood to talk.

She didn't.

Billie trailed behind Charlie like a mother hen. "Well?" Billie asked.

"Well, what?" Charlie burst into the spare room and made a beeline behind the four-paneled room divider and stripped out of her jacket. She froze at the amount of blood splattered on her clothes.

"Aren't you going to tell me where you've been?" Billie needled. "We've been calling everyone we could think of, looking for you."

"Sorry."

"Sorry? That's it?" Billie thundered. "Why didn't you

go to your job interview? Jaleel pulled some strings to get it for you."

Charlie sighed. "I changed my mind."

Billie crossed her arms and waited for Charlie to say more, but when it was clear Charlie wasn't going to add to her explanation, Billie blew a gasket. "That's it?"

Charlie stripped out of her bloody clothes. "Tell Jaleel I appreciate him getting me the job interview, but sitting behind a desk for hours isn't the direction I want to go."

"Why didn't you say something sooner?"

"I know. I'll make it up to him." Charlie slipped on her robe and picked up her bloody clothes from the floor. *Now what?* She grabbed her jacket and wrapped her clothes in it. She left them balled up on the floor behind the divider before stepping out and squeezing past Billie at the door. "I'm going to take a shower."

Billie followed Charlie to the hallway bathroom. "Wait. What are you going to do for a job?"

"I don't know. Maybe I'll go into business for myself." She turned on the shower.

"Business? What kind of business?"

"Now, that, I don't know yet. But anything is better than explaining a criminal record and begging someone for a job."

Billie folded her arms. "You still should have said something sooner."

"I didn't think of it until today."

"You had five years to think about it."

Charlie sucked in a breath.

Billie tossed up her hands. "Okay, but why didn't you answer your phone?"

"Billie, enough. I'm going to take a shower now." Charlie closed the door in Billie's face and locked it. Once underneath the stream of hot water, Charlie's emotions flooded her. She felt everything—except regret.

CHAPTER 14

King Kong and his entourage entered 103.3 WVCX radio station and exchanged dabs, fist bumps, and half-shouldered bro-hugs with the popular morning host and his crew. After the station's music playlist and commercials, the host, Mike Ryan, wasted no time getting to the talk of the town.

"Did you and your crew shoot up the Emperor's Club?"

Kong laughed. "Damn, homey. You're gonna come straight at me like that? What are you, a cop?"

"We keep everything one-hundred around here," Ryan said, pointedly. "The streets are hot. Big Man Ramsey is walled up in some undisclosed location after his birthday party was blasted up. I *know* you at least came here to speak on this."

Kong bobbed his head. "You're right." He stroked his beard. "People are being reckless with my name out there. But you know—hey. Even that shit is part of the game."

"So, you're denying having anything to do with the shooting?"

"I wasn't there."

"You weren't there," Ryan repeated, cocking his head.

"That's right."

"But did you have anything *to do with* the shooting?"

Kong laughed. "That P. Diddy wannabe got enemies in every area code. Maybe dude wouldn't have to dodge bullets if he paid artists. Most of RawDawgs' acts only see money on the first and the fifteenth, if you catch my drift."

Ryan and the crew laughed.

"Ah, damn, Kong," Ryan said. "You're calling him out like that?"

"You keep it one-hundred, right?"

"Yeah."

"Well, then. Ramsey is so broke, he's out here pulling stickup jobs to cover payroll. His label hasn't been shit since Ramsey had Chicago PD cap his partner years ago."

"Oooh." The morning crew all chimed together.

Ryan said, "You're kicking dust off all the old conspiracy theories, now?"

"I'm spitting the truth, man. We all know Hennessey was the genius behind RawDawgs. Since Ramsey's takeover, he ain't done shit but polluted the airways with five-and-dime rappers he picked up out in the pill-popping suburbs. Time is ticking for Ramsey and his fifteen minutes of fame, you hear me?"

"For real?" Ryan laughed.

"Word is bond. But that's all right. He's gonna pay my shit back—*with* interest."

Billie shut off the radio. "Enough of that."

Charlie stewed over her cooling coffee. "What did he mean?"

"Who?" Billie picked up her empty breakfast plate and carried it to the sink.

Charlie frowned. "Kong. What did he mean about Ramsey and the Chicago PD?"

"Psst." Billie rolled her eyes. "Don't pay that bullshit any mind. Kong is spitting some street conspiracy theories. In a minute, he'll say Tupac is coming out of retirement and signing to Gorilla Beats."

Something was way off about the way Billie dismissed Kong. "You heard these conspiracy theories before?" Charlie asked.

"You haven't?" Billie volleyed, surprised. "I mean, there are so many of them."

"I want to hear the ones about Ramsey and the Chicago PD."

"Why? They are bullshit."

"Maybe." Charlie replayed Caruso and his men strolling out of Ramsey's high-rise.

"Maybe?" Billie laughed. "C'mon. I'm not a Ramsey fan, but even *I* know Ramsey and Henny were as thick as thieves. Brothers from different mothers. No way he had anything to do with what happened to you guys on the side of that road. No way. They were like brothers."

"*Like* brothers? Exactly."

"What are you saying?"

"I'm saying Cain killed Abel."

"You believe that mess?"

"I don't know what I believe anymore. I don't put anything past anyone."

"Yeah. But it's Ramsey. We've known him most of our lives. He loved Hennessey. They fought the same fights and dreamed the same dreams. Didn't you go over there and talk to him yesterday?"

"Uh, yeah."

"How is he doing? Is it true he got hit?"

"What?"

"That's the 411 on the streets. They're saying he got popped in the ass." Billie laughed.

"How is it that you always know what the streets are saying? Aren't you ever going to grow out of that bullshit?"

"Hell, no. This is Chicago. Conspiracy theories aside, street news is more accurate than the bullshit on TV."

Charlie rolled her eyes.

Billie returned to the table with a refreshed cup of coffee. "Anyway, the cops have no love for Ramsey, judging by the way they haul his ass in for every little thing. If anything, they're on Kong's payroll."

"What makes you say that?"

" 'Cuz Kong is the real Teflon Don in these streets. Niggas who cross his ass have a funny way of disappearing or being toe-tagged in the morgue. And Kong ain't caught a case yet. He hasn't done so much as a perp walk, though there are plenty of viral evidence crimes being committed on the Internet. Check it. Two years ago, Gorilla Beats' new star, Iron Bars, kicked up a bunch of dust about his contract. He wanted out. Word was, Kong felt some kind of way about him blasting their creative differences on every hip-hop station."

"What happened?"

"Nobody knows. Dude is a black Jimmy Hoffa. Ain't nobody been able to find so much as a hair from his ass anywhere. Some say he's dead. Some say he's chilling on an island with Tupac somewhere."

Charlie let the story sink in.

Billie sipped her coffee and evaluated Charlie. "You know, if I were you, I'd ignore all this shit. It's not going to do anything but rip a six-year-old scab open. You're not going to be able to keep the past behind you and move on listening to any of it."

Charlie leveled her sister with a cold stare. "Move on? Is that what you think I'm trying to do?"

Billie frowned. "Aren't you?"

Sitting on a donut in the back of a black Escalade, Ramsey growled and gritted his teeth while listening to Kong's bullshit on the radio. With each syllable the man spoke, Ramsey's blood pressure elevated. Muthafucka was straight-up lying through his teeth about not having anything to do with the shooting. The way Ryan and his crew laughed and cackled,

Ramsey couldn't tell whether the morning crew was buying in to the steaming pile of shit the rapper–slash–drug lord shoveled or not.

It didn't matter.

Ramsey had something for Kong's ass. He and Dominic sat outside the radio station and waited for Kong's "interview" to wrap up. After forty-five excruciating minutes had passed, Ryan thanked Kong for coming through and clearing the air.

"My pleasure. My pleasure," Kong said. Over the air, listeners heard the slapping of palms before Ryan played Gorilla Beats' latest number-one hit to close out the interview.

Ramsey sent one text: **Get ready**.

Minutes later, the glass door to the radio station opened, and two large men stepped out ahead of Kong while two larger men pulled up the rear. The next thirty seconds passed in a blur.

Ramsey's men, led by Rashid and Trudy, sped down the road, jumped the curb, and sprayed bullets everywhere.

Kong's first two men fell like dominoes.

Kong whipped out his piece and returned fire like a true street soldier—along with the two bodyguards behind him.

But they were outnumbered.

Another car jumped the curb and gave temporary shelter to Kong. It also gave him and his last bodyguard standing enough time to dive into the back seat before it sped off.

"Fuck!" Ramsey shouted, watching the whole thing play out. He couldn't believe his eyes. Kong got away. While he stood, watching the chaos and cries for help, Ramsey's cell phone trilled.

UNKNOWN appeared on the screen.

Ramsey accepted the call. "Yeah."

"You missed, asshole."

CHAPTER 15

"Welcome to the team." Caruso jutted out his hand.

"Glad to be aboard," Karl responded.

Caruso crushed his hand and pumped his arm roughly.

Karl smiled and let his new team leader take his measure. He took Caruso's as well. The man appeared to be everything he'd heard: intense, sharp, and dangerous. There was something about his eyes that set Karl on edge. When the exchange drifted into awkward territory, Caruso released his death grip. The other two task force members, Crews and Graham, also gave his hand a few more pumps and even added a couple of whacks on Karl's back.

"Hope you can keep up."

"Don't worry about me." Karl looked around. "Are we missing someone?"

Caruso looked at his watch. "Yeah. Wallace is running late. He can catch up when his beauty rest is over, I guess."

A knock sounded on the strike team's door before Detective Norman stuck her head inside. "We have a shooting downtown. Possible gang-related. Commander wants your team down there, ASAP."

Caruso sighed. "We're on it."

* * *

Charlie was in the middle of deciding what to do with last night's bloody clothes when Billie hammered once on her door and burst inside. "What the hell?" She tossed the bundled clothes back behind the four-paneled divider and glared at her sister. "If I'm not able to get any privacy around here, I'll have to get my own place," she warned.

"There's been a shooting," Billie announced, ignoring Charlie's words.

"What?"

Billie grabbed Charlie by the wrist and dragged her back out to the living room, where the morning news reporter stood outside of the WVCX radio station.

> *"The chaos downtown has calmed considerably, where minutes ago a mass shooting left three men dead. Eyewitnesses claim the victims were bodyguards to famed rapper and music executive King Kong. Kong was a guest on the radio station this morning, clearing the air on whether he was involved in another mass shooting with label rival RawDawgs at the Emperor's Club Saturday night.*
>
> *"There is no word on whether the music mogul sustained injuries in today's shooting. All we know is that the shooters and the believed target, Mr. Kong, were able to get away. Back to you, Mark."*

Billie muted the television. "Can you believe it? Shit is getting crazy out there."

"You don't think . . . ?"

"Ramsey blazed his ass up?" Billie finished asking for her. "Hell, yeah. And everybody else with any sense believes it, too."

Charlie stood. "I have to go."

"What? Where are you going?"

Charlie didn't answer. Instead, she grabbed her purse and car keys and raced out the door.

The Gorilla Compound

"Muthafuckas took out three of my men and damn-near toe-tagged my ass in broad daylight, and you muthafuckas came here to harass me over some bullshit?" Kong barked at Caruso and his team. "You punk bitches become more of a joke every day."

Caruso hitched up a half smile. "Not as much of a joke as this Biggie/Tupac throwback bullshit you and Holt are kicking up. First of all, neither one of you is that damn talented. Second of all, you're drawing my city into your bullshit. Me and my guys are taking the shit personally."

"Is that right?" Kong chuckled.

"Yeah."

"Let me clue you in on some real shit. I'm a peaceful king, but niggas never stop coming for the crown. *Never.* Now, what would I look like if I let them knock me off?"

Caruso sighed and cocked his head.

"Exactly," Kong stressed, smiling. "I'd look like a false king. I can't have that. Anybody coming for the throne or undermining my kingdom, I gotta handle that shit. Feel me?"

Karl spoke up. "Meaning?"

King Kong swung his gaze to Karl for the first time and sized him up. "Who the fuck are you?"

"Ah," Caruso stepped next to Karl. "This is Detective Nelson. He's a new member of the team."

"Yeah?" Kong stared at Karl. "Why the fuck he eyeballin' me?"

Karl stepped up. "I'll eyeball you any muthafuckin' way I feel like it."

"Oh yeah?" Kong laughed. "I see you, nigga."

"You need to," Karl growled.

"All right. All right." Caruso pushed Karl behind him. "Enough with the introductions."

"Nah, nah. I'm admiring the balls on your new dude here.

Did you guys suck on his nuts before you let him on the team?" Kong cast another look around.

Karl growled, "Check this, I'm not your motherfuckin' bitch-ass mama or your faggot-ass daddy, and I don't give a fuck about you, so pipe your gorilla ass down."

"Now that you two have an understanding, let's move on," Caruso said.

Giving Karl a once-over before turning back to Caruso, Kong asked, "Where's Wallace?"

"Don't worry about it." Caruso squared up with Kong. "Now, are you going to get around to telling us your version of what happened outside the radio station or not?"

"I told you. Ramsey sent his goon squad to mow me down because he couldn't handle the truth I spat on the air. The punk muthafucka."

"And you know it was Ramsey for a fact?" Crews pressed.

"Absolutely."

"Proof?"

"What? Now, you want me to do *your* muthafuckin' jobs? You're supposed to get the proof, right?"

Caruso shook his head. "Just what I thought. Nothing to back it up with."

"I'll take my Spidey senses over your police hunches any day."

Caruso laughed as his gaze swung among his men before returning his attention to Kong. "Ramsey Holt let us in on his Spidey senses yesterday, too."

"Yeah?"

"Uh-huh." Caruso folded his arms across his chest. "His senses are telling him it was you and your gang of goons shooting up his club last night. You want to speak on that?"

Kong's grin wrapped around his face. "No, but I would have *loved* to have been a fly on the wall to see that shit. Word on the street is he took one in the ass."

"I'll confirm it." Crews chuckled.

Kong laughed. "Now, that's what's up."

"This beef ends now," Caruso thundered. "We're not about to let you guys turn the streets into Dodge City."

"This is Chi-raq. I don't go looking for trouble, but when it kicks in my door . . . I have the firepower to protect mine. Feel me?"

Caruso's gaze locked onto Kong. "Yeah, but you're not Teflon on this. We catch you escalating a gang war over this, and you can kiss your kingdom good-bye. You feel *me*?"

Kong smiled. "We'll see about that."

CHAPTER 16

Charlie arrived back out at Ramsey's Gold Coast high-rise building. Once again, news vans and police cars surrounded it. She parked in the same place she did the day before. This time, she stopped by a convenience store and purchased a White Sox cap. After piling her hair on top of her head and covering it with the cap, she slid on her large, mirrored sunglasses and climbed out of the car.

Okay. You can do this. Charlie jogged across the street, her heart hammering against her rib cage. "Excuse me. Please, let me through." She shouldered through the bank of reporters.

"Morning, ma'am." The doorman tipped his hat and opened the door for her.

"Morning." She rushed inside and crossed the marble-floored lobby toward the elevator bay. When the doors slid open, Charlie strolled inside and pushed the button for the fourteenth floor. However, when the door began to close, an older white lady thrust her arm inside to stop the doors from closing.

Charlie tamped her annoyance but stepped aside to give the woman more than enough room to enter the boxed compartment.

The woman's bright green eyes took Charlie's measure while she punched the button for the eighth floor. Once the doors closed, she burrowed herself in the corner and held on to her purse like it held gold bricks.

Charlie sighed and kept her gaze straight ahead. When they arrived at the eighth floor, she laughed at how fast the woman squirreled out of the elevator. On the fourteenth floor, Charlie exited the elevator and walked toward another elevator bay that serviced the penthouse floors.

Ramsey Holt owned the entire eighteenth floor.

When Charlie stepped out of the golden elevator, she approached two large bodyguards posted outside Ramsey's spot.

"I'm here to see Ramsey Holt," she told the men.

"Is he expecting you?" the largest of the two men asked.

"No, but I'm sure he *wants* to see me."

"Name?"

"Charlie Warren."

If the men recognized the name, they didn't let on. However, they did walkie-talkie into the penthouse and passed her name along. Immediately, they were told to let her through. The short man stepped forward.

"Raise your hands for me?"

"Excuse me?"

"Hands."

Charlie sighed but followed his orders for him to complete a quick pat down. When he was through, the other guard opened the front door for her.

"Thank you." She crossed the threshold into the palatial penthouse. Charlie had never considered herself to be materialistic. Money didn't impress her. However, she'd never been in a private residence with so much gold and marble in one place. It looked more like a French museum than a home. Were the RawDawgs rolling like this?

"Charlie," Alexis exclaimed, strutting on heels high enough to make them eye level. "Good to see you again."

"Nice to see you, too." Charlie leaned in for a hug but was surprised to receive kisses on each side of her face. When she recovered, she said, "I hope you don't mind my dropping by, but when I heard about the shootings, I wanted to make sure you and Ramsey were all right."

"Oh, girl. Yes." Alexis waved Charlie's concerns off. "You know how Negroes get when they get too much liquor in them. They can't stand to see anybody having a good time."

Charlie frowned while Alexis laughed.

"So, everything is all right?" Charlie asked.

"Never better," Ramsey thundered as he entered the room. His black gaze centered on Charlie as his smile stretched from ear to ear.

Charlie pulled away from Alexis as she noticed Ramsey's walk. "You're limping."

"Good eye," Ramsey joked. Once he was in front of her, he wrapped his long arms around her. "Looks like you left my party just in time."

"You were hit?"

"It's only a flesh wound." He released her. "How about your sisters? They cool?"

"Johnnie twisted her ankle, but she'll live."

Ramsey sighed. "Send her my love. I hate that shit went down like that. Come on in and sit down." He looked at his girl. "Get us some drinks, Alexis."

"Um, yeah. Sure." Alexis's smile wobbled at her guest before she turned and followed her man's instructions.

Ramsey looped Charlie's arm through his and escorted her to a salon that looked as if it belonged in Versailles. Too much gold, too much marble, and too much glass.

"So, how do you like your boy? A long way from the South Side, huh?"

"Definitely." She took another glance around.

"Go ahead. Sit down," Ramsey directed, but he remained on his feet.

"Any idea who was behind the shooting?"

"Yeah, I have an idea, all right. The same muthafucka who's been sweating Henny and me since back in the day."

"Kong?"

"The one and only. Muthafucka done lost his mind, though."

"Yeah, I heard Kong on the radio this morning," Charlie told him.

Ramsey smirked. "Hmph. You don't believe that bullshit he was spitting on the radio, do you? The shit ain't nothing but fake news."

Charlie didn't respond.

"Anyway, Kong out there writing checks his ass can't cash."

"Yeah, I heard about the second shooting after the interview. Your work?"

Ramsey's eyes narrowed.

Charlie cocked a smile. "Don't worry. Your boys patted me down before I entered."

Ramsey smiled back. "Sorry, but you know how it is. A brother can never be too careful."

Alexis arrived in the salon, beaming. "I hope you like green tea."

"Love it," Charlie said.

Ramsey frowned. "We don't have anything stronger?"

Alexis looked crushed. "I figured since it's not yet noon . . ."

Ramsey lifted a brow.

"I'll fix you a drink." Alexis set the tea tray down.

"Thanks, babe." Ramsey slapped her on the ass when she passed.

Charlie shook her head and filled her teacup. Ramsey's gaze followed her every move. When she glanced up at him, he wasn't embarrassed to have been caught staring.

"It's good to have you back," he said.

"It's good to be back."

He nodded while his smile shrank. "You sure didn't waste any time getting booed up."

Charlie thoughts returned to Karl.

"What was the dude's name?"

"Not your business."

"I'm just looking out. It's what Henny would've wanted."

"Here you go, honey," Alexis singsonged as she returned to the room.

"Thanks, babe." Ramsey took his drink and gestured for her to exit the room. "Give us a few minutes."

Alexis's cheerfulness dimmed as she swung her gaze between Ramsey and Charlie. "Sure, sweetie." She backtracked out of the room while suspicion crept into her features.

"Alexis doesn't look too happy."

"She'll live." Ramsey chuckled. "A little competition would do her some good."

"Competition?"

His grin expanded again.

"It's never gonna happen."

He moved over to the sofa and eased onto the thick cushion next to her. "Haven't you ever learned to never say never?"

"It's *never* going to happen."

"But that Henny wannabe scored, right?" He touched the hickey on the side of her neck.

She flinched away.

Ramsey held up his hands and leaned back. "My bad—but what do you know about this guy?

"I know all I need to know—and so do you."

"All right. All right. I'll let it go . . . for now."

"Boss, the police are here," someone announced over the salon's speaker.

Charlie sprang out of her seat as if the cushion had caught fire. "I have to get out of here."

"Whoa." Ramsey chuckled. "That's usually *my* line."

Charlie's panic escalated. "You got to get me out of here."

Ramsey saw her fear was real. "All right." He stood. "Babe!"

Alexis sprang into the salon like she'd been hovering around the corner.

"Take Charlie to the emergency exit. ASAP."

"You got it, Daddy." Alexis crooked a finger for Charlie to follow her. "Come with me."

Charlie rushed behind Alexis to an in-house studio. Alexis rushed to a paneled wall and pushed something. The panel opened up, and a door appeared.

"It's an elevator," Alexis said. "It'll take you to the building's basement. Hang a right, and it will lead you to the back of the building."

"Thanks." Charlie stepped into the compartment and glanced back up at Alexis.

"We're happy, you know," Alexis insisted. "Ramsey and me."

Charlie struggled to keep a smirk off of her face. "Of course you are."

The door closed.

"Detective Caruso," Ramsey greeted with false warmth. "I must not be living right if I'm seeing your ugly mug in my crib twice in two days."

"That's my consensus, too." Caruso strolled into the penthouse with his blue gang pulling up the rear.

Ramsey's gaze landed on Nelson. "A new recruit?"

Caruso followed Ramsey's gaze. "Good eye. This is Detective Nelson. You and Kong are giving him a crash course in the city's gangster label bullshit. Nelson, this is the RawDawgs' maestro, Ramsey Holt."

"We've met," Ramsey said.

"Yeah?" Caruso's gaze swung between the two men.

Nelson nodded. "Briefly."

Ramsey glared. "We have a mutual friend."

"Is that right?" Caruso frowned.

Ramsey inched toward Nelson and inspected him. A tension built within seconds. "It's uncanny, you know."

"What?" Nelson beat Caruso in asking.

Ramsey chuckled. "Don't tell me you guys don't see the resemblance."

When the other cops looked confused, Ramsey went to the table, picked up a silver-framed photograph, and held it up next to Nelson's face.

The boys in blue stepped closer until a light clicked on over their heads.

"Fuck," Caruso said. "Damn near a spitting image—except for the hair."

"Exactly."

"Are you related to Hennessey Rawlins?" Graham asked, frowning.

Nelson pushed the frame from his face. "Nah, no relation."

Suspicion remained on the cops' faces.

Nelson frowned. "My family roots are out of Georgia. But you know . . . slave trade. Anything is possible."

Caruso hitched up a corner of his mouth and returned his attention to Ramsey. "We didn't come here to sketch out Nelson's family tree."

"Nah?" Ramsey returned the frame to the glass table. "What did you come here for?"

"So, we're playing dumb now?"

"I don't know. Are we?"

"Someone sprayed bullets all over downtown, trying to take your man, King Kong, out."

Ramsey's lips twitched.

"Now, this is the part where you lie to me and tell me you had nothing to do with it."

"I had nothing to do with it."

"That's what I figured."

The cops snickered.

"Tell you what," Caruso said. "Why don't we take a trip downtown and you can tell us where you were this morning?"

Graham's cell phone trilled.

Caruso glared at Graham for the distraction.

Graham held up a finger and turned his back to answer the call.

"I went out for a drive," Ramsey answered Caruso's question.

"Downtown?"

"I may have passed through there, but I didn't shoot nobody."

"All the same. Let's take a ride." Caruso removed his handcuffs.

"Uh, Vic," Graham interrupted.

"What?"

"This is gonna have to wait. We're going to have to get over to Wallace's."

Caruso frowned.

"He's dead."

CHAPTER 17

"It's so good to see you, baby." Betty Rawlins wrapped her arms around Charlie and squeezed. "I didn't think these old eyes would ever get to see your sweet face again."

"It's good to see you, too."

"C'mon in. Let's get you out of the cold." Betty stepped back and allowed Charlie to enter the house.

The warm, familiar sights and smells of Betty's home stirred old memories of hanging out here most of her childhood years. When Charlie hung her coat in the closet, she remembered her first kiss, playing Ten Minutes in Heaven during Henny's twelfth birthday party. In the living room, or what was once referred to as the playroom, she couldn't count the number of Monopoly and Domino games they'd played on the coffee table. And the couch, which must have been a family heirloom from the seventies, was where so many Netflix-and-chill nights went down before it was ever called that.

As she took her seat, she sniffed the air. "Ginger cookies."

Betty grinned. "Just took them out of the oven. Would you like some?"

"Do you have to ask?"

Betty laughed as she patted Charlie's shoulder before walking to the kitchen. "Would you like some warm milk or tea?"

"Tea would be nice." Charlie stood back up and looked at the photographs on the tables and walls. It was a colorful timeline of Betty Rawlins's life and the husband she'd lost in the Gulf War. Hennessey, her only son, she'd raised on her own. Charlie was on the wall, too—for the three proms Hennessey had escorted her to. Emotions rumbled around like tumbleweeds inside of her chest.

She entered Henny's old childhood bedroom and smiled at all the posters of sports and rap icons taped to the wall. On his dresser were more pictures of Charlie: Senior pictures, Valentine Day dates, and endless candid shots. She had all the proof she needed of how much she meant to him.

Charlie swiped away tears. If only she could turn back time . . .

"Charlie, baby? Your tea is ready," Betty called up the staircase.

"Oh, okay. Here I come." Charlie set down a photograph and took a step toward the bedroom door when she noticed a dip in the floorboard. Frowning, she stepped back and looked down. She pressed her foot on the board again, and it dipped. "What the hell?" Charlie squatted down and inspected the board. It wasn't even with the rest of the floor. She pulled at it until the board came up. "What the hell?" She pulled out a rusted metal box and opened it. Inside were bundles of hundred-dollar bills . . . and a gun.

Caruso and Crews dispatched Graham and Nelson to Wallace's place ahead of them while they listened to Ramsey's denials about having anything to do with the drive-by shooting outside of the radio station. With nothing concrete to hold Ramsey on, Caruso let him go with a warning.

By the time Caruso and Crews made it to Wallace's yellow-taped home, another set of news vans greeted them.

Caruso and Crews flashed their badges to the homicide team and were allowed past the yellow tape.

"What the hell happened?" Caruso asked Graham.

"Somebody speared him in the gut."

"Stabbing?"

"Yep. Wallace managed to squeeze off a shot, but he missed."

"So, what? A home invasion that went south?"

"That was my guess, but it doesn't look like anything was taken."

"Murder weapon?"

"Clean. Whoever it was, was smart enough to stick the damn thing in the dishwasher and cleaned it. I doubt we'll be able to get any prints off of it."

Crews hissed, "What about the . . ." He rubbed his fingers to indicate money.

Graham slapped Crews's hand down and glanced over his shoulder to make sure they were out of earshot of Nelson. "What the fuck, man?"

Crews insisted on an answer. "Well?"

"Nothing yet." Graham lowered his voice. "But if he stashed his cut in the house, it's only a matter of time before they find it."

The men shared worried looks.

"Is everything all right?" Nelson joined the men's huddle.

Before anyone had a chance to answer him, the forensics team ordered them out of the way so they could carry Wallace's bagged body out of the house. And five minutes later, the lead homicide detective, Jack Sturgis, carried a duffel bag filled with money out of Wallace's bedroom and plopped it on the coffee table in the living room for everyone to see. "Now, where in the hell would Detective Wallace get this kind of money?"

★ ★ ★

Karl made it to the Den Theatre with a bundle of roses in time to catch the last act of his sister's play. The moment she saw him backstage, she lit up.

"You made it." Kacie threw her arms around her brother's broad shoulders and allowed him to spin her around.

"Of course, I made it. No way was I going to miss my baby sister's opening night."

"You better not." She slapped him on the chest and introduced him to her thespian friends. When Kacie extended an invitation to an after-party, Karl declined and glanced at his watch.

"I have to meet up with some fellas on my new team. I told them I'd join them for a beer. If I rush, I might catch them before they leave."

"Are you saying my friends aren't cool enough?" Kacie laughed.

"Nah, you know how much I love hanging out with the theater crowd." He pretended to hang himself with a noose.

"Oh, see." She waved her finger at him. "You ain't right. Wait—there she is." Kacie gasped and clutched her brother's arm.

"There who is?" Karl craned his neck to scan the crowd.

"Johnnie Blackburn," Kacie whispered, excitedly. "She's one of the play's producers. She saved our asses on this production. I hope she liked it. C'mon."

Karl's gaze settled on the woman approaching them, and he choked on his drink.

"Hi," Kacie greeted her. "I hope you enjoyed the play."

"Enjoyed it? Are you kidding me? I loved it." Johnnie laughed. "You guys were great."

Kacie squealed as she threw her arms around Johnnie for a quick hug.

Karl stared.

"I hate that my husband wasn't here to see it." Johnnie

pulled out of Kacie's embrace. "He's in London on business for the rest of the month. But I'm FaceTiming him later to let him know how well everything went."

Husband? Karl couldn't believe what he was hearing.

"Oh, I almost forgot." Kacie smacked her head. "Where are my manners? Mrs. Blackburn, this is my brother, Karl. Karl, this is Mrs. Blackburn."

Johnnie cast her gaze toward Karl and froze.

Karl smiled. "I believe we've met."

Johnnie shook her head. "I don't think so."

Oh, she's going to play this game.

"There you are," a voice interrupted the awkward group. "I left you at the bar."

"Ah, Charlie." Johnnie accepted an offered drink. "I was just talking to the playwright and her brother, Karl."

Charlie looked up and froze.

"Karl, I'd like for you to meet my twin sister, Charlie. Charlie, this is Karl."

Karl wasn't aware when his mouth fell open, but he appreciated it when Kacie pushed up his chin to shut it.

Charlie smiled. "Yes, I believe we've met."

Kacie laughed. "Oh, I get it. You two met before, and you thought Johnnie was her sister."

Karl blushed. "My apologies. I—I thought I'd met all your sisters at the Emperor's Club."

Johnnie laughed. "Sorry, there is a handful of us. And since my husband tends to keep me knocked up, I never get to do anything as exciting as hanging out at clubs anymore."

The small group laughed.

"It's nice to see you again." Karl kept his gaze leveled on Charlie. "I didn't get a chance to say good-bye the last time."

Charlie's cheeks darkened. "Yeah, sorry about that."

Kacie took Johnnie by the arm. "Mrs. Blackburn, I hope you don't mind, but there are a few more people I'd like for you to meet." With that, Karl and Charlie were left alone.

"I might have made my sister uncomfortable."

Charlie chuckled. "Wow. That's a low bar. It would take an awful lot to embarrass any of my sisters. Believe me, I've tried."

Karl chuckled. "I would offer to get you a drink, but I see you already have one."

"It is an open bar."

"Damn, I was about to buy a round for the whole room."

"Ah. Big spender."

"Hardly." He glanced around. "What are my chances of whisking you away so we can—"

"Do a repeat performance?"

"—so we can talk," he finished.

"Talk?" she repeated, blinking.

"Yeah. I hear it's what people do when they want to get to know each other—vertically—with their clothes on."

"Sounds boring."

Karl laughed. "It'd be fun . . . with the right person."

Charlie sipped her drink. "I don't know if I'm ready to trade fantasy for reality yet."

"No?"

"Reality has been kicking me in the ass for a while now. I want simple. Easy."

"No strings attached," he filled in for her.

"Can you handle that?"

Karl smiled. "I can . . . for now."

CHAPTER 18

At Dugan's the next night, Caruso and the gang were back at their booth, huddled over frosted mugs and trying not to shit bricks over the amount of heat rolling their way.

"What the hell happened?" Graham asked Caruso. "A burglary that went south?"

"A burglar who doesn't steal anything?" Caruso asked. "I doubt it."

"A hit?" Crews asked.

Caruso rolled his shoulders and swiped the beer foam from his upper lip. "I'm not sure. Everybody on Kong's crew prefers bullets. In my experience, knives tend to be more personal—and a killer usually brings their own weapon."

"Where does that leave us?"

Caruso gave another roll of his shoulders. "I'm not sure. Was he seeing anyone?"

Graham and Crews's gaze scattered over to the blond-Afroed waitress and back to each other.

"He hasn't mentioned anyone special to me since Barbara and the kid moved out to her parents in California," Graham said.

"Why the fuck did he keep the shit in the house?" Crews wondered aloud.

"Maybe he thought it was safer than a bank," Graham defended.

"Not by much," Crews argued. "Please tell me you don't have your cut lying around the house, ready to declare to the whole world you're a thief."

"No, I'm saying Jace probably hadn't had time to stash the shit. That's all." Graham glanced over his shoulder. "Is Nelson coming?"

Caruso shrugged. "I invited him."

Crews shook his head. "A new team member couldn't have come at a worse time."

"Everything is going to be all right if everyone keeps their cool."

Crews laughed. "You believe that?"

"I do. We've gotten out of stickier jams with the department."

Graham nodded.

Crews shook his head. "It's not the department I'm fucking worried about. It's King Kong. When reports of the money hit the news, how long will it take Kong to put two and two together?"

"Are you back for another burger?" Bianca, the Afropunk waitress, asked before she flashed her perfect teeth.

Charlie pulled her gaze from the huddled cops and stared at the woman. "What?"

Bianca lifted her pad. "Your order. I figured since you didn't finish the one from the other night, you were back to try again."

"Oh, um, sure. And some water, please."

"Water?"

Charlie blinked.

"This is a pub. Alcohol is kind of our specialty."

"A beer," Charlie corrected her order.

"I didn't mean to pressure you." Bianca twirled a lock of hair around her finger. "I can get you the water if you want."

Charlie smiled though she was annoyed. "The beer and burger are fine. Thanks."

"All right. Coming right up." Bianca wrote down the order and drifted away from the table.

Charlie's gaze zoomed back across the pub to the huddled cops—but one of them was missing.

It was late by the time Karl made it to Dugan's. As he pulled into the parking lot, a face behind the wheel of a black Camry caught his attention. *Charlie?* He stopped at the parking lot's entranceway as she pulled out of the lot.

He honked his horn—but her attention was elsewhere, and she went ahead and hung a right into traffic.

"Shit." He wanted to back up, but there was a car waiting to turn into the pub's parking lot as well. Karl pulled ahead and circled in the lot to pull back out into traffic. However, Charlie, if it was her, was long gone. "Damn." Giving up, Karl returned to Dugan's.

Caruso grinned. "Look who decided to show up."

"Better late than never, eh?" Crew asked.

"Sorry, I'm late," Karl said. "I got here as soon as I could."

"Ah, a new member of the gang," the waitress said. "What can I get you to drink, handsome?"

Karl blinked at the size of the waitress's blond Afro. "Um, yeah. A beer would be good."

"You're in luck. I had a customer dip on me, so it's on the house." She set a frosted mug in front of him. "Hungry?"

"A burger is fine."

The waitress smiled. "Today is your lucky day." She plunked a burger down in front of him with a wink. "Bon appétit."

"Talk about fast service." Karl laughed and glanced at Caruso. "I can see why you guys like this place."

Caruso and Crews cocked uneven smiles at him.

"So, um, where is Graham?"

"He called it an early night," Caruso said.

"Yeah. He and Wallace were pretty tight," Crews added.

Karl nodded. "Yo, man. I'm sorry about your boy. Pretty fucked up. Heard anything else about what could have gone down?"

Caruso shook his head. "So far it looks like a burglary gone wrong."

Karl bobbed his head, but he wanted to ask about the money. However, his instincts told him not to. Instead, he let Caruso and Crews grill him. In the next hour, the two men learned everything there was to know about him. He was a third-generation cop, served three tours in Iraq, in his seventh year on the force, and he'd recently passed his detective exam.

It was a fishing expedition, and he had a hell of a time avoiding their hooks.

Charlie followed Detective Graham to Paulie's Auto Shop. Since it was the middle of the night and the place was closed, she couldn't imagine what the cop was doing there. But she hung back and waited.

After ten minutes, Charlie's patience waned. She retrieved Henny's gun from the glove compartment. When she climbed out of the car, she was a soldier again, on the move.

Ramsey called Billie for the fifth time that night. "Is she in yet?"

Billie sighed. "No, she's not. Why don't you tell me what this is about? You're making me nervous."

"You know if she's out with dude again?"

"Dude? Oh, you mean the guy from the club?"

Ramsey's grip on the phone tightened. "Yeah, that fake Henny wannabe muthafucka."

"I don't know—but I'm sure she'd tell both of us it's none of our business."

"I wouldn't be too sure about that," he grumbled.

"What do you mean?"

Ramsey sighed. "Have her call me when she gets in—or you could give me her cell number?"

"If she wanted you to have her number, she would have given it to you."

"What's up with you, Billie? How come you've never liked me?"

"'Night, Ramsey," Billie said. "I'll tell Charlie you called—again." Before he could say anything else, she hung up.

Ramsey pulled the phone from his ear and stared at it. "Ain't that about a bitch?"

Alexis stewed with her arms crossed on the other side of the bed. "What's so important you have to keep calling Charlie in the middle of the night?"

Ramsey set his cell phone down on the corner of the nightstand before easing into bed. "She needs to know that nigga from the club is a cop."

"Ain't that her business?" Alexis snapped.

He noticed her anger. "What's with you?"

"What the fuck do you think?" She did a full cobra neck while her gaze speared him. "The bitch ain't been out the joint a hot minute, and she already got your nose wide open."

"Don't." He pulled Alexis into his arms. "I'm only looking out for my man's girl. I know she don't want nothing to do with a pig after what happened to Big Homey. I'm tryin' to let her know what time it is. That's all." Ramsey nuzzled her neck.

Alexis stiffened and turned her head.

Her jealousy made his dick hard. He palmed one of her

breasts and shifted gears toward the weak spot behind her ears. "C'mon, baby. You know you're the only one for me."

As he predicted, Alexis softened.

It didn't matter he was spitting some bullshit to get some pussy today. Tomorrow, he'd reevaluate squashing the engagement. Since Charlie's return, all he could think about was how to get her into bed. He'd been in love with her forever—with Henny gone, why shouldn't he make his move?

Ramsey slid in between Alexis's legs, but it was Charlie who remained on his mind.

Karl tumbled into bed exhausted, but as soon as he closed his eyes, his cell phone rang. At first, he told himself to let the call go to voice mail, but the nagging voice in the back of his head warned him the call could be important. Sighing, he shot an arm from underneath his perfumed pillow and grabbed the phone without reading the screen.

"Yeah?"

"I like a man who plays hard to get."

Karl peeled open a single eyeball at the familiar voice. "Charlie?"

"Ah, you *do* remember me," she teased.

Karl sat up in bed. "Of course, I remember you. You're the chick who likes to hit it and quit it."

"Mind if I hit it again?"

"You're direct." He laughed.

"Is that a yes or a no?" she pressed.

He glanced around his disheveled but empty bedroom. "I could do with some company."

"Good."

His doorbell rang.

"Answer your door," Charlie told him.

"You're here?"

"I took a chance you'd say yes," she said. "But if you prefer I come back at another time . . ."

"No, no." Karl leaped out of bed. By the time he snatched open the front door, he was out of breath. "Hi there."

Charlie disconnected the call and slid her cell phone into her jacket. "Hello. Mind if I come in?" She strutted across the threshold and into his apartment.

"Make yourself at home."

"Don't mind if I do." Charlie unbuttoned her coat and let it slide to the floor. Underneath, she wore a sexy, red and black thong and garter set, and a smile bloomed across Karl's face as he closed the front door.

Charlie wasn't in the mood for small talk. She was still high off her second kill. In combat, it was called appetitive aggression or a lust for violence.

When Karl moved into her personal space, she jumped him.

"Whoa, whoa." Karl pushed her back a bit. "Slow down. What's the big rush?"

Charlie swiped his hands from her shoulders. "What can I say? You bring out the animal in me." She attacked him again, but this time Karl didn't put up any resistance, and they tumbled to the floor.

He watched her with a bemused grin as she raked his boxers off his hips. His dick sprang up like a titanium pole. Her devilish look melted the smile off his face.

"Don't hurt me," he warned.

"Oh, I'm not going to hurt you . . ." She crawled back up his body to straddle him. ". . . much." She shifted her thong to the side and slid down his cock, squeezing her pelvic muscles.

Karl rolled his head back. "Oh my God." His hands roamed over her hips and inched around to cup and squeeze her ass.

Once Charlie hit the base of his cock, she worked her hips into a figure eight a few times before sliding back up and down. She rolled her head back and called on the Almighty.

Karl's hands moved yet again. He placed the pad of his thumb against her clit while she bobbed up and down. Within seconds, Charlie released a strangled cry as her body exploded with the night's first orgasm.

Karl took control and flipped her around and beneath him. In no time, they'd worked up a sweat and wore a few more patches of rug burns on their knees. It was much later before they made it up to his bedroom for a few more rounds.

Charlie needed to go; however, after the fourth orgasm, she collapsed, exhausted.

Chuckling, Karl snuggled up beside her while planting kisses across her back.

Charlie quivered. "That tickles, Hennessey."

Karl froze, but instead of questioning her, he listened to her breathing even out as she fell fast asleep.

CHAPTER 19

Charlie pried her eyes open before dawn. She wiped the sleep from her eyes and stared at her new lover. It still unnerved her how much Karl looked like Hennessey, but when it came to lovemaking, there were differences between the men. They weren't bad—just different. Either way, being with Karl came with a heavy dose of guilt. She had never been the type of person to use someone before, but in this case, she couldn't help herself. God help her.

It wasn't as if Karl was without his charm and talent. Far from it. But she wasn't in the headspace of thinking of a long-term relationship. She needed a Mr. Right Now—and he more than fit the bill.

Charlie untangled from Karl's muscular arms and tiptoed from the bed. She reclaimed her shoes and coat downstairs and, like before, let herself out the front door.

Mike Ryan and the morning crew arrived early and set up in Ramsey's undisclosed location to give him a chance to respond to King Kong's allegation and to squash rumors about whether he and his crew had anything to do with the shooting outside of the WVCX radio station.

"C'mon, man. I'm not going to dignify that with a response." Ramsey laughed. "If Kong is out there dodging bullets, it ain't got shit to do with me."

"Sounds like a response to me."

"You can take it how you want." Ramsey grinned. "I'm a legit businessman, emphasis on *legit*. I'm grown about my shit. I ain't tryin' to run a boardroom *and* the streets. Kong is talking mad shit about what's going on over at RawDawgs, but let me assure everyone that the ends are meeting like a muthafucka. Bills stay paid, and every muthafucka I fuck with is feasting daily. You hear me? But if homies wanna roll over to the Gorilla compound and catch a few cases for street bullshit, you go right ahead."

Ryan and his crew chuckled while bleeping out most of the interview.

"You got anything to say to the charge that you had something to do with Hennessey Rawlins's passing?"

"I got plenty to say on that shit." Ramsey inched closer to the microphone. "Fuck Kong for that foul shit. Fo' real. Matter of fact, that nigga needs to keep my brother's name out his mouth. That shit was more than reckless, and the next time the nigga come across my path, I'm gonna see him for it. Hennessey was a real nigga. Straight up. I owe everything I am to my brother, and there isn't a day that passes I don't miss him. I ain't tryin' to hear from no nigga who don't know shit about the real between me and my boy. You hear me? Hennessey Rawlins was my best friend. We walked through fire and brimstone together, and any muthafucka who say otherwise don't know shit."

"Respect." Ryan lifted his fist.

"That's what's up." Ramsey bumped Ryan's fist and finished out the rest of the interview.

Charlie clicked off the car radio. She'd arrived home but remained in the car and replayed Ramsey's interview in her head. She also compared it to what Kong had said the other day. Sure, she and Ramsey had clashed in the past, but it felt odd questioning his loyalty. Though she had always known Ramsey had a thing for her, she'd never questioned his loyalty to Hennessey.

Had that been a mistake?

Karl woke up in an empty bed. "Fuck." He hung his head. Hadn't he known last night when Charlie showed up at his door that she would pull this stunt again? He glanced at the nightstand and made sure she hadn't left money for services rendered.

His cell phone trilled. Karl snatched it up but recognized the department's number on the screen. "Yeah?"

"Get your ass down here in my office, pronto," Robinson ordered and then hung up.

"What the hell?" Sighing, he tossed the phone onto the bed and peeled out from under rumpled sheets. It was going to be another one of those days. However, before climbing out of bed, he grabbed the phone again and scrolled through his contacts to find Charlie's number. His thumb hovered over the call button. *Is it too soon?*

Probably—but he hit the button anyway. Karl waited through four rings before being transferred to voice mail.

"Hey, Charlie. It's me—Karl. I, um, had a great time last night. I wish you'd stayed for breakfast. I swear I make the best pancakes in Chicago." He laughed. "All right. Call me." He set his phone down and stared at it. Did this chick pull his man card?

Karl stood and headed off to the shower. Good thing he had to work, or he'd be sitting by the phone all day waiting for her to call back. He rushed off to the shower, hating having to wash off Charlie's scent. But after he replayed last night's events in his head, one name crashed his morning high. "Hennessey."

CHAPTER 20

Laundry day.

Billie drifted through the house, emptying hampers and carrying them down to the laundry room. She entered the guest room and searched around for clothes that needed washing.

Then she found the bundled jacket and clothes behind the room's paneled divider. "What the hell is this?" She unzipped the jacket and jumped back. Even though the ugly splatters were an oxidized brown, Billie knew blood when she saw it. "Oh, shit."

Billie dropped everything and sprinted out of the room to find a phone.

After watching Karl's call go to voice mail, Charlie climbed out of the car and headed into the house.

"Look who the cat dragged in." Johnnie looked at the clock. "It must be a buyers' market if they're showing houses at all hours of the night."

"Ha-ha." Charlie marched past the kitchen.

Johnnie cocked her head as Charlie walked by, then followed. "Do you have any clothes underneath that coat?"

"Hovering, *Johnnie.*" Charlie marched toward her bedroom.

Johnnie took affront. "I don't hover." She followed her twin. "Is this the same dude from the club the other night or . . . are we letting our inner ho out?"

"I plead the fifth," Charlie teased.

The phone rang, ending Johnnie's interrogation.

Johnnie picked up on the first ring. "Do you know what time it is?"

"Johnnie, is Charlie there with you?" Billie asked.

"Yep, she just walked in—believe it or not."

"She was out all night again?"

Johnnie looked around and lowered her voice. "Yeah, I think she was with Karl again." She chuckled as she returned to the kitchen.

"Are you sure?"

"I can't be one hundred percent sure." Johnnie laid strips of bacon into a skillet. "I'll know for sure if she shows up at the breakfast table with more hickeys on her neck." She laughed.

Billie fell silent.

"Is there something wrong?"

"Do me a favor and keep her there. I'm going to call the girls. Emergency family meeting."

Johnnie frowned. "What's the emergency?"

"I'll tell you when I get there. Don't let Charlie leave."

"But—"

"Hog-tie her if you have to." Billie hung up.

Stunned, Johnnie pulled the phone from her face. "What in the hell got into her?"

There was a knock on the front door before a key twisted in the lock.

"Solomon?" For a brief moment, she was excited at the idea of her husband returning home early from his business conference, but when she made it to the door, it was only Michael entering, wearing her morning workout clothes. Johnnie relaxed. "What are you doing here?"

"Have you seen the news?" Michael asked.

"No, I'm still trying to get breakfast ready for the kids—and Charlie."

"Turn it on." Michael made a beeline to the living room and found the remote control. When she powered on the television, Johnnie followed her to watch.

"An off-duty police officer, forty-one-year-old Detective Thomas Graham of the city's Twelfth District, was shot and killed at the Paulie's Auto Shop in downtown Chicago last night. Officers were called to the scene when the shop's owner, who happens to be the officer's older brother, discovered the body this morning when he came to open for business.

"According to Superintendent Eddie Whitehead, Graham, a twelve-year veteran of the force was shot multiple times and was also in the same Special Task Force as yesterday's murdered police officer, Jace Wallace. There are no current suspects for the murders . . ."

Michael muted the television and looked at Johnnie. "What do you think?"

"Holy shit."

"Shit." Kisi giggled.

Johnnie spun. "Kisi, what did I tell you about listening to grown folks' business? Have you finished making your bed?"

Kisi shook her head.

Johnnie spun Kisi by her shoulders and gave her a swat on the behind. "Go."

Kisi raced off, giggling. "Shit. Shit. Shit."

Johnnie's attention returned to Michael. "Are you thinking what I'm thinking?"

"Depends. *I* think your twin came back home as a serial cop killer," Michael said.

"Okay. We *are* thinking the same thing." Johnnie plopped down on the sofa and buried her head.

There was another rap on the door.

"Are you expecting someone?"

Billie rushed inside, clutching a garbage bag. "I got here as fast as I could." She sniffed the air. "Is something burning?"

"Shit! My bacon!" Johnnie sprang to her feet and rushed off to the kitchen. The smoke detector blared. "Shit!"

The kids came squealing back into the living room with their hands covering their ears.

"Everybody calm down," Johnnie ordered, searching around for a stepladder.

Billie looked at Michael and shouted, "I tried to call you."

"Sorry. I left my phone in the car. Have you seen the news?" Michael unmuted the television and surfed to another local channel reporting Detective Thomas Graham's murder.

Suddenly, Billie needed to sit down, too. "This is bad." She hugged the garbage bag to her chest.

Johnnie shut off the smoke detector and returned to the living room. "What's that?" She pointed at the bag.

"Evidence," Billie mumbled.

Johnnie and Michael frowned.

Charlie rushed out of the bathroom. "What's going on out here?" She coughed as she passed the billowing white smoke from the kitchen. "Are you trying to burn the place down?" She made it to the living room and stopped. "What are you guys doing here?"

Teddy burst through the front door shouting, "Oh my God, Charlie is a cop killer!" She screeched to a stop when she noticed Charlie standing in the center of the room. "Oh, hey, Charlie."

CHAPTER 21

Captain Robinson paced his office like a caged lion. "I'm not here for the bullshit, Caruso. Two of your men have been found dead with bags of cash in the vicinity, and you want to sit here and tell me you don't know anything about it?"

Caruso shook his head, his face scrubbed of all emotion.

"What do I look like to you, a fuckin' idiot?"

"I can only tell you what I know, Captain."

"Bullshit."

"If you're accusing me of something, sir, this conversation should hit pause until I can get my union representative down here."

Robinson stopped pacing and narrowed his gaze on the detective. "Do you *need* a union rep, Caruso? What kind of bullshit are you and your men about to drag this department through? As if I don't have enough to deal with."

Caruso shook his head with his perfected poker face.

"Get the hell out of my office before you need a paramedic instead of a union rep."

Caruso pulled himself out of the chair. When he was on his feet, he hovered two inches above his captain.

Robinson refused to be intimidated. He stepped forward and jabbed a finger into Caruso's chest. "Let's get one thing straight: If I get proof that you and your men are dirty, there's not a fuckin' union rep in this country that's going to protect you from my wrath. Put that shit in a pipe and smoke it. Now, get the fuck out of here."

Anger crept onto Caruso's face, but he suppressed the instinct to lash out and marched out the door.

Chris swung up from a chair as Caruso exited Robinson's office. "What did he say?" he asked.

"Crews, get in here," Robinson bellowed.

"Oh, man," Chris whined, looking like he was ready to shit his pants.

"Hey, stay cool, man. Everything is going to be fine."

"CREWS!"

"Ah, shit."

Caruso grabbed his buddy's arm and hissed, "Stay cool."

Crews hesitated but nodded before he headed off to face Robinson's wrath.

Caruso cast a futile glance over his shoulder toward the captain's office and watched Robinson tear into Crews. At this point, he could only hope his longtime colleague kept it together—at least long enough for them to figure out what in the hell was going on. Somebody had it out for his team, but common sense said it couldn't be Kong. No way he or his guys would have left the bags of money behind. One thing for sure, the department wasn't going to be able to keep the discovered cash out of the news for long—which meant Kong would find out about it and would come gunning for them, too, sooner rather than later.

Karl made it to the precinct in record time, despite having stopped for coffee. After listening to the radio on the drive over, he was no longer in the dark about why the captain had barked orders for him to get down here this early. First Detective Jace Wallace and now Thomas Graham. Somebody had the Special Task Force in its crosshairs.

"Let me guess," Caruso said, appearing out of nowhere. "The captain called you in, too?"

"Yeah, I see being on this strike team is going to be hell on my beauty rest," Karl joked.

Caruso grinned. "You'll survive."

"NELSON," Robinson shouted.

"It looks like it's your turn." Caruso slapped a hand across Karl's back. "Good luck."

"Thanks. It looks like I'm going to need it." Karl shared an uneven smile and a wink before he headed up the stairs. He had no idea what Robinson thought he could tell him. Surely Robinson didn't think he had anything to report this soon.

As Karl climbed the staircase to the captain's office, a red-faced Detective Crews descended. Karl stopped and watched the man rush the rest of the way down the steps and race around the corner.

Caruso followed behind Crews.

"NELSON!"

Karl groaned and resumed his march up the staircase. "You called, Captain?"

"Come in and shut the door," Robinson ordered.

Karl complied.

"Have a seat," Robinson added.

Karl sat.

"I'm reassigning you," Robinson announced.

"Sir?"

"The strike team is disbanded until further notice."

"Um . . ."

"Did you hear about Detective Graham this morning?"

"Yes, sir. It's all over the news. It's, um . . ."

"Fucked up," Robinson filled in for him. "That's what it is." He sighed. "You worked with Graham yesterday. Did you notice anything?"

Karl frowned. "Like what, sir?"

"I don't know. Was he behaving oddly?"

"I just met him, sir. I wouldn't know whether he was behaving oddly or not."

Robinson grew frustrated.

Karl added, "He was upset about Wallace. They all were."

Robinson crossed his arms and leaned against his desk. "And were you guys there when they found the money?"

Karl nodded.

"And how did they react?"

"They seemed"—Karl thought about it—"pissed."

Robinson's phone rang. "I'm in a meeting. What?" He stood and glanced out his office window. "Shit. All right. Thanks."

Karl frowned and followed the captain's line of vision out into the department. "Whitehead."

Robinson hung up the phone and straightened his tie. "We'll continue this conversation later. After I get my ass chewed out again."

In the clubhouse, Detective Crews hissed to Caruso as he made a beeline to his locker, "I'm getting the fuck out of town."

"What?" Caruso laughed. "Where are you going?"

"As far as my half of the money will take me," Crews snapped. "If you were smart, you'd do the same damn thing."

Caruso shut the clubhouse door to ensure they weren't overheard. "Calm down. You're not thinking straight."

"No. For the first time, I *am* thinking straight—and thinking for myself. We've opened up a can of worms somewhere, and someone is out there knocking us off one by one. You can stay here and wait for the muthafucka to put a bullet in your head like Graham or gut you like Wallace if you want to, but I intend to live a bit longer."

"This whole thing isn't going to disappear. Not with Robinson crawling up our asses. You run, and it's going to make us look guilty."

"We *are* guilty," Crews shouted.

Caruso's eyes narrowed. "What did you tell Robinson?"

"Nothing!"

Caruso stared. He didn't believe him.

"Nothing, I swear," Crews stressed before adding, "though I'm not too sure he bought it. He's shutting down the strike team's operation until further notice."

"He didn't tell *me* that." Caruso inched closer to Crews. "What else did he say?"

"That's it. He'll shift us to desk duty or to homicide until the department has a better handle on this cop killer."

"Anything else?"

"He asked about the money."

"Shit."

"But I didn't tell him anything."

Caruso shook his head.

"Help me out. If we're not running, what the hell *are* we doing?" Crews asked.

"I'm thinking."

"I mean, we got to come up with a plan, right?"

"A plan only works when you know who you're going up against," Caruso barked. "Somehow we've got to find out who's behind this—and fast."

Charlie laughed. "What's this about me murdering cops?" She swung her gaze among her sisters, but none of them appeared to find the situation funny.

Billie lowered her hands from her face. "Are you denying it?"

"Of course I deny it." Charlie's laugh sounded like a misfiring muffler.

"Oh?" Billie opened a plastic bag and pulled out Charlie's bundled clothes. "Then what are these?"

Charlie's eyes widened before she marched over and attempted to snatch the clothes and the bag from her sister. "Are you going through my things now?"

"This isn't a privacy issue," Billie snapped. "It's a murder issue."

Johnnie hissed and looked around for small, prying eyes. "Will you please lower your voices?"

"Let go." Charlie wrestled her clothes from Billie's tight grip before Michael latched on to Charlie's arm and spun her toward her. "Tell us we're wrong about this shit. You're not out there killing cops—are you?"

Charlie hesitated.

Her sisters gasped.

Charlie snatched her arm free. "I didn't plan it." She shook her head. "It just happened."

Billie lifted a brow. " 'It just happened'? What are we supposed to do with that?"

"You don't have to do shit. None of you. It doesn't involve you guys."

Teddy spoke up. "How can you say that? What happened to you didn't happen in a vacuum. True. We will never know *exactly* what it's like to go through what you went through. But we love you, and when you hurt, *we* hurt. Don't think for one second we don't hate those raping, murdering bastards, too."

"So, what's the problem?" Charlie challenged.

Her sisters were at a loss for words.

Michael croaked, "They'll turn this city upside down looking for you."

"Then I better not get caught."

"Now I need to sit down," Johnnie said, but before she could, the telephone rang. "Shit." She grabbed the phone. "Hello. Oh, hello, *Ramsey*." Johnnie glanced over at Charlie.

She frowned.

"Yeah, she's, um, standing right here. Hold on." Johnnie held the phone out to her sister. "He wants to talk to you."

Charlie shook her head.

"He must've called six times last night," Johnnie informed her. "Maybe it's important?"

Charlie frowned at the offered phone and then at her expectant sisters. They looked as puzzled as she felt. She took the phone. "Hello."

"Hey, Charlie." Ramsey laughed. "You're a hard woman to catch up with."

"You know how it is."

"Yeah? Did you catch me on the radio this morning? I was on with Mike Ryan, addressing Kong's ridiculous accusations."

Charlie shook her head and lied. "Nah, sorry. I've been, um, pretty busy."

Ramsey laughed. "That's one way of putting it."

The hair on the back of Charlie's neck rose.

"I caught the news. You've been a *naughty* girl."

Silence.

"We need to talk."

CHAPTER 22

King Kong stared at the texted images from his connect within the police department. He'd been played. Ramsey hadn't jacked him. The cops did.

"Muthafuckas." He set his phone down next to his plate of barbecue, leaned back, and braided his fingers together as his gaze swung to his cousin Alexis. "It looks like you may be right about the pawn shop heist."

Alexis crossed her arms. "I told you. Now, you call this whole war thing off before more bodies drop."

Kong shrugged.

"You are going to call it off, right?" Alexis needled.

"Maybe—in time." He gave her another careless shrug. "What can I say? Gorilla Beats has had a surge in a music streams, CD sales, and even selling out bigger arenas. You couldn't buy this kind of publicity."

"David!"

Kong rolled his eyes at the use of his government name. "I'll get back to you." He glanced over to his man by the door, who then moved behind Alexis to let her know her time was up.

Alexis got the message and shoved her chair back before

bouncing to her feet. "I'm warning you, David. Don't ruin this for me."

"Or what? You're going to call my grandmother?" He laughed.

"Damn right." Alexis turned on her heel and shoved Kong's man out of the way.

Kong laughed as he watched her go, knowing it pissed her off. But once she was out the door, his attention returned to his phone. He picked it up and reviewed the picture of his money again.

"Problem, Unc?" Birdie asked.

"Always." Kong sighed. "But it's nothing a few bullets can't fix."

"Are there any particular names on these bullets?"

"A couple of cops."

"Are you Detective Nelson?"

Karl turned away from Caruso. "I am."

"You're with me," Bennett informed him. "Let's roll."

"Right behind you." Karl slapped a hand on Vic's shoulder. "It was good while it lasted—catch you later." He pushed up a half smile and rushed to catch up with Bennett, who was already heading out of the door. By the time Karl caught up with Bennett, the detective was behind the wheel with the engine revving.

Karl's butt had barely touched the seat before Bennett shifted into DRIVE.

"Whoa!" Karl shut his car door. "Where's the fire?"

"Paulie's Auto Shop. The owner may have captured something on the surveillance tapes after all."

"That's good news." Karl secured his seat belt.

"The sooner we get this maniac off the street, the sooner a lot of our guys can sleep easier—especially the guys on your strike team," Bennett added.

"Yeah."

Bennett pulled his gaze from the road for a few moments to glance at him. "Any idea who may be behind this?"

"Nah, but the guys are shook up, though."

"Yeah, I don't blame them. They've stomped on plenty of toes out here."

Karl frowned. "I keep hearing that."

Bennett laughed. "Thank your lucky stars you were only on the team for days—or you'd be looking over your shoulder constantly." They arrived at the crime scene.

Bennett killed the engine, and together they climbed out of the car.

Quickly, they maneuvered through the crowded street, ducked under the yellow tape, and entered Paulie's Auto Shop. Given the size of the place, the forensics team was still there, snapping pictures and dusting for prints.

Karl followed Bennett to the auto shop's office. There were already two cops posted by the door when they entered.

"Mr. Williamson?" Bennett inquired.

Paul Williamson pulled his large, bearded face from an eight-inch screen on the corner of a banged-up metal file cabinet. "Yeah?"

Bennett slapped palms with the owner and introduced him to Karl as an addition to the case.

"I finally remembered the password and pulled the digital file from last night," Williamson said.

"Mind if we take a look?" Bennett asked.

Instead of answering, Williamson moved away from the screen and plopped down into a chair behind the desk.

Bennett's smile tightened. "We're going to need some privacy."

"Oh." Williamson sprang to his feet. "Sure, sure. I'll, um, leave you two alone."

Karl met the man's gaze for a fraction of a second, then looked away. The man was hurting.

"All right. Let's see what we have here." Bennett took Paul's place before the eight-inch screen while Karl leaned against the corner of the desk for a better view. Bennett hit the PLAY button.

On the screen, Detective Thomas Graham crept into view.

Karl frowned as he craned his head. "Where is this?"

"The back of the shop."

"And he had a key?"

Bennett bobbed his head. "Williamson and Graham are brothers—stepbrothers. Graham used to come in and work on his days off, fixing up and pimping out motorcycles as a hobby."

Karl's gaze scanned outside the office and over to a distraught Williamson, who looked like he didn't know what to do with himself.

"Now, who do we have here?" Bennett asked.

Karl returned his attention to the small screen and zeroed in on a second figure moving in the shadows. He squinted and moved closer. "Who is that?"

"That's the million-dollar question." Karl hit the PAUSE button and then rewound the tape.

Onscreen, Graham removed loose cement blocks from a wall, then removed a large duffel bag. Meanwhile, the shadow in the background grew closer.

"He doesn't see or hear the guy behind him," Bennett noted and cocked his head. "Or her," he corrected.

Karl nodded in agreement and leaned in close. The killer lifted a gun toward the back of Graham's head, bringing part of the killer's coat and hand visible to the camera.

Karl froze. *I know that coat.*

CHAPTER 23

After arguing with her sisters that they didn't need to come with her to meet with Ramsey, Charlie settled into the back seat of the Escalade. As Dominic pulled out of the driveway, her sisters lined the porch, waving with worried lines grooved into their faces. She wanted to shout that they would see her again, but the words caught in her throat behind a stone, which then sank to her gut.

How the hell could she assure anyone of anything? The night she crept through Detective Wallace's window, her fate was sealed.

"This isn't the way to the Gold Coast."

Dominic glanced into the rearview mirror. "We're not headed out there."

Charlie tensed. "Where are we going?"

"Relax." He smiled. "With the heat being what it is, my man got a crib off the grid for such special occasions."

The explanation didn't calm Charlie's nerves, but she sat quietly as Dominic traveled south. Twenty minutes later, Dominic arrived at an old brownstone in Riverdale.

"This is it?" She frowned.

"This is it." Dominic winked.

A large, at least four-hundred-pound man stomped across the cracked sidewalk and opened Charlie's door.

"Tiny will take you in," Dominic informed her before nodding for her to get out.

Charlie slipped her hand into the pocket of her leather coat, reassuring herself she still had Henny's gun for protection before she climbed out of the back seat. As she marched in front of Tiny, eyes from around the dodgy neighborhood followed her.

"Downstairs," Tiny ordered.

She followed the command despite her gut twisting into knots. As she descended, a foul smell rose up to greet her. Halfway down, she stopped, but Tiny's gut bumped her from behind and propelled her forward. She kept moving until she reached two more men standing outside of a metal door. To her relief and surprise, she was ushered in without a pat down.

However, the interior of Ramsey's off-the-grid crib was different from what she expected. In fact, it was an extension of the Palazzo Versace style from his Gold Coast apartment. Only, instead of marble floors, Charlie's shoes sank into a white shaggy, deep-pile carpet.

Ramsey rounded a corner and stretched out his arms. "Ah, if it isn't the lady of the hour. You've been busy." Ramsey smirked, handing Charlie a drink.

"Am I supposed to know what you're talking about?" she asked coolly.

"This may surprise you, but sometimes I catch the news and learn stuff."

"You're right. It *does* come as a surprise," Charlie volleyed.

"Please have a seat."

Charlie hesitated and looked around.

"Don't worry. It's just the two of us." He grinned.

"Is that supposed to make me feel better?"

Ramsey's smile dimmed. "Of course. We're friends, aren't we?"

Charlie held his gaze, then took the offered drink without answering the question and sat down.

"I see." He eased down onto a strategically placed donut on the couch next to her. "Anyway, I'm on to you." He leaned close.

Charlie leaned away. "What are you talking about?"

Ramsey's smile stretched. "Don't worry. Your secret is safe with me. After all, we're family." He went for a kiss.

Charlie sprang from her seat. "What the fuck? Where's Alexis?"

Ramsey chuckled. "Where else? Shopping." He patted the empty cushion next to him. "Sit."

"I'll stand."

"C'mon. I don't bite."

"No? I do."

Ramsey grew excited. "Oh, tell me more."

Charlie frowned. "What are you doing?"

"Nothing." He leaned back and stretched his arms across the back of the couch. "I just wanna talk."

"We have nothing to talk about. This is *never* going to happen."

"No? Don't even want to talk about how you plan on getting away with your murder spree?"

She lifted a brow.

"Enough with the cat-and-mouse game. I know it's you. And if I can connect the dots, so can the cops—especially Caruso. He's an evil muthafucka, but he's not stupid."

"This may come as a surprise to you: I'm not stupid, either." She met his gaze head-on, and it took him a moment to notice she'd leveled a gun at him. When he did, he laughed.

"What are you going to do? You shoot, and my boys will run in here to mow you down."

"You'll still be dead."

Ramsey's cocky smile melted as he eyed something on the table.

"You'll be dead before you reach it," she warned.

He turned the charm back on. "What's this, Charlie? I thought we were family?"

"Nah." She shook her head. "I've been playing Kong's radio interview over and over in my head—"

"Kong?" Ramsey laughed. "You gotta be fuckin' kidding me."

"The thing is, Ram. He was making an awful lot of sense. I mean, look at you, living Henny's dream."

"*Our* dream," he corrected. "Henny and I built this shit together. We were like brothers."

"You keep saying that."

His brows collapsed in confusion.

"Henny wanted to be the music mogul, and you wanted to run the streets—even when the music popped off, you didn't want to let it go. Just like Kong. God." She shook her head. "It was in front of me the whole time. You didn't love Henny. You hated him. You were jealous."

Ramsey laughed. "Jealous? Who? Me?"

Charlie nodded, convinced she was on the right track. "The guys were loyal to Henny—not you. The label was nothing more than a convenient way to launder the drug money. When Henny wanted to start the next chapter of his life with me, he wanted out of the drug game, didn't he? That's what you guys fought about that night."

"Okay, now you're talking crazy."

"Am I? You two disappeared together for a while. When Hennessey returned, there was blood on his cuff, and when I saw you again, you had a busted lip and eye. After Hennessey whupped your ass, you called your dirty cops on the payroll, didn't you?"

Ramsey's mask fell for the first time. "You believe Kong over me?" Ramsey asked. "You believe I could have turned on my brother?" His eyes hardened. "You don't know me at all." Emotion thickened his voice.

Charlie regarded him again.

"I loved Hennessey. Him and his mother. I've made sure Mrs. Rawlins hasn't wanted for anything since his death. I show up for every birthday and holiday and reminisce about the old days."

Charlie said nothing.

"At Henny's wake, I, um, didn't choose my words right when we talked. I didn't mean to give you the impression that I didn't support your fight against those asshole cops. It's just—I knew the bastards would get away with it. It's how the system works."

"And how does the system work for *you*?"

"That's not fair."

"Since when the fuck is life fair?"

Ramsey lifted his chin and chewed on his words instead of spitting them out.

"They're dirty cops," Charlie pressed.

"They are hardly the only ones," Ramsey snapped.

"You do business with them?" she asked.

"Of course." Ramsey looked up. "Hennessey did, too."

Charlie's heart dropped to the pit of her stomach.

"That surprises you?" A corner of Ramsey's mouth curled. "Ah, that's right. Hennessey Rawlins could do no wrong in your eyes. He never bent the rules, lied, or crossed over to the dark side to get what he wanted. He pinned it all on me. You think *I* could tell Hennessey what to do—talk him into shit that went against his principles? He was the brains behind *everything*. Always had been."

Charlie kept shaking her head.

Ramsey laughed. "Hennessey had been a drug dealer since we were in junior high. You were too blind to notice. But your father had his ass pegged. That's for damn sure. He knew what was up the moment Hennessey figured out he could do more than pee with his dick. I never saw a man happier than when you told him you were enlisting and heading out to war instead of sticking around for my man's slick-talking ass to put a ring on it. But it was temporary, wasn't it?

"You never wondered how Henny and his mother were able to live so well out of the hood after his pop died? Sure, he hid the money he was making at first. He stashed money everywhere. And when the bills stacked up, Momma Rawlins asked fewer questions."

"You're lying," Charlie snapped, even though her gut said he was telling her the truth. How had she ignored what was right in front of her all this time? "But Caruso—"

"Caruso and Hennessey had an arrangement," Ramsey filled her in. "They had been business partners for years—until Hennessey wanted out."

Charlie lowered the gun and dropped into the chair behind her.

"Hennessey knew wifing you and having a kid meant he had to clean up his act. Go legit."

"So, everything they said at the trial . . ."

"Was mostly true," Ramsey confirmed. "Except that his drug partners were the police. Hennessey used the profits from the streets to put himself through college and launch RawDawgs. When he opened the Moonlight Club, he used it to launder money. When he wanted out, Caruso somehow caught wind of it before he finished devising an exit plan. Caruso and his guys didn't want the money train to end."

"What about you?"

"I had my man's back," Ramsey said. "Whatever he wanted to do, I was down with it. When Caruso and his gang showed up at the engagement party—"

"He was there that night?"

Ramsey nodded. "*They* had a brief disagreement. But I guess Caruso wasn't finished making his point."

A long silence lapsed between the old friends.

"And now you're doing this crazy thing." Ramsey leaned over.

Charlie stiffened and leaned away.

"C'mon, you have to know how crazy I am about you. After all these years?" He erased another inch. "If there was anything I was jealous of Hennessey having—it was you."

She laughed.

The hope in Ramsey's eyes dimmed. "What's so damn funny?"

"You." Charlie continued laughing, swinging a finger between them. "This right here will never happen."

"What the fuck is wrong with me? I'm rich, successful—and pretty damn good-looking."

"And engaged."

He waved off the comment. "Forget about that. Alexis is—wrong for me. I realized that when you returned. When you stepped into the Emperor's Club, all these feelings I have for you came rushing back. I was about to make the biggest mistake of my life."

"I . . . see." Charlie stood again.

"Do you?" Ramsey groaned and climbed to his feet. "I can protect you."

"I don't need your protection."

"Like hell you don't." He laughed. "Like I said. It's a matter of time before the police connect the dots—especially that pig you're fucking."

Charlie froze. "What did you say?"

Ramsey's grin returned. "That's right. That Hennessey lookalike you've been dicking down is *Detective* Karl Nelson. He's one of Caruso's new boys."

"You're lying."

Ramsey cocked his head. "Am I?"

CHAPTER 24

At the first chance he had, Karl crept away from Paulie's Auto Shop's crime scene and called Charlie. Once again, the call went to voice mail. "Charlie, it's me—um, Karl." He glanced around and ensured no one was ear-hustling in on his conversation. "We need to hook back up today. It's important I talk to you. Call me as soon as you get this message." He wanted to say more but didn't know where to begin. "All right. Talk to you soon."

He disconnected the call and stared at the phone, hoping it would ring. He needed reassurance that it wasn't Charlie on the surveillance footage.

Stones settled in his stomach while the questions circled in his head. His head kept telling him something his heart didn't want to hear. But why? There was a hell of a lot of missing pieces to this puzzle, and he needed to find them fast.

Charlie stared at the screen as Karl's call transferred to voice mail.

Ramsey smiled. "Is that him?"

Charlie's gaze snapped up. "That's none of your business." She shoved the phone back into her pocket. "I have to go."

Ramsey lifted a brow. "Just like that? I'm supposed to forget you had a gun in my face a few minutes ago?"

Charlie rolled her eyes and spun on her heels toward the door. "You'll get over it."

Ramsey laughed and limped after her to cut off her path. "I wasn't finished talking about us." He backed her up against the living room wall and brushed his hand against the side of her face.

Charlie laughed. "There is no you and me." She shoved at his chest, but he refused to budge.

"There could be." He leaned in. "I'd give you the world if you'd let me."

She shoved at his chest again. "Ramsey."

He inched even closer. "C'mon, Charlie. I'm serious. Don't you feel this thing between us?"

The intensity in his eyes made Charlie uncomfortable. She had to do something, because he was coming in for a kiss. Her hands braced against his chest. "Ramsey, wait."

The basement door opened. "Ramsey, baby. I'm"—Alexis froze—"home."

Ramsey sprang back from Charlie as if her touch had become a hot poker. "Alexis, baby. You're home."

Alexis's fiery gaze swung between Ramsey and Charlie. "What the fuck is going on here?"

"Nothing," Charlie barked, seizing the opportunity to get the hell out of there. "I was just leaving." She rushed toward the door, but Alexis didn't move. "Nothing happened," Charlie insisted.

Alexis's gaze darkened, but she stepped away from the door.

Charlie bolted out into the hallway and didn't look back.

During the entire ride back to Johnnie's place, Karl kept blowing up Charlie's cell phone. After receiving numerous looks from Dominic in the driver's seat, she placed her phone on vibrate and watched each call go to voice mail.

A cop.

She shook her head. What kind of joke was the universe playing on her? Charlie pulled her gaze from the phone's screen to glance out of the window at the passing scenery. It all whizzed by without her seeing it. She was overwhelmed with conflicting emotions—especially a rising sense of betrayal. Of course, that didn't make sense. The man hadn't done anything to her. In fact, he'd been exactly what she'd needed and wanted at the time.

And he was funny.

And kind.

But he was also a cop.

A fucking cop.

"We're here," Dominic announced.

Charlie blinked out of her stupor to see she was in front of Johnnie's house. "Oh, thanks," she mumbled before gathering herself and climbing out of the back seat of the SUV. As she headed toward the front door, Charlie's phone vibrated in her coat pocket. At this point, she didn't bother looking at the screen. She knew who it was; she just didn't know what to do about him.

Johnnie snatched open the front door, but it was Michael and Teddy who grabbed her and dragged her into the house.

"What happened? What did Ramsey say? What does he know?" The questions fired off before she could register which sister asked which question.

"Nothing," she lied. "He just wanted to talk."

Billie frowned, not buying her bullshit. "Talk about what? The weather?"

"No. Um . . ." Charlie forced out a lie. "Believe it or not, he wanted to talk about his feelings for me."

Her sisters all wore matching confused expressions.

Billie folded her arms. "He didn't want to talk to you about the dead cops?" she pressed.

"No," Charlie lied, shaking her head and threading her way through her sisters to the living room. "It was nothing like that."

Silence followed in her wake.

Johnnie was the first to break it. "*We* need to talk about it."

The baby cried from upstairs.

"Shit," Johnnie swore. "I'll be right back. You girls don't start without me."

Everyone nodded, but within seconds of Johnnie taking off upstairs, the sisters turned toward Charlie.

"What were you thinking?" Billie fired off.

"I was thinking that those bastards got away with murder," Charlie snapped. "Hennessey, my baby—daddy! And on top of that, they stole six years of *my* life on some trumped-up drug charges. And I'm supposed to just let it go?"

"Charlie, you could get the needle for this," Michael fretted.

Teddy shook her head. "No. Illinois repealed the death penalty."

Charlie smiled. "Thank you."

"But you could end up behind bars for the rest of your life," Teddy added somberly. "Is that what you want?"

"I want justice." Charlie's hands clenched at her sides. "Why is that so difficult to understand? I'm sick and tired of feeling helpless and hopeless—of reading every day about another 'justified' homicide by cops. Our lives mean something. Hennessey's life meant something—even if he wasn't perfect. Even if he . . ." She sniffed and wiped away tears. "Even if he was guilty of some of the things they accused him of in court. He didn't deserve to be killed on the side of the road as if he was trash. I wasn't trash—and my baby was wanted and loved—even if I never got to see his face." Her tears fell harder and faster. She gave up wiping them away.

Billie, Michael, and Teddy looked at each other and hung their heads.

Michael said, "We understand where you're coming from."

"Do you?" Charlie's face crumpled with doubt. "Then why are you even questioning me?"

"Because we don't want to lose you again," Billie said. "If you're caught—"

"I'm not going to get caught."

Teddy rolled her eyes. "No one *ever* thinks they'll be caught."

"If I'm caught, it was worth it."

Her sisters gasped.

"I can't make you understand, and I'm not asking you to go along with it. But I'm not going to stop. I won't stop until each of those bastards is in his grave."

Johnnie rushed back into the living room and took one look at their faces. "Damn it. What did I miss?"

CHAPTER 25

Vic Caruso refused to feel like a caged animal. If he was indeed in the crosshairs of some serial cop killer, he wasn't going to go down without a fight. The muthafucka was going to work to take him out. Fuck Chris's punk ass. Caruso grabbed his sixth chilled beer mug and downed it as quick as the previous five, which didn't go unnoticed.

"Rough day on the job?" the bartender asked.

"You could say that," Caruso grumbled without looking up. "Another."

"I think you've had enough for one night—at least, enough for one hour."

"What the fuck? Are you my babysitter now?"

Unintimidated, the bartender braced his arms on the bar and met Caruso's hard stare. "No. I'm your bartender, and I'm cutting you off."

"Are you fucking kidding me?"

"I'm afraid not."

Enraged, Caruso jumped off his stool and swung his arm across the bar, sending his empty mug flying toward the bartender, who ducked out of the way. The mug exploded on the floor.

Everyone in the bar stopped.

The bartender maintained control. "You should leave."

"Who's is going to make me?" Caruso growled.

Bianca came up behind Caruso and placed a hand on his shoulder. "Vic."

Without thinking, Caruso spun and popped the waitress in the mouth. A gasp went up when she stumbled backward. Before Caruso could process what he'd done, other cops came to her rescue.

"What the fuck, Caruso?" someone barked as an army of bodies became a muscled wall around him.

He caught sight of the waitress cupping her bleeding lip, but pride prevented him from apologizing.

"Leave," the bartender repeated.

"Fine. I was going anyway," Caruso snapped, but not without giving a few of his *brothers*-in-blue an evil glare.

Everyone's angry gazes followed him to the door, where he slammed into Detective Nelson, who was entering the pub.

"Hey!"

"Hey, yourself," Caruso sneered and kept walking.

Karl remained rooted at the door as he watched his ex–team leader walk a crooked line out to his car. "Should he be driving?"

"Probably not," Elliot said. "If you wanna go be his Uber driver, be my guest."

While Karl contemplated offering Caruso a ride, Elliot entered the pub and ordered a much-needed drink.

Karl watched Caruso start his car and peel out of the parking lot before joining his old partner inside. While Karl caught Elliot up about his crazy few days with the strike team, Bianca served them frosted mugs of beer and an insane-sized platter of steak nachos.

"Look." Elliot looked over his shoulder and leaned over his plate of nachos. "I don't like talking bad about other cops, but . . ."

"But?"

"Caruso and his guys." Elliot shook his head. "Let's say they aren't much better than the criminals running the streets. I'm willing to bet my pension the reason the members on the strike team are dropping like flies is because they crossed the wrong muthafucka out there somewhere, and now the chickens have come home to roost."

Karl lowered his gaze. "You think so?"

Elliot nodded. "A lot of cops think that. What I can't figure out is the money."

"You heard about that?"

"Are you kidding me? A million and a half between the two of them recovered? C'mon. Unless they won a lottery no one knows about, where the hell did they get that kind of money?"

"You got me."

Elliot leaned forward and lowered his voice. "I have a theory."

Karl lifted a brow. "You do?"

Elliot nodded.

"All right. I'm all ears."

"A couple of weeks back, this place called Lenny's Pawn Shop was hit. It made the news because the muthafuckas used explosives and shit. But what didn't make the news was that the folks in the neighborhood claimed the place was pretty shady. Men were always going in and out of it at strange hours of the night. Get this. They were always carrying huge duffel bags. Kind of like the ones recovered at Wallace's place and the auto shop. The owner of the pawn shop is a cousin of King Kong's."

"The rapper?"

"And rumored drug dealer. Word on the streets is the explosion was a diversion. The crime was a heist."

Karl snapped the pieces together and scooched forward in his seat. "You think the strike team robbed the place?"

Elliot nodded as his grin grew. "I'd bet my pension on it. It was the same night the Emperor Club was hit. Real money. Kong thought it was his nemesis, Ramsey Holt, behind the hit—hence the shooting at the club. And Ramsey retaliated by doing a drive-by outside of that radio station."

"Damn."

"I know, right?" Elliot scooped up another loaded nacho chip. "Maybe I should take the detective exam, too."

"You should. You'd be a great detective."

"Maybe. In the meantime, watch your back," Elliot warned before shoveling more nachos into his mouth. "I'd hate to see your toe tagged down at the morgue."

"I, um, have been transferred from vice to homicide."

"Hmph. Count your blessings."

Karl seized the opening. "You're a hip-hop head, right?"

"RawDawgs for life. Woof-woof."

Karl frowned. "Oookay. What can you tell me about Hennessey Rawlins?"

"Your doppelganger." Elliot laughed. "What, did Caruso give you a hard time?"

"Not exactly."

"I'm surprised. He had to think you were a ghost. Especially considering he and his boys were charged with Hennessey's murder."

"Come again?"

"Yeah, Caruso and his shadows were dragged into court over a traffic stop gone wrong."

Karl sat back. "Fill me in."

Elliot launched into the whole story. It was more from a fan's point of view than a cop's, but he had Karl's full attention.

"Of course, the union pulled out all the stops to save their asses, which couldn't have been easy, especially going up against Rawlins's old lady, who claimed they'd also raped her."

Karl's blood went cold.

"You want to know what the fucked-up part was?" Elliot asked.

"What?"

"The prosecutor's office flipped the script on Henny's old lady. There were drugs in their car, and they charged her with trafficking and convinced a jury that she and Henny were involved in a drug deal gone bad—that it was these mysterious dealers who had killed Rawlins and assaulted her."

"But you don't buy it?"

Elliot lowered his head. "Nah. His old lady was pretty credible, if you ask me. And she was a real looker, too." Elliot picked up his phone and typed. "Here's a picture of her." He handed over his phone, which showed an image of Charlie Warren smiling in Hennessey's arms.

Karl stared. He *did* look like Hennessey Rawlins.

Bianca replaced their drinks. "Oh, I know her," she said pointing at the picture. "She's been in here a couple of times."

Karl twisted his neck. "What?"

"Yeah. She's been in here twice—but she never gets around to eating anything." Bianca laughed. "She just sits and watches the cops during the happy hour crowd and then leaves in a hurry."

Twenty-four hours later, Karl was once again transferred to voice mail. Instead of pleading for another call back, he disconnected the call and swore a blue streak. After his talk with Elliot about the Hennessey Rawlins murder, he'd spent the rest of the evening Googling everything he could find on the matter. There was a ton of information on the web. Also on the Internet was his fiancée's courageous fight against the city of Chicago and the police. Charlie had lost both her fiancé and their child. When Karl stumbled across the leaked images of Charlie's battered face after the incident, something shifted in him.

Reading Caruso and his men's shifting explanations made

Karl's blood boil. He knew the routine. Denial. Denial. Denial. Mayors will back the police force, and the police departments will always defend their officers—even when they are wrong. And the citizens, unfortunately, lived in an undeclared police state.

Karl read how within days of Charlie Warren's campaign for justice, the city went after her with everything they had. Caruso and his men were found not guilty, and Charlie was sent to prison for five years. She must've been released recently, even though he couldn't locate a single article about it.

It has to be her.

Karl glanced at his phone again before shoving it into his pocket and heading out to the precinct. At the department, he learned there had been a police shooting. The officer was with another precinct, and it might have been gang-related, but not knowing what they were dealing with, the department wasn't willing to dismiss it as being unrelated to the Wallace and Graham murders. One thing was for sure: Everyone in the precinct was on edge—notably Caruso and Crews.

"Hey there. How you guys doing?" Karl invaded their private huddle.

Caruso and Crews pushed up tight smiles.

"Hey, Nelson. What's up?" Caruso slapped palms with him. "How do you like Homicide?"

"So far, so good. If they transfer me in a few days, I'll know the problem is not them, it's me."

They laughed, even though it didn't sound natural.

"Any news?" Crews asked. "You guys have any idea who may be behind this?"

Karl hesitated before shaking his head. "Nah, not yet."

Caruso frowned. "I heard there was surveillance footage."

"Yeah. A pretty bad one. The killer pretty much stayed in the shadows. Bennett sent it over to the tech guys to see if they can clean it up. We still have to go through family and friends. You know, rule out the usual suspects."

"You'll let us know if and when they learn something, right?" Crews asked.

"Fo' sure," Karl lied. They exchanged fist pounds before Karl broke away and headed toward his new department. As he walked away, the weight of their stares followed him.

Karl and Bennett spent the day interviewing Wallace and Graham's family members and friends. No one could think of anyone who wanted to harm the officers, and no one could explain the duffel bags filled with cash. For a few hours, Karl reconsidered Charlie being the murderer. The money meant something. It could lead them down a different path—until you factored in that the killer, at both criminal cases, had left the money behind.

"Could it be a frame job?" Bennett mused at the end of the day.

"An expensive one." Karl shook his head.

Heading out the door, Karl caught sight of Caruso and Crews huddled together again. Crews was upset.

Karl climbed into his car, but instead of starting it up, he watched as Caruso and Crews seemed to exchange heated words.

Crews tossed up his arms and marched off to his car. When he started his car, Karl did, too. As he followed Crews across town, he kept questioning what he was doing. The short answer: He was following a hunch.

CHAPTER 26

Caruso powered down his window, hoping the night's cool breeze would help sober him up. During his drive home, he replayed the scene at the bar at least a dozen times. During each instant replay, he'd change the embarrassing incident with *would'ves*, *should'ves*, and *could'ves*. The last thing he needed was for people down at the precinct talking about how much he was losing his shit. Robinson and the superintendent would think they'd done the right thing by giving him desk duty.

Him. Shackled to a desk. Internal Affairs would sit on them for the next decade, waiting for them to fuck up—and fucking up was coded in Crews's DNA.

Caruso swung into his driveway and killed the engine. He wasn't any more sober than when he first got into the car. He weighed whether to sleep off his buzz right where he was or to go inside and grab a few Heinekens from the fridge and try to black out his shitty day.

The lure of more alcohol won the debate. His cell phone rang. "Yeah."

"You got something that belongs to me," Kong growled over the line.

Caruso's grip tightened on the phone. "I'm not sure I know what you're talking about."

"I'm not in the mood to play cat and mouse with your ass," Kong warned. "I want my money—*all* of it. Even the bags in evidence lockup."

Silence.

"Good. You *do* know what I'm talking about. You have twenty-four hours."

"Wait," Caruso barked.

"Don't waste my time, telling me it wasn't you who jacked Lenny's. I'm not that big a fool—especially now that half of my money is in police lockup."

Silence.

"Bring me my money."

"I-I need more time."

Kong hung up.

"*Fuck!*"

Stumbling out of the car, Caruso headed toward his side door, struggling to maintain a straight line. Despite being inebriated, his senses seemed sharpened somehow. At the slightest breeze, the hair on his arms stood at attention. The rustling of the fall leaves and the few mewlings from neighborhood cats played in surround sound in his head. For no discernable reason, he unsnapped his holster and reached for the door.

It was unlocked.

Reality was like a splash of cold water, sobering him.

Had the city's cop killer finally showed up to visit him?

God, he hoped so. He was itching to put a bullet in the muthafucka's head for fuckin' up all his plans. Caruso palmed his weapon and inched his way through the house. When he made his way to the living room, he was caught off guard when the room's light clicked on and revealed a beautiful woman, sitting on his couch with a weapon leveled at him.

She smiled. "It's about time you showed up."

* * *

"What the fuck is he doing?" Karl wondered. Parked two houses down from Crews's house, Karl squinted over the wheel, trying to make out what Crews and his wife were dragging out of the house. "Is that luggage?"

Crews argued with his wife while he opened the trunk of his car and tossed in their bags. He glanced around his dark neighborhood, and Karl crouched down in his seat.

Satisfied he wasn't being watched, Crews climbed into the car with his wife.

Karl waited until the Crewses cornered off the block before starting his car. "All right. Let's see what's up." He pulled away from the curb and followed.

Fifteen minutes later, Crews led Karl to a private storage facility—one that required a code to enter the property. Karl hung back, again, staying in his car across the street. He still didn't know what was going on, but his gut told him that Crews was running—but running from what?

Karl parked and waited.

BOOM!

The earth shook as a ball of fire lit up the night. Karl stared in openmouthed shock at the storage facility embroiled in flames.

CHAPTER 27

Caruso lowered his weapon. "What are you doing here?"

Alexis's thin smile expanded. "Your fuckup is back in town and is ruining everything I've worked for the past six years."

Caruso frowned. "What the fuck are you talking about?"

"Ms. Charlie Warren. Ring any bells?"

Caruso rolled his eyes. "That bitch."

"Yeah. *That* bitch." Alexis stood. "She was released from prison last week, and Ramsey can't think of anything other than replacing me with that G.I. Jane wannabe. You were supposed to body that bitch six years ago."

"Put your man on a tighter leash. I have bigger problems to deal with right now."

"Oh, so fuck me, huh? Maybe I should place a call to Kong and let him in on who jacked his crew down at Lenny's Pawn Shop?"

"You wouldn't," he sneered.

"Wouldn't I?"

Caruso cocked his head as he evaluated her. "You got your cut."

"And you got your cut to handle Charlie *and* Hennessey—only you did a half-ass job, and I don't remember getting a fucking partial refund." Agitated, Alexis tapped her gun against the side of her leg as if she was still weighing whether to shoot his ass.

Caruso slid the safety back off on his own weapon. "You've been offing my guys as payback?"

She barked out a laugh. "You're slower than I thought." Alexis slipped her gun into a dainty cross-purse before strolling toward him. "Think *harder* about what I'm telling you?"

Caruso frowned.

Sighing, Alexis filled him in. "Charlie Warren is more than just a pretty face. She's ex-military with a chip on her shoulder. Your men started dropping the same time she came back to town. Do I need to draw you a picture?"

The final puzzle pieces snapped together, and Alexis could see it in his eyes. "Ahh, there we go. We're on the same page now. The question is, what the fuck are *you* going to do about it?"

Thump!

"What was that?" Caruso asked.

"Why are you asking me? This is your place," Alexis sneered.

He palmed his weapon again and crept toward the hall. "You came alone?"

"Of course. You think I'm an idiot?"

"Stay right here," Caruso ordered and turned to investigate.

Alexis ignored the order and instead crept with him down the hall. Caruso clicked on a light in the first bedroom they came across.

"Is this where you came in?" Caruso walked toward the open window.

"No. I came in through the back door."

Caruso shoved his head out of the window and looked out into the night. His gaze focused on a few broken branches. "Someone was in here." He ducked back into the room and shut the window.

"I better go."

"That's right. If you can't handle the heat, get out of the kitchen." He smirked.

"Whatever. Just make sure you take care of our little problem. I've put in too much work for this shit to go south now."

"I'd say. Six years, and Ramsey still hasn't given you his last name? Kind of makes you wonder what he's waiting on—or *who* he's been waiting for."

"You're worried about the wrong damn thing." Alexis's face morphed into stone. "Fix this shit. *Now.*" Alexis stormed out with Caruso's laughter ringing in her ears.

When she made it to her car, four houses down, she slipped in behind the wheel and peeled out of the neighborhood as fast as she could. Angry, she cursed herself for trusting Caruso and his thugs to handle a job she should've handled herself. *I can still handle myself.* A smile curled at the corners of her mouth while she came up with a backup plan. When she shifted her gaze to the rearview mirror, her heart dropped.

Charlie sneered. "Hello, Alexis."

"Goddamn it. Where are you, Chris?" Caruso tossed his cell phone over to the passenger seat while his heavy foot jammed on the accelerator. He was a fool. He'd long forgotten about Charlie Warren. After he and his men took care of Hennessey Rawlins, she had been a thorn in their sides. But once she'd been shipped off to prison, he'd put her out of his mind.

Now she was back, and everything made sense. Warren sought revenge—vigilante justice. She didn't give a damn about the money she'd left behind.

Caruso jetted up Crews's driveway. Where was his car? He shut off his engine and jumped out almost in the same motion before racing to hammer on Crews's front door. The lights were out, and the only sound in the neighborhood were dogs barking in the distance.

Crews could be out at a bar or out with Bernice for all he knew—or he could be lying inside the house gutted or with the back of his head blown off. He'd been to Crews's crib enough times to know the spare key was hidden beneath a rock in the hedges. Caruso scrambled for it and jammed the key into the lock.

"Chris," he yelled, rushing inside and swiping on the light switch.

Silence roared back at him.

Quickly, he darted from room to room. Nothing was disturbed. Caruso forced a sigh of relief, but something still wasn't right. He marched back to the master bedroom and threw open the closet door.

Caruso stared at rows of naked clothes hangers. His blood pressure shot up. "*Fuck!*" Next, he stormed over to the dressers and snatched the drawers open.

Empty.

"Goddamn it, muthafucka!" Caruso raced out of the house. He started up the car and dialed Crews at the same time. The call went straight to voice mail. "Chris, where the fuck are you? You better not be doing what I think you're doing. Running isn't going to solve a damn thing. It's going to make things worse." He cornered a sharp right, ignoring a stop sign.

Horns blared, and tires screeched, but Caruso avoided an accident as he sped across town. More alarm bells went off at seeing the place so dark, and after breaking in, he discovered it was almost as empty.

"Fuck!" He rushed back to his car.

His cell phone trilled.

"This better be you, goddamn it." Caruso scooped the phone out of his jacket but frowned at seeing the name of Captain Robinson on his screen. "Hello."

"Caruso. Thank God. Where are you?"

"I'm, um . . . headed home," he lied. "What's up?"

"Bad news. Detective Crews is dead. You need to come in ASAP."

CHAPTER 28

Johnnie kissed her daughter good night and crept out of her bedroom. She had thirty minutes to shower and get ready before Solomon FaceTimed her. However, the moment she headed for the shower, someone pounded on the front door.

"Who on earth?" She marched down the staircase. As she drew closer, the hammering intensified. "I'm coming. I'm coming." She gazed through the peephole and gasped. *Caruso.*

Before Johnnie could react, Caruso burst through the door, splintering the frame.

Johnnie turned to run, but Caruso grabbed a fistful of her hair. "Now I've got you, you bitch." He snatched her back.

Johnnie stifled a scream and flailed out her arms, slapping Caruso's face. "Let me go!"

"I don't think so." He kicked the door closed and slammed her against it. "You've been a naughty girl, Charlie. I should have put it all together sooner."

"Let me go, muthafucka! I'm not Charlie!"

He grabbed her face and squeezed. "What? How big of a fool do you think I am? You think I don't remember our last time together?" He leered into her face and jammed his other hand in between her legs.

Johnnie kneed him in the groin. When he doubled over, she landed a perfect right hook. It hurt her hand, but it gave her enough time to make a second dart toward the staircase.

After she'd taken a few steps, Caruso tackled her to the floor. "Where do you think you're going, bitch?" He wrestled to flip her back around to face him.

"Let go of me," Johnnie cried.

"I don't think so." Caruso locked Johnnie's arms down.

"Mommy?" Kisi queried from the top of the staircase.

The wrestling stopped as Caruso and Johnnie glanced up.

"Go back to your room," Johnnie begged while tears spilled from her eyes. "And lock the door."

Kisi didn't move.

"Go, now!"

At last, Kisi unrooted herself from the top of the staircase and ran to her room. A few seconds later, her door slammed.

Caruso's face twisted in confusion. "You're not Charlie."

"Get off me." She wrestled her hands free to shove him off her.

"You're one of her sisters. The twin," he said, catching up.

"No shit, Sherlock." Johnnie scrambled from underneath him.

Caruso adapted and went for his gun. "Fine. Change of plans."

Johnnie went cold at the sight of the gun pointed at her head.

"Call her. Get Charlie over here, or I swear to God, what I do to you will be nothing compared to what I'll do to that sweet angel locked upstairs in her room."

Johnnie's eyes bulged.

"Call her! Now!"

"You don't have to do this," Alexis whined as Charlie forced her to walk into a weed-filled patch of grass under the CTA train tracks at the west end of a Costco's parking lot.

"Please, can't we talk about this?"

Charlie's brows dipped together. "Do you think you're going to talk your way out of this?"

"I . . . I want to explain."

"Oh, I heard enough. I heard how you had your buddy Caruso pull Hennessey and me over that night, and how you wanted both of us dead so Ramsey could take over everything. And how, once he married you, you'd be the queen of the RawDawgs' empire. Did I miss anything?"

Alexis cried harder.

"Quit with the fake tears. Your whack-ass performance ain't doin' nothing but working my damn nerves."

The sniffling stopped.

"You can stop right here."

"Here?" Alexis glanced about, trembling.

"Here is perfect. Now, turn around."

Alexis turned and met Charlie's dark gaze beneath the moonlight. Suddenly, her anger and contempt loosened her tongue. "I was so close," she said.

Charlie lifted her chin. "Close only counts with horseshoes and hand grenades." She clicked off the safety and aimed.

"You didn't even want it," Alexis spit out. "You didn't even know who the fuck you were marrying. You were clueless about the real drug empire Hennessey and Ramsey built out in the streets. But both of them were crazy about you. The sun and the moon rose and set on your bougie, black ass. I *deserved* to be queen. I put in the work. Who the fuck you think warmed Henny's bed while you were out playing soldier in the Middle East. Huh? *I did.* I tried to fuck and suck every memory of you out of his head. But the moment you came back to Chicago, Hennessey flung me out like trash—like I was nothing. Here it is, six years later, and Ramsey has yet to give me his last name. And here you come, marching out of jail, and he *still* wants your ass. He's ready to toss me aside if you signal he has a chance with you. *I've* been the ride-or-die chick for them every step of the way. And what did I get? Nothing."

"Wrong. You get a bullet." Charlie fired one shot into the center of her forehead and watched Alexis's small frame bolt backward before crumpling to the ground. "Bitch." She turned and stopped. Pivoting back, she walked over to Alexis's fallen body, then squatted down and removed the diamond ring from her finger. When she shined a light inside the band, she read the inscription:

Forever starts today—Hennessey

CHAPTER 29

"She's not picking up," Johnnie informed Caruso. "It's going to voice mail."

Caruso growled, "Where the fuck is she?"

"I don't know!"

Caruso whipped his hand across her face with a hard *slap!* Johnnie slumped, but she didn't fall.

Caruso grabbed her by her hair. "You know something. Maybe we should take a trip upstairs and tuck your little girl into bed? I hear it's never too early to train bitches how to please a man."

Johnnie attacked, screaming. She pummeled him with everything she had. She landed a few hard blows and raked her nails down the sides of his face before he knocked the shit out of her again.

"I swear, you Warren girls know how to make a man's dick hard. But first things first." He grabbed the phone again. "Call her back. And you better hope to God she answers this time."

Charlie took a bus, a train, and then another bus. The whole time, she replayed Alexis's confession in her head. It was the missing piece of an old puzzle. Now she couldn't get the images of Henny and Alexis coupled up out of her mind. A scorned lover. That was what all this was about? A bitch who'd decided that if she couldn't have Henny, then no other woman would? How cliché.

Charlie emitted a sad chuckle and drew a few stares from the other passengers. She straightened her face and pretended not to be a crazed serial cop killer until she arrived at her stop and walked the rest of the way back to her car. Once she was behind the wheel, she had the almost-insatiable desire to swing by Karl's place for another quickie—until she reminded herself he was one of the bad guys.

A cop. Charlie still had a hard time wrapping her head around it.

Traffic slowed to a crawl and then stopped altogether.

"What the hell is going on?" She leaned forward to see over the car in front of her. There was an orange glow off in the distance. Had a car or something caught on fire? She sighed and sat back in her seat, deciding she should call Johnnie and tell her not to wait up. Charlie grabbed her phone, which was off but still attached to the car's charger. After she turned it on, a series of pings went off, and she saw she had over a dozen missed calls.

"What the hell?" She went to her voice mail and hit PLAY.

"Charlie, it's Johnnie. Where are you? I need you to call me back as soon as you get this message."

In the second message, Johnnie's voice was a few octaves higher. "Charlie? Where are you? I need you to call me back. *Now.*"

The third message from Johnnie's phone wasn't from Johnnie, but Caruso. "Hello, Charlie."

Charlie pulled out of traffic and into the emergency lane before jamming her foot onto the accelerator. More cars snaked into the lane with her, and she had to lay on her horn to get people out of her way. Her heart pounded while adrenaline shot through her body, making her jittery in her seat. Horrific scenarios of what Caruso might have done to Johnnie and the kids played, one after another, in her head.

What have I done? She clenched the steering wheel. *I led him to my family.*

Never once did she consider Caruso coming after them, which was stupid. She'd seen what the man was capable of doing.

"*What happened to you didn't happen in a vacuum.*" Teddy's voice echoed in her head.

I need backup. Charlie picked up the phone again and dialed Billie.

"Do you know what time it is?" Billie groaned.

"Johnnie is in trouble."

"What?"

"Call Michael and have her call Teddy."

In no time, the Warren girls were on the line, and Charlie filled them in on what was happening.

"I knew this shit was going to blow up in our faces." Billie swore.

"I take full responsibility," Charlie cut to the chase. "Right now, we've got to save Johnnie and the kids. Are you guys with me?"

"You're damn right we're with you," Teddy responded without hesitation.

"You got it," Michael agreed.

"We're going to have to open Dad's old bunker," Charlie told them.

Fifteen minutes later, Charlie took a bolt cutter to the chains around the door to her father's old bunker. The military and gun enthusiast kept a cache of weapons underneath their childhood home. Once the dead bolt came off, the Warren girls snatched AR-10s and AR-15s from the walls as well as 9mm Berettas and Glock .45s.

When Teddy reached for a couple of hand grenades, Michael stayed her hand. "Whoa. What are you going to do with those? We aren't trying to level the place."

"Better safe than sorry." Teddy hooked the grenades onto her vest. "We don't know how many people Caruso's got over there."

"She has a point," Charlie said.

"Didn't you take out his other guys?" Billie hissed.

Charlie thought about Karl. "Doesn't mean he hasn't recruited more."

"In that case . . ." Michael grabbed a grenade, too.

Charlie shook her head. "Let's roll."

CHAPTER 30

Karl peeled away from the blazing crime scene downtown. His concern was for Charlie's next target: Victor Caruso. He was the last man standing. It was only a matter of time before Charlie set her sights on him. If she hadn't already.

Karl hopped into his car with his mind scrambling on what he should do. As he worked his way into the crawling traffic, he picked up his phone and called Caruso. The line rang. "C'mon, Caruso. Pick up."

The call transferred to voice mail.

Karl almost hung up, but his gut churned and stopped him. "Hey, Caruso. It's Karl. Look, man. I know this may sound strange, but I think I've figured out who is killing members of your crew. It's a long story on how I figured it out, but I think she's coming after you next. I believe . . . she's already taken care of Crews tonight. Please call me back as soon as you get this message." He disconnected the call—and wondered whether he'd done the right thing. For one thing, it didn't make the sick feeling in his gut go away. What if he was wrong? There was a chance—albeit a small one—that he was wrong about who was behind the murders. As Elliot said, Caruso and his guys weren't angels.

Karl picked up the phone again. This time he called Charlie.

* * *

As the Warren girls neared Johnnie's place, Charlie's phone rang.

"Is it him?" Teddy inquired before Charlie scooped the phone out of her pocket. But when she looked at the screen, her heart hammered against her chest.

"Charlie?" Michael inquired from behind the wheel.

"No. It's Karl."

The vehicle fell silent while the phone trilled.

"Are you going to answer it?" Billie asked. "He could be with Caruso. Right?"

Charlie answered the phone before the call transferred to voice mail. "Yeah."

Silence.

Did he hang up? "Hello?"

"Charlie," he stuttered. "You answered the phone."

"Look, if you and Caruso harm one hair on my sister or her kids' heads, I swear there will be nowhere on this earth you can hide from me."

"What? What's this about your sister?"

"Don't play me," Charlie snapped. "You're a cop, and you work with Caruso."

"I *used* to work with Caruso—for a few days. Now I've been assigned to *Homicide*."

Silence.

"What? You don't have anything to say?"

Silence.

"I saw the tape, Charlie."

"What tape?"

"At Paulie's Auto Shop. It was you, wasn't it? *You* killed Detective Graham and Detective Wallace, and tonight you killed Detective Crews."

Crews? She kept silent.

"What? You're not going to deny it?"

Billie rolled to a stop a few houses down from Johnnie's place.

"I have to go," Charlie said.

"Wait, Charlie," Karl barked.

"What?"

"Where are you? You have to let me bring you in. It would be better that way."

"Better for who?"

"For all involved. You can't believe you'll get away with this? You've killed *three* cops."

"Three?"

"You're going to tell me you didn't plant the bomb at that storage warehouse tonight?"

"I don't know what the fuck you're talking about, and I don't have time to debate you right now. I have to save my twin sister from your deranged colleague. And if you're involved in this, heaven help you." She ended the call and looked at her sisters. "Are you guys ready?"

Teddy shrugged. "As ready as we'll ever be."

After Charlie disconnected the call, Karl stared at the phone. The conversation circled around in his head a few times, and half of it still didn't make sense. What the hell did she mean about Caruso and her sister? He pulled over to the side of the road. He remembered her twin sister's name was Johnnie. In no time, he was able to find a Johnnie Blackburn related to a Charlie Warren. Two seconds later, he had an address.

Vic Caruso paced in front of a distraught Johnnie. She sat straight in an upholstered wingback chair with her hands tied behind her back, glaring at him. Occasionally, he glanced out through the Venetian blinds and wondered aloud for the millionth time, "Where the fuck is she?" When he turned back to face Johnnie, the window exploded with a series of rapid-fire shots.

He and Johnnie dove toward the floor. After which, Caruso whipped out his .45, and Johnnie wormed out of the living room as fast as she could.

Caruso swiped glass from his face and fired.

The front door was kicked off its last hinge.

Spinning on his back, Caruso changed the direction of his targeted fire and blew three holes into the wooden door. There was a moment of silence—and then all hell broke loose.

Bullets flew from every direction. Glass and wooden shrapnel were as dangerous as the bullets zooming by his head. He needed a shield. *Where did that bitch go?* Caruso belly-crawled his way out of the living room to search for her. But the bitch had disappeared.

"Where the fuck?" *Upstairs—with the kids.* It was the only logical answer. However, Caruso had serious doubts as to whether he could get up the stairs without the gunfire making minced meat out of him. But at this point, he didn't have a choice.

Once Karl got out of the downtown crawl, he jetted across town with his foot like a brick on the accelerator. The scenarios in his head grew worse with every passing moment. If Caruso had figured out who was killing his crew, would he be crazy enough to do something to Charlie's family? Each time he posed the question to himself, the answer kept coming back with a resounding *yes!*

When he was within a mile of the Johnnie Blackburn's home, he heard the unmistakable sounds of gunfire. "Oh, shit."

Charlie and Billie scaled the lattice in Johnnie's backyard while Teddy and Michael open-fired through the front of the house. When they got to the second level, they searched for an unlocked window to get into the house. The only one they found was in the upstairs bathroom.

Charlie climbed in through the window first and then helped Billie.

"Shit," Billie swore. "I'm a bit rusty."

"You're doing fine," Charlie assured her and led the way out the bathroom. In the hallway, they looked both ways before creeping out. The hail of gunfire downstairs had them on edge, but they kept to the mission and headed toward the kids' bedroom.

The boys' rooms were empty. Kisi's room was locked.

Charlie rapped quietly on the door. "Kisi, baby? Are you guys in there? It's Aunt Charlie and Aunt Billie. We've come to get you out of here." She pressed her ear against the door but couldn't make out any sounds.

"Are they in there?" Billie whispered.

"I don't know." Charlie tried the door again.

"Break it down," Billie suggested, keeping her eye and her gun trained on the hallway.

Charlie knocked again. "Kisi, sweetheart, please. If you're in there, open the door. We don't have much time."

"Mommy told us to stay here until she comes for us."

"It's okay," Charlie assured her niece. "She sent us to get you out of the house, but we have to go now. Unlock the door."

After another moment of hesitation, while both Charlie and Billie tapped their feet, the doorknob jiggled and twisted before opening.

One of Kisi's large brown eyes stared up at her aunts as the last check to make sure it was indeed safe.

Charlie smiled and pushed open the door. Kisi held Amir and behind her, huddled in the corner, were her four brothers. "Great. Let's get you out of here."

"But where is Mommy?"

Charlie hesitated. "Don't worry. Everything is going to be

all right. Let's get you and your brothers out of here. C'mon." She kept a smile on her face while she and Billie led them back to the bathroom.

"We're not supposed to go out on the roof," Jaxon told them.

"It's all right this one time." Billie handed her weapon to Charlie and took the baby from Kisi. The boys were out the window lightning-fast.

Billie gave Charlie a departing look. "Handle your business."

Charlie slung the backup weapon over her shoulder. "I'm on it."

Caruso was pinned down, and he knew it. Again, his gaze swept toward the staircase, and he weighed his chances of making it up to the second level. He told himself he had a 50/50 chance, but that was generous. "Fuck it." He went for it. Though he moved as fast as he could, time seemed to slow. It took forever to get to the first step and then another millennium to get halfway up. Something moved at the top of the stairs.

When he looked up, it was straight into Charlie's angry face.

"Shit." Caruso lifted his weapon.

But it was too late. Charlie's weapon was already aimed, and her finger was on the trigger. He didn't feel the blast to his chest, but he was aware of being lifted off his feet and reeling backward. Another bullet interrupted his fall, slamming into his shoulder and knocking him into the wall on his way down. Once he landed on his back on the staircase, he fired off a shot.

Charlie cried out as Caruso's bullet pierced her left shoulder and spun her away from the banister. Quickly, she gathered herself together and got to her feet. When she returned to the top of the staircase again and looked down, Caruso was gone.

* * *

Teddy and Michael stopped firing. Police sirens filled the night, and Charlie only had a few minutes to track this son of a bitch and put him down. She rushed down the staircase as Teddy and Michael raced inside.

"Where is he?"

"I don't know," Charlie told them, "but he has to be around here somewhere."

"The police are coming," Michael said.

Charlie noticed the direction of a swipe of blood across the floor and followed it. It went through the kitchen and toward the basement door.

Michael grabbed one of the grenades on her vest.

Teddy stopped her. "Wait. There are *two* trails," she pointed out.

"Johnnie," Charlie and Michael concluded at the same time.

"Fuck." Charlie reached for the door.

Michael stopped her. "He's gotta have the door covered. The moment you poke your head through, he's going to start blasting."

"Do you have a better plan?"

Her sisters looked at each other.

"Go cover the back door," Charlie ordered. "If he goes out that way, empty everything you've got into him."

"You got it." Teddy raced toward the front door.

Michael kept a hand on Charlie's shoulder. "Be careful—and get Johnnie back from that bastard."

"I got this." Charlie pressed a kiss to Michael's cheek before she raced after Teddy.

Charlie glanced back at the basement door, drew a breath, and went for it.

Karl clipped the corner of the Blackburns' driveway, demolishing the mailbox before slamming on his brakes. After killing the engine, he bolted out of the car and raced to the front door. The place looked like a war zone. He took it all in before the sound of more gunfire made him jump. Withdrawing his gun, he raced to investigate. He flew through a kitchen and toward an open door.

Charlie held her hands up while Caruso kept his gun aimed at her head. Both of her weapons had been placed on the floor, inches from his feet. He kept Johnnie clutched underneath his other arm, choking her as she struggled to wriggle free.

"We meet again," Caruso growled. "You've been a busy bee since you got out of prison."

"Let my sister go," Charlie ordered. "This is between you and me."

Caruso tightened his hold. "By hurting her, I'm hurting you."

Karl raced through the open basement door.

Caruso turned his weapon toward the staircase and fired.

Ducking, Karl lost his balance and tumbled down the steep staircase.

Charlie dove for her .45.

Caruso swung his aim back at Charlie, loosening his grip on Johnnie.

Johnnie elbowed Caruso in the ribs, causing his shot to go wild before she darted away.

Charlie dropped and rolled, and when she came up, she fired.

Caruso reeled back and hit his head on the water heater before collapsing to the cement floor—but he was still alive and breathing. Charlie aimed again, this time at his head.

"Charlie, no," Karl shouted, dragging himself to his feet. "You don't want to do this."

"Like hell, I don't," Charlie growled.

Caruso grinned. "Go ahead. Pull the trigger."

"No," Karl shouted again. "He's not worth it. Let the courts decide his fate. He broke in here. He threatened your family. That's enough to put him away."

Charlie laughed. "Ha. You can't believe that. I know how the *justice* system works. It's just *us* against them. His badge gives him *protection* from the law."

"Charlie, you *have* to trust me on this. He will pay for what he's done here tonight. I promise."

Tension thickened the air as the police sirens sounded as if they were on top of them.

"Tick-tock." Caruso winked. "My buddies are coming to rescue me. I can't wait to see what they'll do to you once they learn you're their serial cop killer. They might reverse the death penalty just for you."

Charlie's hand tightened on the gun.

"Don't do it," Karl begged. "Don't listen to him. Please. Trust me."

Rushing feet pounded on the basement ceiling.

Charlie's trigger finger trembled, but at the last second, she swore and lowered the gun. "Fuck."

"Stupid bitch." Caruso picked up his gun and aimed.

"No!" Karl shoved Charlie out of the way and fired.

Johnnie screamed and clutched Charlie close.

Again, Caruso slammed backward, dropping his weapon. When he hit the floor this time, he was dead.

EPILOGUE

Five months later

For the second time in her life, Charlie walked out of prison. But eighteen months was a deal compared to what she could've gotten—had she been charged with murdering Detectives Wallace and Graham, and of course, Alexis Glover. As it happened, she only had to serve time for a probation violation for staying in a house with weapons. To her surprise, Detective Karl Nelson didn't rat her out.

Caruso was blamed for the murders of his own team members. Detective Crews's wife admitted to every media camera available that she believed Victor Caruso was behind the murder of her husband. Detective Crews had told his wife how he and the strike team had robbed a drug dealer, and they were in the middle of getting out of town when the place where he'd stashed his portion of the cash had blown up.

In the effort of closing the case, the mayor and the police superintendent cast guilt for the police murders on Caruso, who had gone crazy and sought revenge on Charlie and her family when he learned she'd been released from jail. Mrs. Crews also confessed that her husband had told her about murdering Hennessey Rawlins years ago. Weeks after Mrs. Crews's bombshell, the money recovered from both Wallace and Graham's crime scenes went missing, and Caruso's cut was never found. The prison grapevine reported that the money belonged to King Kong, and that his snitches on the inside got his shit back for him. It was even rumored he'd gotten his money back from Crews's hiding place before booby-trapping the place to explode when Crews came looking for it.

Charlie didn't give a shit about any of it.

She was vindicated. Her eighteen months' parole violation was cut short. Currently, a petition to the White House demanded to have Charlie's drug charges overturned and erased from her record. Charlie was happy to be out again. After she and her sisters shoved their way through a horde of reporters, she was surprised to see Detective Karl Nelson leaning against his car parked at the curb—a single red rose in his hand.

Charlie stopped in midstride.

Her sisters closed ranks around her.

Johnnie said, "You know, despite him looking like Henny and being a cop, he seems like a nice guy."

The other sisters nodded.

Michael added with a shrug, "At least he's not a snitch."

True. Karl could have dropped a dime on her for the Detective Graham killing. He knew it was Charlie on the grainy security tape, and yet he'd said nothing.

Karl's smile grew as he stared at her.

She could feel him willing her to come to him and give love another chance. She touched her visibly pregnant belly. *Why not?*

"Tell you what, girls. Don't wait up." Charlie swaggered away from her sisters and walked toward the next chapter of her life.

About the Author

National bestselling author **De'nesha Diamond** wrote dozens of books, and her Divas series was featured in *Essence* magazine. The Divas series has been described as a hard-hitting tale of crime in Memphis. Her writing has been featured in a myriad of national publications. The new Parker Crime series tackles D.C.'s dirty politicians.

PSEUDO

Briana Cole

PROLOGUE

The body was discovered just after one on a Friday afternoon—1:13, to be exact. It wasn't like that piece of information was important on its own. In fact, Detective Jamie Warren would have easily filed that away in his mental evidence portfolio if it wasn't for his partner's comment. "Thirteen-thirteen," Bernard said, his voice sharp with thirty-plus years of military command as they climbed the stairs together.

Jamie glanced at him. "What?"

"Thirteenth hour. Thirteenth minute. Today is Friday." Bernard shrugged off further explanation, but Jamie had to admit, the coincidence left him slightly uneasy. But nine years on the force and the title of lead detective hadn't come because of superstition, so he quickly dismissed the thought.

The apartment was flooded with typical crime scene chaos. Cops scoured the rooms for any shred of evidence, snapping pictures, jotting notes, picking over this, that, and the other. Red had been the woman's favorite color, he noticed almost instantly. Splashes of red adorned every swatch of furniture, from the deep-set throw pillows on the beige couch, to the lampshades, to the accent rug swallowing the rich hardwood floor. He nodded in approval. Subtle, yet dominating.

Jamie lifted his hand in greeting to a few idle officers and stooped to the shards of glass prickling the floor. Absently he lifted the aged picture discolored to a sepia hue, eyeing the bright-eyed college graduate whose smile was obstructed by broken glass.

"Detective." Jamie turned and nodded toward the young officer who gestured toward him. "Could you come here a sec?"

He followed him across the hall into the bedroom. Jamie hated feeling like they were intruding. He looked past the burgundy satin sheets, the purely feminine smell-good bottles scattered on the dresser. This was strictly business.

Another officer lifted the yellow crime scene tape fencing in the bathroom and Jamie ducked his head under to enter the en-suite. The woman lay in the middle of the floor, turned on her side with an arm sprawled out to the side of her body. Death had colored the woman's chocolate skin a bluish hue, and a curly mane of hair fanned around her face. *She looks like she's made of crystal.* He was surprised at his own comparison, but it seemed to fit—both in her fragility and in her pallor. Professionalism masked his face as he scanned the corpse down to her bare feet. But he couldn't help the stroke of grief that tugged at his heart. The victim couldn't have been any more than twenty-five. His own daughter had just turned twenty. He had never seen this woman a day in his life, but he certainly felt like he knew her. She, too, had been someone's daughter.

Jamie used a gloved hand to lift the woman's hand, a small butterfly tattoo on her inside wrist exposed by the tattered sleeve of a satin green blouse. *Blouse and navy slacks.* He made a mental note of the attire. He rose as the forensics photographer continued to bend and angle to snap pictures around him.

"No signs of forced entry." Another officer was bringing everyone up to speed as Jamie reentered the bedroom. "The person had a key somehow."

"Or she let them in because it was someone she thought she knew," Jamie murmured. "Or someone who knew her. Who is the landlord?"

The officer began flipping through the pages on his mini spiral pad. "Vernita Allen," he read. "Age fifty-eight. She and her husband purchased the building twenty years ago. Recent widow, as he died of lung cancer six years ago, so she's been running the place herself ever since."

Jamie nodded. "Find out where she was and what she was doing," he instructed. "Also get a list of employees. Maintenance, whoever. I want to know everyone who might have had access to keys to this building." He stepped toward the dresser, ignoring the strap of some sexy lingerie piece peeking from a drawer. He glanced over the perfume and hair products, noted the antique jewelry box shoved against the mirror. Rubies glittered from all sides, encased in gold framings of intricate swirls. Expensive, indeed. Anybody with eyes and half a shred of common sense could look at the box and know it could at least go for five thousand dollars on the black market. He pulled a pen from his pocket, used it to gently lift the lid, and had to swallow a chuckle. Not strings of pearls or other fancy trinkets, but loose change—mostly pennies—paper clips, gum, and was that a scratch-off ticket? He closed the top.

"So, our assailant didn't take anything," he concluded, walking toward the window. He parted the blinds a bit and glanced at the pedestrians three stories below.

"Doesn't look like it," his partner, Bernard, confirmed. "And she had plenty to take. Lots of little gadgets and expensive stuff he could've snatched."

Jamie let the blinds snap closed. *If that was the motive.*

"Cable man found her," Bernard was saying, nodding his

head in the direction of the bathroom. "Says she had an appointment, and when he arrived, the door was open. We should know more after the autopsy."

Jamie nodded and turned to head back into the living room. "Cable guy?"

"Paul from AT&T," Bernard said. "They took him down to the station. Young guy. He was a little shaken up."

"Hell, I would be too after finding a dead body." *Especially at 1:13,* Jamie wanted to add, but he knew the timing would've been bad for their friendly banter. Plus, his partner didn't play about his signs. Even still, Jamie couldn't shake the tug of familiarity. Maybe there was a little bit more under the surface. More than met the eye.

CHAPTER 1

Washington drummed his fingers impatiently on the table, a half-empty glass of Crown Royal at his elbow. He couldn't believe Lisa was pulling this shit again. Here he was, having spent all day planning a nice anniversary dinner, and her ungrateful ass didn't even have the decency to call and say she was going to be late.

On a stifled groan, he eyed the flames of the candlelight flickering shadows on the walls. The plates had already been set, displaying the wide array of gourmet dishes he'd had the chef prepare before he had sent him home for the evening. Lisa's gift, a surprise that had taken him weeks to find, was situated in a small, wrapped box at her end of the table. A light jazz tune wafted through the hidden speakers and poured a soothing ambiance into the dining room.

A beam of headlights spilled through the sheer curtains, and Washington glanced over expectantly, only to hiss in annoyance when the lights did a turnaround maneuver before the car disappeared. He couldn't believe he had been foolish enough to think this woman loved anyone but herself. She damn sure didn't mind expressing her love when he was handing over his credit cards for her to purchase clothes or jewelry. He had even broken down and given her a key to his mini mansion, something he couldn't remember ever doing for a female. All to keep her close. But something about this young, vibrant, outspoken woman rocked his world and left him pining for her.

He had met Lisa Brown a few months ago. She was an obvious new face around the bank that he frequented, a fact she had confirmed when he struck up a conversation and she admitted to having just moved to South Jersey. When this mystery woman continued to entertain his advances, he had to admit, it came as a slight surprise.

Washington didn't consider himself a handsome guy. In fact, no one had ever used his looks as an identifying factor. He was pretty plain-looking with a milk-chocolate complexion and more age lines than he cared to acknowledge. He kept his hair short in a style that seemed to downplay the peppering of gray strands in his hair and goatee. He wasn't skinny, fat, or muscular. Just average in body stature. But he did fall a few inches shorter than most in the height department, which seemed to work well with Lisa, because she wasn't all that tall herself, even with heels. But what he lacked in looks, he made up for in other areas.

As a plastic surgeon, Washington knew his money was his main attraction, which actually gave him the confidence to approach women. So, he had no problem striking up a conversation with little Miss Lisa Brown that day in the bank as she handled his business transactions. He had been eyeing her for a while, so he was happy to finally make his move. She had kept the conversation professional, and he honestly figured she would just discard the business card he slid in her deal tray underneath the glass window. But she did call about a week later, and they had spent a lot of time on the phone before she actually agreed to go out with him.

Washington couldn't help but find Lisa intriguing. She was very reticent about her past. Her parents had died when she was young, and she had no family to speak of other than an older sister. She rarely spoke of herself, instead always steering the conversation back to him. In one breath, she carried a shy innocence that mesmerized him. But the longer they dated, the more she seemed to blossom.

His mother didn't care for Lisa much. Not that he was too surprised. She didn't care much for anyone. But she had especially made it known on several occasions that Lisa was too sneaky, too young, and he was too good for her. Washington frowned in his glass at the distasteful thought. The fact that he was forty-nine to her mere twenty-four years didn't help the situation, either.

He liked to think Lisa was different from all the others. She definitely acted like it when she was around by making him feel like a king. *When* she was around. More often than not, she made a habit of not answering her phone and not calling back for days at a time. When she finally did pop back up, she gave half-assed excuses, acting as if nothing was wrong. Frankly, he tried to swallow that flaw of hers because it paled in comparison to all her positive attributes. Besides, with his long and crazy hours at work, he knew how important trust was in a relationship. Lisa had never given him a reason not to trust her. So, he stopped bringing up his views on these little incidents altogether to keep the peace. He really should have known better, though. He wasn't stupid by any means.

But it was times like this, when he was sitting alone waiting for her to show up while his repeated phone calls went straight to her voice mail, that he knew something was up.

Washington knocked back the rest of the alcohol and rose to make himself another drink. It was enough to calm his nerves for the moment. He stood at the bar, eyeing his cell phone, almost willing it to ring, when he heard the jingle of keys in the front door. Her heels clicked on the hardwood floor entrance in rapid succession, as if she were stumbling into the house. Then calmer footsteps as she moved, unhurried, toward the dining room.

He had gone so far as to lay a trail of rose petals that led her way, and he figured, with the only light coming from the candles on the table, she would eventually make it there. In the meantime, he poured himself another drink and reevaluated what he was about to do. Earlier that day, he had been so sure. Now, with Lisa strolling in almost four hours late with no call or concern, he didn't know.

"Hey," she greeted, appearing in the doorway.

Washington took her in as her eyes swept over the elaborate display. She was dressed casually in a skintight black dress and a cropped blue jean jacket. She wore knee-high black boots and a gray infinity scarf around her neck. A black and silver Coach bag, a gift from him, dangled from her shoulder. Her burgundy bob had grown out quite a bit, and now the front fluttered flirtatiously at her shoulders while the back was layered and tapered to reveal the butterfly tattoo on the back of her neck.

He had to admit, her body was beautiful. He should know, he had operated and paid for it himself. Her breasts were larger and perky enough to peek from the necklines of her shirts. Her butt was bigger, too, and filled out a pair of jeans perfectly. She had also requested some facial contouring: a slimmer nose, larger lips, longer eyelashes, and a slight cheek restructuring to get rid of her "fatty face," as she so eloquently put it. He was definitely the best in the business, and the multiple procedures had only defined and enhanced her beauty.

"Hey," he responded, his voice equally as unenthusiastic. She didn't even seem fazed by the rose petals, the candles, or the dinner. And here he was thinking he had gone above and beyond to make her feel special.

"Sorry I'm late," Lisa said finally, entering the rest of the way into the dining room. She plopped down in her seat and leaned over to begin unzipping her boots. "I got held up with Andrea. You know that girl can talk." She kicked off her shoes, picked up her fork, and immediately dove into the braised chicken.

"You knew we had plans, Lisa," Washington said. "I told you earlier this week I wanted to do something special for our anniversary. The least you could've done was call. That shit is inconsiderate."

Lisa paused long enough to look up. "I said I was sorry, Washington. What do you want me to do?"

Washington bit back his anger and crossed over to the table once more. He sat down beside her and could only watch as she continued picking at the food without so much as a "thank you." His eyes flipped to the gift at her elbow. He was still torn.

"Then I got a call about a friend of mine coming into town this weekend," Lisa said as she lifted the glass of wine to her lips. "I haven't seen him in forever. So, I'll probably be hanging with him until he leaves."

"Is that some kind of hint not to mess with you?" Washington tried to keep the agitation out of his voice, but he was failing miserably.

Again, Lisa didn't seem to notice. Or care. She placed her hand over his, the fresh manicure making her nails stand out against her bronzed complexion. "I didn't mean it like that, sweetie," she said with a soft smile. "I just meant it'll be great to see him after so long, so I'm going to want to spend as much time with him as possible."

"Duly noted."

They ate in silence for a moment. Well, Lisa ate. Washington tried to eat, but he had definitely lost his appetite. When she'd cleaned her plate, she sat back on a sigh and tossed him an appreciative smile. "This was all so sweet of you," she said.

Her eyelids drooped, and it was then Washington realized she was under the influence of a lot more than the one glass of wine she had just consumed. The faint smell of vodka seemed to linger underneath the Flowerbomb fragrance she wore. "I don't tell you as often as I should how much I love and appreciate you, Washington," she was saying, her finger lightly stroking the back of his hand. "You're a good man."

She licked her lips, those now-luscious lips of hers, and he felt the crotch of his slacks tighten. It was his fault he had made her so damn irresistible. To hell with the hesitancies. He wasn't getting any younger, and he was ready. And frankly, this opportunity was as close as he was going to get. "Lisa, I have something for you," he murmured.

"What is it?"

He reached for the gift, and with a small sigh, he lifted the lid of the velvet box. The ring's brilliant diamonds cast streams of glitter between the folds of the white leather pillows in the box. He heard her sharp intake of breath as her eyes rounded in shock.

"You complete me, Lisa Brown." Washington hadn't rehearsed his proposal. Whether fueled by the alcohol or anxiety, fear, or all of the above, the words seemed to tumble from his lips before he had time to think or stop them. "You and all of your craziness. I want to spend the rest of my life with you. I know it seems sudden. I know we have our little rocky moments. But I can't help that I've fallen in love with you. Will you marry me?"

Lisa's eyes never left the ring. She let out a breath and blinked hard, as if trying to clear a mirage. "Wow," she whispered. "You don't waste any time, do you?"

"Is that a yes?" he pressed, his heart nearly stopping at her behavior. He had expected screaming, hugging, jumping around feverishly, and a quick, non-hesitant "yes" as soon as he flipped open the box. Why was she so damn calm about this situation when his nerves were rattling like crazy?

She never verbalized her affirmation. She merely nodded her head and held out her hand for him to slide the ring on her finger. Again, it wasn't quite what he expected, but it worked for him. At least she hadn't messed it all up with a flat-out "no."

CHAPTER 2

Kennedy lay in bed, quietly listening to Washington's congested snore. Her mind was reeling from the day's earlier events. But she needed to see the confirmation. Lifting her hand in the air, she spread her fingers wide to watch the diamond engagement ring wink in the darkened room. Kennedy had to admit, it was absolutely stunning. But then, did she really expect any less? One thing Dr. Washington Bell had going for him was great taste. Now, whether she would actually go through with the marriage was another issue altogether.

He wanted to marry Lisa Brown. But she was as fictitious as an Aesop's fable.

It wasn't just the acrylic nails and body work, either. Nor was it the contacts or the contoured makeup she often wore that sharpened her cheekbones and widened the doe eyes that Washington absolutely adored. No, it was her. All of her. Just a few short months ago, Lisa Brown didn't even exist. Well, not this version, anyway. And pretty soon, she wouldn't anymore.

Sighing, Kennedy angled her head to look at him. Washington was actually a very nice guy. Never married, no kids, with the exception of a son he said he'd lost contact with years ago. So, his vulnerability and lack of ties had made him a prime target. He had money and lots of it. But now he was looking for someone to settle down with. She hadn't even been surprised by the proposal if she had to be honest with herself. But she definitely wasn't looking for another husband.

Kennedy had done the marriage thing before—well, twice before, if she counted the fake one under another alias. But that was just long enough to get her hands on some of his workers' compensation settlement and sift a few thousand dollars into a private account. Kennedy had just been starting out then, a little petty fraud to stay afloat. She'd thought that marriage was the only way she could manipulate men out of their money. They questioned girlfriends all the time. Rarely did they question their wives. *Boyfriends are smart. Husbands are stupid.* Words her older sister, Deven, had relayed once. At that time, Kennedy didn't get it. But now, three years in the game, shit made perfect sense. She had managed to master the art of deception so well that sometimes even she couldn't distinguish the blurred lines that separated her true reality from the reality she made up.

Kennedy's last identity before she'd had to assume the role of Lisa Brown, was as an LA yoga instructor named Shaye. But the real Shaye had caught on to the scheme quicker than most and started filing disputes on the fraudulent charges. So, Kennedy had abandoned that identity fast. This Lisa one wasn't too bad, though she really didn't have too much. Just a few assets tied up in stocks, which Kennedy had already withdrawn and depleted. Her credit was fair enough, so Kennedy had been able to open and max out a few credit cards. Plus, thanks to some broke college student who needed fifty dollars, she had been able to get a business plan written up for some fake home health agency. A few more forged documents, and she had walked out of the bank with an approval for a small business loan that was going to be deposited any day now.

All that was well and good, but the "big fish" was Washington. Kennedy had been grooming and polishing him since she had eyed his accounts that day he visited the bank to make a deposit. And now, it looked like she was finally about to cash in on that investment. About damn time.

Kennedy moved slowly, sliding her naked body from underneath the sheets and shivering against the chilly air that bit her skin. She made her way into the adjoining bathroom, the new iPhone Washington had purchased already in hand. It was late, but she knew her sister would be up. She didn't know why she felt compelled to call Deven, but Kennedy was already punching in the ten digits and listening to the ringing echo in her ear before she had even given it a second thought. For good measure, she nudged the door closed, leaving a crack just big enough to see Washington still reveling in his deep slumber.

As expected, Deven picked up on the third ring, sounding just as wide awake. "Girl, what are you doing up this time of night?" she greeted.

Kennedy took a seat on the lip of the whirlpool tub. "Couldn't sleep, sis."

"What's wrong?"

A confession played on her tongue before she swallowed it. Kennedy had never told her sister about her little hustle. It wasn't like Deven was judgmental or anything. To be honest, Kennedy was somewhat ashamed. Somewhat. As long as she kept the truth to herself, she didn't have to reflect on her indiscretions. But it was times like this, when it weighed heavier on her heart, that a part of her wished she had someone to talk to about it.

"Nothing's wrong." Kennedy opted to comfort her sister with a lie rather than hurt her with the truth. "Just a little nervous."

"I know you ain't nervous about Benji," Deven said on a light chuckle. "Don't tell me your nose is still wide open for that boy."

Kennedy was glad her sister was on the phone rather than talking in person. Surely, she would have commented on the sudden embarrassment coloring her cheeks at the true statement she still refused to acknowledge.

Deven loved to boast that Benji was the "one that got away." Kennedy had loved that boy something serious ever since high school, but he hadn't so much as given her the time of day. Kennedy had had to swallow her discontent and flaming jealousy as he entertained every cheerleader, groupie, and popular chick at Lyons High while she had to resort to being his "homegirl."

They had managed to stay in touch after graduation, especially since they were more alike than Kennedy had realized. Like her, Benji was crazy-smart, but he didn't bother applying himself, instead opting for fast-money hustles and illegal schemes because the stiff, blue-collar jobs didn't pay enough for him. Which was why she often relied on him for assistance when it came to stealing her identities. Benji had a plug for everything.

Kennedy didn't realize she was grinning like an idiot until she caught a glimpse of her reflection in the mirror. She had to shake her head at her own giddiness. Benji had moved to Atlanta while Kennedy had decided to stay in Jersey. He was flying back in a few days to visit family, and she had readily volunteered to pick him up from the airport. Just the thought of seeing him again gave her butterflies.

"Benji is just my friend," Kennedy said, her lie almost wistful. "It'll be good to see him again. That's all."

"Uh-huh." Deven's murmur was laced with doubt, but she didn't bother pushing the issue. She knew Kennedy better than the girl knew herself. "Well, if it's not Benji, what's got you so nervous?"

"I just wanted to share some news."

"Good news?"

Kennedy paused, not really sure how to answer the question. It was going to be good—hell, great, actually—as soon as she cashed in. She thought for a split second before responding. "Something like that."

"Is it about Washington? How is he, anyway? Haven't heard you mention him lately. Is his old ass even still in the picture?"

Kennedy rolled her eyes at the offhand comment, shaking her head when she heard her sister chuckling to herself. "As a matter of fact, he is. He proposed."

Deven's pause was so heavy Kennedy could almost feel her disbelief. "I know you're lying," she said, finally.

Kennedy flexed her fingers, eyeing the engagement ring once more. It looked even bigger and more brilliant under the fluorescent lights of the bathroom's vanity lamps. "I'm serious."

"Oh, damn, girl." Deven broke the awkward silence following her sister's admission. "What are you going to do? Did you say 'yes'?"

Kennedy sighed. "I just don't know if I'm ready to get married," she admitted honestly. "We have fun. Washington is cool, don't get me wrong. But marriage?" One secret she had never told her sister was about her first real marriage, if it could be called such a thing. She had met Lewis online, then gone to the courthouse after just six months of social media and phone dating. Her intention was really to make Benji jealous, but the shit had backfired. Lewis was controlling and abusive, and Kennedy had rushed to get an annulment before the ink had fully dried on their marriage license. Thanks to Benji forging Lewis's signature, she was once again a single woman within the same year, and she had moved on without even a backward glance.

Not saying it would be like that with Washington. The man didn't have a violent bone in his body. But realistically, knowing her intentions, did she even want to waste his time?

"Just think about it," Deven was saying, pulling Kennedy's attention back to the conversation. "Seriously. I always told you that guy was too old for you, and I figured it would only be a matter of time before he was ready to settle down. Do you even love him?"

Kennedy remained quiet as she mulled over her sister's words. One thing about it, her sister was only twenty-five, but Deven had the wisdom of someone well beyond her years, and her maturity often manifested when she spoke her logic. Kennedy could only agree with her. In a normal circumstance, it would make sense. But Kennedy's circumstances were far from normal.

After Deven mentioned needing to stay with her for a few days while her carpet was being replaced, they hung up and Kennedy headed back to the bedroom, her mind even heavier with the burden of uncertainty. If she pulled out now, all her hard work would go to waste. But if she married Washington, she would at least get something out of the arrangement first. That would make the last few months well worth her trouble. Keeping Lisa's identity was risky, she knew. But hopefully by the time the creditors even bothered to investigate whatever fraud allegations Lisa had filed, Kennedy would be long gone. She would just try to lie low for a while longer, only spending what she needed to, and making sure to milk Washington for everything she could.

Kennedy got back into bed and turned over, but insomnia had her wide awake. Needing something to do, she picked up her cell phone once again and began navigating to one of her favorite jewelry websites, Shane Co. She scrolled aimlessly, looking for pieces that caught her eye, and because it was Lisa's credit card saved in her shopper profile, not even bothering to glance at the prices.

After settling on a fourteen-carat white-gold diamond tennis bracelet and pear-shaped sapphire and diamond earrings, Kennedy purchased the items and had them shipped to Washington's house. Lately, she had been spending more time over here than at her condo anyway. She then turned her attention to the TV, immediately stabbing the VOLUME DOWN button to make sure the noise didn't wake Washington.

It was the image that caught her eye first. Kennedy jolted upright in bed, the sheets falling to pool at her waist. That green blouse. She had been wearing it the last time Kennedy saw her. The real Lisa Brown.

She snuck a glance over at Washington, and confirming he was still sound asleep, upped the volume just a bit to catch the end of the newscaster's commentary. ". . . *body of the woman found in her Atlantic City apartment has been identified as twenty-five-year-old Lisa Michele Brown. Police are ruling this death a homicide . . .*"

CHAPTER 3

"Seriously, girl, something crazy is going on," Lisa said, sliding a glance to the window.

Kennedy feigned confusion as she, too, looked to the window. Lisa was usually soft and quiet, sure. But today she clearly seemed shaken up. "What do you mean?" she asked.

Lisa sighed and turned her head in the direction of the galley kitchen. "You want a drink?" She was almost pleading.

Recognizing that she just wanted something—anything—to do, Kennedy nodded and followed her.

Lisa plucked a mug from the dishwasher and began to collect the makings for coffee. Kennedy already had a feeling why the woman was so nervous, but instead of voicing it, she remained quiet. She watched her take extra care with scooping the sugar, pouring the milk, and stirring the liquid until it turned caramel brown.

For a while, all that could be heard was the spoon clinking against the sides of the mug with every swirl. Finally, Lisa turned and handed Kennedy the cup. "Sorry I don't have anything stronger." She offered her a weak smile. Kennedy accepted the drink, and because Lisa was looking, took a healthy swallow. Lisa turned, braced herself against the laminate countertop, and sighed. "I feel like someone is stalking me," she started.

Kennedy was thankful she had the coffee mug in her hand so Lisa wouldn't be able to see her tense up. "Why do you say that?"

"I mean, first the fraud on my accounts, the missing money, and every time I change my passcodes, I still get hacked."

Kennedy dismissed the comment with a shake of her head. Of course she knew all that was happening. She was the one doing it. But still, stalking? That was a bit extreme. "I think you're overreacting a little, Lisa," she said. "People get hacked all the time. Doesn't mean they're being stalked. Plus, your bank opened that investigation—"

"No, it's not just that." Lisa crossed the kitchen to lean on the pub table alongside Kennedy. She lowered her voice as if the two weren't the only ones in the room. "Someone followed me home yesterday."

Kennedy frowned at the new information. "Who?"

"Hell, I don't know. It freaked me the hell out."

"Did you call the police?"

"Yeah, but they couldn't do anything. I don't have any proof."

Lisa gripped her wrist and used her thumb to massage the butterfly tattoo, as if it gave her strength. "I'm thinking of getting a gun."

Kennedy laughed and placed the coffee on the table. "I think you're doing the most you can," she assured her. "You need to relax and get some rest. I'll give you a call tomorrow, okay?"

It was clear Lisa was still apprehensive, but she pursed her lips and nodded. "You mind staying for a little bit longer?"

Kennedy glanced at the clock on the stove. "I can't, girl. I'm already late. Washington is supposed to be doing some-

thing special for me at the house for our anniversary." The fear was still evident in Lisa's eyes, so Kennedy pulled her in for a hug. "Hey," she murmured. "You're going to be fine. Lock up when I leave and take a bubble bath or something."

Lisa nodded.

Kennedy touched the satin green blouse Lisa wore, and just because she knew it would make her smile, added, "And wash this for me. I want to borrow it next time."

It must have been a coincidence.

Kennedy tried her best to convince herself as she drove to the airport. She had tried her best to shake the anxiety, but the news story circulating about Lisa's murder was clawing at her stomach so deep it was nearly making her sick. Especially considering she had been the last person to see her alive.

She didn't consider Lisa a friend, by any means. She was sure if someone had asked Lisa, it would have been a completely different story. But to Kennedy, the woman had just been a target. That friendship was a means to get closer to her so she could secretly sift money from right under her nose.

Lisa had been a bank customer, like most of the other victims. Kennedy's teller position allotted her the opportunity to see bank accounts, CDs, credit scores, and enough identifying information to use at her discretion. Lisa had been in for a withdrawal one day a few months back when Kennedy saw a huge settlement deposit for a car accident. Lisa worked in payroll for the hospital, so it wasn't like she was rich. But she had enough money and social personality to make her easy to befriend.

Kennedy had Benji forge a few documents for good measure. The thing was, the fake birth certificate he gave her put the women at the same hospital at birth. Same high school attended, same college, same accounting major. Then suddenly, Lisa Brown was murdered.

Kennedy glanced at the clock in her truck, realizing she

had only a few minutes left before Benji's plane arrived. She didn't know whether to ask him about it or just leave the subject alone altogether. Part of her didn't want to know, out of fear of the truth. The other part, the suspicious part that had been nagging at her since she'd first heard the story, well, that part needed his advice on what the hell to do next.

The airport was crowded as usual. Not wanting to chance going inside, Kennedy parked in one of the garages and whipped out her phone to text Benji with her location. Then she settled in to wait.

Without thinking, Kennedy reached into her pocket and pulled out the driver's license she had been carrying around. It was weird seeing her old face. The plastic surgeries had definitely redefined her, mentally and physically. But this, this young girl was ripe in youth, despite the makeup and the hair. And the features were so much like her mother, whom she despised, it was almost sickening.

Kennedy turned the driver's license over, then held it up to the light. She wasn't exactly sure what she was searching for. Maybe if she looked close enough, some evidence of Lisa's murderer would manifest itself.

The knock on her window snatched a gasp from her throat while the license slipped from her fingers. She glanced to the passenger side window, and sure enough, there he was.

It was as if time had stood still. Benji had always been sexy as hell, and though it had been a couple of years since his last visit, his presence now still had that same stimulating effect. His locks had grown in nice and luxurious. He had the top half pinned into a ponytail while the bottom half gently caressed his shoulders. His facial hair had also grown, and he kept it trimmed to form a neat fuzz outlining a full set of lips. It looked as if the edges of a tattoo kissed the muscles of his arms and poked out from underneath the sleeves of his polo. The man was still damn fine.

Kennedy flicked the button to unlock the doors and

watched as he slid into the car, bringing with him the familiar Cuban musk of his cologne. He reached behind her to put his suitcase in the back seat, then looked at her as she stared, almost dumbstruck.

"Damn, girl." A startled smirk formed at the corners of his lips. "I see New Jersey has been treating you good."

Kennedy relaxed into a smile, still breathless from the feelings tumbling around in her chest. "It's been a long time," she said. *A year and a half, to be exact.* Sure, they spoke often on the phone, but actually seeing him always reignited those feelings she tried her best to bury.

Benji leaned over the middle console and pulled her into a hug, and Kennedy could all but feel herself quivering right there in the car. "I know," he said, leaning back. "How have you been?"

"Good. What about you?"

He nodded and stroked his goatee. If Kennedy didn't know any better, she could detect lust in those eyes that were so casually studying her. "Everything is everything," he answered, finally. "I appreciate you coming to pick me up."

"It's no problem." Kennedy exited the garage and navigated the truck toward the airport exit ramp. "Where am I taking you? Your aunt's house?"

"Yeah, a little later. Why don't we go grab something to eat first so we can talk."

Kennedy nodded. That was exactly what she would have preferred, but she was relieved she didn't have to suggest it.

They stopped at Denny's near the airport for breakfast. The restaurant was not crowded this time of day. The hostess seated them in a quaint little corner booth toward the back. Benji slid into the booth space opposite her, and their knees bumped companionably under the table.

"So, what's been up?" he said with a grin after the waitress had taken their orders.

Kennedy gave a half shrug and absently fingered the Pandora charm bracelet adorning her wrist. "Not much of anything," she said. "Just working, the usual."

Benji took her hand and angled her wrist toward him so he could get a better view of the striking piece of jewelry. "Flashy," he murmured, and Kennedy wasn't sure if that was a compliment or if there was a hint of jealousy in the one-word phrase. "Who you fucking for this kind of thing?"

"Excuse me?"

"You heard me." He hadn't bothered to let go of her hand as his eyes lifted to hers. "Who you got buying you jewelry like this?"

Offended, Kennedy snatched her hand back and rolled her eyes. "How you figure I didn't just buy this myself?"

Benji grunted in response and leaned back, casually tossing his arm across the back of the booth. "Okay, well, then, who you fucking for the new face? New titties? New ass? You bought all that yourself, too?"

Now it was Kennedy's turn to roll her eyes. She didn't know why the interrogation was beginning to piss her off. "Why you so worried about who I'm with?" she said.

"I'm just trying to look out for you."

"Oh, please, Benji. Since when? You never cared about me."

To her surprise, the statement had him laughing. "How the hell can you say that? I'm always calling you, texting you, trying to make sure you good. Even had my family looking out for you, girl. How can you say I don't care?"

Because you never came to see me, Kennedy wanted to say, but embarrassment had her pursing her lips shut. *Because you don't love me like I love you. Because you only think of me as a friend, even though you know I want something more.*

"Just don't get too serious," Benji said, leveling his eyes. "You don't need complications."

Kennedy thought about the engagement. She had made sure to slip the ring off before leaving the house that morning, and it was now hidden in the side pocket of her Louis Vuitton purse. For some reason, his little comment had a jealous twinge attached to the words. The thought brought her enormous pleasure. "Why shouldn't I get too serious?" she asked, taking a sip of her fruit punch and studying him as he took his time answering.

"Because it gets too messy," Benji said. "For real. You don't need to complicate anything. Just keep doing you. I don't want to have to say 'I told you so.'"

She rolled her eyes. "That's because you think you're always right."

Benji shrugged. "I usually am."

She knew he was insinuating it was because of the deceptive lifestyle she was in, and her heart fell a bit. It was still a concern but not in the way she craved. Kennedy wondered what he would say if she told him she had been dating and it was working out just fine. She didn't know if he would be angry, though. So instead, she said, "Well, none of that matters. Trust me, I'm not about to let you say *I told you so*. I've been good. As you can see. Still got my place, and you see I got my new car."

"Yeah, I see," he said with a nod toward the white Range Rover parked out front. She watched him swipe the screen on his cell phone and begin keying in something.

"What about you?" Kennedy asked. "What have you been up to?"

"Nothing much. Just working. Living. Making it."

"How is Atlanta?"

Benji chuckled as if he was thinking of some secret joke. "It's straight," he answered, simply.

Kennedy cocked her head and lifted a curious brow. "Just *straight*? Nothing else?"

"Nah."

"So, why do you stay? Come back home to Jersey. Your family is up here." *I'm up here*.

Benji looked up from his phone then, a grin playing on his lips. "I'm good where I'm at."

Disappointment had a frown creasing Kennedy's face. When was he going to stop playing these damn games with her? It wasn't like he was leading her on or anything. Benji had always been straight up and direct with her, and though she hated his candor, she appreciated it. But every time he reached out, even as a friend, a part of her got her hopes up. Deven was right. She was still pining away over this boy, a high-school itch that had never been scratched.

Kennedy's mouth was suddenly dry, so she lifted her glass and took another sip of her drink. It went down without any taste. "I haven't been to Atlanta in a minute," she murmured. "Maybe I should come down there for a visit soon." She expected him to respond to her self-invite. He didn't.

The waitress came back with their food and began setting the plates down on the table. She left again and Kennedy dove into her French toast, sighing in satisfaction as she chewed. She couldn't remember the last time she'd eaten at Denny's. Her lavish lifestyle afforded her five-star restaurants and chef-catered meals. Her palate had grown accustomed to the gourmet dishes so that now she had a newfound appreciation for a a simple plate of French toast and eggs.

They finished their meals, and Benji paid for both without hesitation. As they were leaving, he turned to her with a wink. "So, tell me about Mr. Wonderful."

Kennedy ignored how the gesture had her heart fluttering. "What are you talking about?" she stalled.

Benji nodded toward her bracelet again. "Must have some money."

"He's nobody," she admitted. But the thought that he kept inquiring thrilled her. Just maybe he did have some feelings for her. He was just so damn unreadable.

They slid in the car, and Kennedy didn't immediately move to crank it up. She sat back in her seat, debating on whether to go ahead and mention what she had been so anxious to discuss. "Benji, I may need your help with something."

"What's up?"

"I probably need some paperwork for a new identity."

She caught his nod out of her peripheral. "I got you," he agreed.

She breathed a sigh. She knew he would help with that part. No questions asked. Benji had always been there for her in that sense. It was obvious she still had more to say, though, and she felt Benji's eyes on her in a questioning stare.

"What is it?" he prompted when she made no move to speak again.

Kennedy thought about the news story of Lisa Brown. No way should it be linked to her, but the fact that she had appeared to be her "friend" and she was at her place shortly before she was murdered, well that shit was making her feel uneasy. Her mind flashed to the coffee she had been drinking while Lisa poured out her concerns about a stalker. She had been telling the truth. And now she was dead. Kennedy knew she should have felt more grief about that. But all she could think about was that damn mug sitting on Lisa's kitchen table. The mug with her fingerprints on it. Would she be a suspect?

"Have you seen the news lately?" When Benji shook his head, Kennedy continued. "You know the stuff I asked you for a while back, for a Lisa Brown?"

"Yeah."

"Well, the real Lisa Brown, the one whose identity I've been stealing, she's dead."

The air seemed too quiet around them, and Kennedy looked for some sort of reaction from Benji. His face remained expressionless. "Okay," he said finally. "What does that have to do with you?"

"That doesn't seem like a coincidence to you, Benji?"

"Hell no. There are plenty of Lisa Browns. That name is common as hell."

"There's more," Kennedy murmured. "I was there at her house. I think it was the night she died."

"Why the hell would you be over there?"

"I was . . . kind of acting like her friend. She mentioned something about how she thought she had a stalker because of the identity theft, so I thought she was just being paranoid. I didn't think—I never thought . . ." Kennedy clenched her fists to stop her hands from shaking. "Benji, what if they think I did it?"

"Hey, it's cool." Benji pulled her into his arms for a reassuring hug. "Don't worry about it."

He sounded calm. Way too calm. Kennedy didn't like how he was just brushing this off. Something wasn't sitting right with her. But she couldn't read him. She doubted Benji would have anything to do with this situation. But why was he so calm about the news? Almost as if he knew something?

Kennedy shook her head to try to dispel the crazy thoughts. Now who was the one being paranoid? Why would Benji have anything to do with Lisa's murder? Plus, hadn't she just picked him up from the airport—meaning he'd flown in from Atlanta only hours before? But then again, he knew people in Jersey . . .

Benji released a frustrated sigh as Kennedy continued to sit in silence. "Listen, everything is going to be fine," he said. "Nobody will suspect you had anything to do with it. In a few days, the whole case will blow over and you won't even hear about it anymore."

"How can you be so sure?"

"Because that's how the news works." Benji paused for a bit, then added, "Why are you stressing anyway? Has somebody contacted you?"

"No."

"Okay, then." His words carried that *end of discussion* tone, and he gestured toward the ignition. "Can we leave now?"

Kennedy watched Benji turn his attention back to his phone. For some reason, she couldn't shake the nagging feeling that something was going on. And Benji sure as hell wasn't letting on that he knew what it was.

CHAPTER 4

The ride to Benji's aunt's house was tense. By the time they arrived, Kennedy was grateful for the reprieve. Not to mention Benji's aunt Gloria, or Glo as everyone called her, was the family member she was especially close to.

Aunt Glo's house was an older historic home not too far from the downtown district. When they pulled up, a collection of vehicles was already stuffed in the short driveway and spilling out onto the street. Kennedy maneuvered her truck in an awkward parallel park, and they walked to the house.

Sure enough, the living room was filled with people scattered on the floral-print furniture. Someone had some music playing even though the TV was on, and the smell of a soul food dinner wafted from the adjoining kitchen. Kennedy greeted them as they came in, then left them all to flock around Benji. It had been years since he had been home, so some kind of homecoming party was expected. She found Aunt Glo and Uncle Bernard in the kitchen. Seeing Benji's uncle had her pausing at the entryway, her blood chilling a few degrees.

In all the chaos, she had totally forgotten Bernard was a detective. And now, standing here in his presence was suffocating. He stood at the counter dressed casually in some slacks and a polo shirt, the neck of a Corona between his fingers. He gingerly took a sip of his beer and nodded his greeting in Kennedy's direction. That familiar smile of his should have relaxed her. Bernard had known her for years, for as long as she'd known Benji. Instead, it only heightened her anxiety, her muscles so tense they were nearly aching. She glanced away when Bernard's detective badge seemed to wink at her from his belt loop.

Aunt Glo was the first to break the brief silence. "How have you been, Kennedy?" she asked, turning from the pot on the stove.

"I've been good," she answered. Needing something to do, she crossed to the refrigerator to pull out the lemonade. *Was Bernard watching her? Did he know something?* No, there was no way. She had nothing to do with it. Lisa was very much alive when Kennedy left the apartment. She tried her best to push the sudden thoughts of the dead Lisa Brown from her mind. If it came down to it, Uncle Bernard would have to be on her side. He would know she would never murder anyone. The identity theft . . . well, that was another story. But just because she was a thief sure as hell didn't mean she was a murderer. He would understand that, right?

"Thanks for picking up Benny from the airport," Aunt Glo said, wiping her hands on her apron. "Heavens knows it's about time that boy made it back home. Always complaining about being so busy in Georgia. What could he possibly be so busy doing?"

"Don't start, Glo," Bernard chastised. "That boy is grown, and he can move anywhere he wants to."

Glo rolled her eyes. "I still don't have to like it," she grumbled. Kennedy sipped her lemonade, swallowing the urge to agree.

A notification from Bernard's cell phone pierced the air, and Kennedy held her breath as she watched him pull it from his pocket and swipe the screen to eye the message. His face remained stoic and completely unreadable. So much like Benji.

"I'll be back, babe," he said before downing the rest of his drink.

Glo frowned. "What's wrong?"

"Work stuff," he said simply, then pecked a kiss on her cheek. "Be back in a few hours." He lifted a hand in Kennedy's direction. "Talk to you later. Good to see you again." He was gone before Kennedy had a chance to respond, and she let out the breath she had been holding. His words echoed in his absence. *Talk to her later? Was that meant to be literal?*

Kennedy turned to walk toward the bar where Glo had various bottles of liquor, vodka, and wine organized on display. She reached for the Cîroc and without hesitation, popped the cap and poured some into her glass to lace with her lemonade. She needed something to take the edge off, and she was praying like hell Bernard didn't come back home later with suspicions, or even worse, handcuffs.

Kennedy spent the next hour helping out in the kitchen and mingling with Benji's cousins. Friends were coming in and out, helping themselves to plates of food and partaking of the festivities. A game of Spades was going on, and the fellas had started shooting dice against the garage. All the while, Kennedy was trying to enjoy herself, but she couldn't stop throwing expectant looks at the door. It felt like a ticking time bomb, waiting for Bernard to arrive. But it had now been three hours since he'd left and still no sign that he was returning anytime soon. She should have been relieved, especially in the midst of the party. But she couldn't relax at that point if someone had paid her. Plus, she knew she would have to hear Washington's mouth later because he had been calling her all day.

"What's wrong?" Benji asked while not taking his eyes off the cards in his hands. Kennedy was sitting between him and his cousin Shawn at the card table. She would have been engrossed in the Spades game taking place if she wasn't so distracted by her cell phone's constant vibrating.

Kennedy pulled the phone from her pocket for the umpteenth time and swiped the screen to see the notifications. Nine missed calls and four text messages were from Washington, of course. On a sigh, Kennedy powered off her phone.

"Nothing's wrong." She feigned ignorance as she slid the phone back in her pocket.

"Yo' man been blowing you up all day," Benji teased, tossing out a card. "You may want to call him back before he come looking for your ass." That prompted a chuckle from the rest of the people around the table.

"Sounds like you jealous," Kennedy said with a gloat.

"Yeah, big homie," Shawn agreed with a smirk. "It does sound like you a little too interested in who calling her."

"Man, kill that noise," Benji said. "Kennedy is like my little sister. I got to look out for her."

Kennedy frowned at the association. She didn't want to be thought of as his "little sister." She sure as hell didn't think of him as her brother. She wanted so much more.

"Yeah, your fiancée would kick your ass anyway," the other woman at the table said with a laugh.

Kennedy frowned. She couldn't possibly have heard correctly. She glanced around as the others joined in on the laughter. Everyone except Benji. He kept his eyes on his cards.

"Whose fiancée?" she asked.

"Your boy," Shawn said, nodding toward Benji. "Wanted to pull a punk move and get cuffed. Only he would do some shit like that, because I ain't trying to get married. That's for damn sure."

Kennedy felt light-headed. She would have wanted to say this was some joke—some inside family joke that probably stemmed back to before she even came in the picture. But not the way Benji was avoiding her looks. Not the way he seemed to be entirely too interested in the cards in his hand. She knew it was true. Her breath caught in her throat, and suddenly needing air, Kennedy pushed back from the table and half-walked, half-ran for the front door.

She bypassed the other people clustered on the porch and willed her feet to move even though they felt like lead. All she could think about was Benji getting married. Even worse, he hadn't even told her.

"Kennedy!"

She had made it all the way to her car before she heard his shout, followed by the pounding of his shoes on the pavement as he ran in her direction. Kennedy didn't turn around, but she froze at the car door, her hand gripping the handle. She closed her eyes against the tears that were threatening to fall.

Benji stopped at arm's distance, not bothering to reach out to her. "Listen," he said, "I didn't want you to find out like this."

So, it was true. Hearing his lack of denial cemented the hardened truth even more. "Why?" Kennedy's voice broke as she spoke, and she cursed herself.

"Don't ask me that," Benji murmured. His voice was closer, but still, he didn't touch her. "I don't want this to change anything between us. I don't want you to be mad at me." Now his voice was at her ear as he lowered it to a whisper. "Please don't be mad at me, Ken."

Kennedy shuddered. Hearing his compassion had her wanting to crumple to the street and cry like a baby. But she couldn't. She had to be strong. Even though she was hurting inside.

Once she was sure the tears wouldn't fall and betray her, Kennedy turned around and glared at him. "And how could I be mad at you, Benji?" she said, her voice icy. "I'm just a *little sister*, right? Do what you got to do because that's what I plan to do."

His face registered confusion at her words. He didn't bother stopping her as she slid into the car. Kennedy fumbled around in her purse before pulling the engagement ring from the side pocket. She jammed it on her finger with enough force to invoke a sting of pain with the movement. When she glanced back to the window, Benji wasn't there. Whether he had seen it or not, it didn't even matter. He had warned her about not getting too serious. About not complicating her life. But Kennedy didn't give a damn anymore. If he could do what the hell he wanted, so could she.

CHAPTER 5

The body was badly decomposed. The water and bacteria had eaten at the man's flesh until nothing more than rotting muscle and bone were exposed. DNA analysis and dental records had confirmed the identity of the corpse.

Jamie flipped through the pictures. He wasn't emotionless at all, but his job had given him slight immunity to the gory details he was often subjected to. And instead of cringing at the graphic photos and scientific jargon of lacerated neck abrasions and blunt force trauma, he planned to use his emotions to find out just what had happened.

Jamie moved that folder to the side and turned his attention back to the case of Lisa Brown. He had read the reports so many times the ink had begun to blur into a jumbled mess. There was surveillance from a nearby ATM showing Lisa entering her building Thursday evening. Residents trickled in per usual "end of work" traffic. Residents had key cards they used to buzz themselves into the building, and despite the huge sign that indicated visitors must call up using the call box next to the door, people would often hold the door open for others approaching. So, Jamie didn't know if they were residents or guests, which definitely made it harder to decipher between who was and was not supposed to be at the apartment.

One of the elevator's cameras was broken, which, after viewing the footage from the only working camera, Jamie had to deduce that was the one that Lisa and the perpetrator used to go up to the apartment.

She was scheduled to be off that Friday, so no one found it out of the ordinary when she did not show up for work. On Friday afternoon at about 12:52, Jamie did see the cable man arrive, his company logo on the breast pocket of his blue button-up. He buzzed using the call box, and surveillance showed he made a call on his cell, which corroborated with Lisa's phone records. He had been attempting to call when she didn't answer the call box. It looked like he was about to leave until another resident opened the door to exit the building and held it open for him, granting him access inside. That was when he discovered the body.

Reports estimated she died sometime between 8:00 p.m. and 8:00 a.m., a wide window for someone to show up, strangle her, and leave. Jamie had read the reports and watched the surveillance tapes so many times, but he still couldn't shake the feeling that Lisa's killer was right there in his face.

Jamie yawned, rubbing his eyes. There were only a handful of people at the station at one in the morning. He should've been at home in bed himself, but his impending divorce and custody case was stressing him out and giving him insomnia. Rather than go home to the dismal reality of spending yet another night in the guest bedroom, he found comfort in engrossing himself in his work.

"Still at it?"

Jamie didn't bother glancing up at his partner, Bernard, but he instantly felt the warmth from the mug of coffee being placed at his elbow and sighed in relief. He lifted the mug to his lips, allowing the bitter liquid to sting his tongue.

"I think I need something a little stronger than the nasty-ass coffee you make," Jamie said with a grin.

"We got a few kilos of coke in the evidence room," Bernard joked, and both men chuckled.

"Too strong. Too strong." Jamie sighed and began straightening the papers and pictures strewn across his desk.

Bernard watched his partner's weary movements, saw the stress lines creasing his face. "Man, go home," he suggested. "Seriously. You've been here seems like for a week straight looking at this stuff. I thought you called in some favors."

He had. But so far, nothing. No leads, nothing that could point him in the right direction. He hated being stuck.

Somewhere in the station, the whir of the fax machine echoed, and a distant police scanner rattled off some inaudible verbiage.

"I should be asking you the same question. Why are you still here?" Jamie finally looked up at his partner just in time to see Bernard smirk.

"I got a date."

"You're married. Is it even still called a date when you're married?"

"Hell, yeah. Glo don't play about that. The day I stop dating her is the day I need to pack my shit."

Jamie slid his eyes to the digital clock on his desk. "At one twenty-three in the morning, though?"

"Those are the best ones." Bernard tossed him a knowing grin before sliding his hip off the desk and headed for the door. "Go home, Jamie. Shit, shower, shave, and come back in a few hours so we can look at that case."

Jamie didn't bother responding as his partner left him alone once again. Bernard was right. He needed some kind of work/life balance. But with both being so stressful right now, it wasn't like a balance would make that much of a difference.

Absently, Jamie got to his feet and walked toward the fax machine. Maybe if he went to the back room and stretched out on the cot for a few hours of sleep, he would be more focused. Right now, he was coming up blank and it was frustrating the hell out of him. He picked up the two single sheets of paper on the machine, surprised to see someone had scribbled it out to his attention at the top.

On the first page was a scanned copy of a Social Security card and a driver's license belonging to Lisa Michele Brown. He eyed the driver's license. Everything matched up to the copy of the license he had in his file. Except the picture. That picture wasn't of the Lisa Brown he had seen. The second page was a copy of a profile for a jewelry company, Shane Co. A diamond bracelet and earrings had been purchased using Lisa Michele Brown's credit card just last week. Hard to believe Lisa was purchasing jewelry after being murdered.

Jamie carried the papers back to his desk to put in the file. Suddenly that cot in the back sounded even more attractive. He would catch a few hours of sleep and as soon as morning hit, make a few phone calls.

CHAPTER 6

The casket was pink. Not rich pink, but more like a pastel rose, as if someone had watered the polished wood down a bit, trying to achieve the same effect with an appropriate subtlety. From her position in the back of the church, Kennedy could see Lisa nestled in velvet cushions of the same hue, her lids lowered so long lashes kissed each caramel cheek. It seemed to fit her perfectly.

On a sigh, Kennedy tried to focus on the task at hand. Even though her relationship with Lisa had been completely fraudulent, it wasn't making the service any less upsetting. She continued to sit, head bent, eyes scanning the wilted grievers behind sunglasses that hid half of their foreheads and cheekbones. The fact that no one noticed her, Kennedy took as a blessing. She couldn't afford to be recognized, not when she was so close.

When Kennedy first saw the details about Lisa's "homegoing service," she'd had no intention of going. But the more she tossed the idea around, the more she felt compelled to make an appearance. It had nothing to do with Lisa and everything to do with finding her killer. Not that Kennedy was planning on doing some Nancy Drew shit, but she could not afford to be on the police's list of murder suspects.

She had no idea what she expected to find. It wasn't like Lisa's killer would be sitting in the front row in a hooded black cloak with a scythe in hand like the Grim Reaper. But maybe, just maybe, she would be able to get some evidence of what happened, or who could possibly have had a motive to kill Lisa. A jealous ex-boyfriend, a jealous friend, *something*. Then just maybe it would point the police in that direction and keep them off her ass.

Kennedy made an educated guess on the number of people in attendance and scribbled it down in the small pad that rested beside her thigh on the pew. She then tried her best to decipher the true mourners from the fakers, the ones who appeared genuinely distraught versus the ones who carried more nonchalance. She continued to search among the faces, mostly obstructed by hands and soiled tissues.

"Oh God, why?"

The desperate shriek had Kennedy zeroing in on a woman, half-collapsed on the floor and struggling to be controlled by a man at each side. Kennedy glanced at the woman's face, and then behind her to the framed eight-by-ten portrait of Lisa on the altar, and hastily tucked her small notepad in her purse. The resemblance was uncanny. A few less wrinkles, and this woman could have passed for Lisa's twin sister. So, either she was Lisa's mother or someone else close enough to give her more intimate details about Lisa. Either that or she was just one hell of an actress.

"It's okay," Kennedy said, while stooping to help the woman, now sprawled on the floor of the aisle. She continued to wail at her feet, her sobs muffled by the carpet. Kennedy glanced up at the men, who clearly looked unsure of how to handle the situation. "I'll take her to the restroom," she offered and was met with twin looks of relief. They helped her get the woman off the floor, and Kennedy all but carried her to the doors to the lobby. She couldn't have weighed more than 150 pounds, but the weight of her grief made Kennedy feel like she was pulling a charter bus.

For a second, she felt bad for taking advantage of the woman when she was so clearly vulnerable. But there was no other way to get the information she might need. Kennedy kept this in mind as she pushed the door to the restroom open.

They were alone. But just to be sure, Kennedy quickly checked the stalls after she had positioned the woman to rest on the marble sink. Satisfied, Kennedy came back to her side, removing her sunglasses and perching them in the wild mane of natural curls of the wig she had opted for. The woman's loud sobs had died down to a soft whimper with the occasional hiccup. She used a shaky hand to wipe the tears from her flushed cheeks and sighed.

"Thank you," she said with a strained smile, and Kennedy nodded sympathetically.

"I'm so sorry for your loss."

To her surprise, the woman chuckled. "You don't have to say that," she said. "Everyone just says that because they feel they should. No one understands what it's like to lose a child." Kennedy rested a hip on the counter. So, she was right. This *was* Lisa's mother.

"You're right. I don't understand," Kennedy agreed. "But I'm still sorry." The woman looked at Kennedy then. She studied her so long that Kennedy thought she surely recognized her face from somewhere. Had Lisa mentioned her? Shown her mom a picture?

"Do you have any children?" the woman asked, and Kennedy shook her head. "She was my one and only. I had never wanted children, you see. And now I don't have any anymore. I guess God has a sense of humor."

Kennedy watched the woman look at herself in the mirror.

"I don't know who I am anymore. You ever felt like that? Like life is not worth living?"

Kennedy recognized the question was rhetorical and kept her lips pursed.

"I know it's silly, right? My daughter was a grown woman. But I worried about her constantly. That was my baby." Lisa's mother appeared to be drawing into herself again, reflecting on her own words, so Kennedy rested her hand on the woman's shoulder.

The swell of guilt swam in her gut, urging her to leave this woman to mourn the death of her daughter. She shut her eyes and swallowed. "You shouldn't blame yourself," she said, and because she figured the woman expected it, added, "God doesn't make mistakes. He just called one of his angels home."

Lisa's mother nodded but didn't respond. Silence lay suspended between them, both women tied into their own thoughts. When she didn't readily make a move to speak again, Kennedy chanced further inquiry.

"Do you know anyone who would want to hurt Lisa?" she asked. "I mean, I think we're all just in shock because she was such a sweet person."

She shook her head on a sniff. "Not at all. No one would want to hurt Lisa. She didn't have a mean bone in her body." Kennedy leaned over to grab some paper towels from the dispenser, then handed them to Lisa's mother, who took them gratefully. "To make it so bad, I didn't believe her about the stalker . . ." she trailed off as she blotted her face with the rough paper.

Kennedy nodded. *Make that two of us.* "Who in the world would want to stalk Lisa?" she pressed. "She never mentioned anything to me about anyone she was scared of."

"Who are you again?" The woman's question was sudden as she narrowed her eyes. "I'm sorry, I didn't get your name. Are you a friend of Lisa's?"

The lie was already falling from her lips before Kennedy

had time to formulate it. "Yes," she said. "I'm Tanya. Lisa and I worked together at the hospital."

Lisa's mother nodded, satisfied, and cast her eyes down. She turned on the faucet, let the water pool in her cupped palms, and leaned over to splash it on her tearstained face. She stood up, and feeling compelled, Kennedy grabbed more paper towels to offer. "I just don't know." She accepted the napkins and patted her face, her eyes wet and swollen as they met Kennedy's in the mirror. "I guess you never really know what some people are capable of. Especially the ones who smile in your face." Kennedy ran an unsteady hand through her hair as the woman started for the door. "Thank you so much for coming," she said. The door closed with a quiet *click* behind her, and Kennedy glanced to the balled-up paper towels littering the countertop.

"Touché," she murmured, her voice a whispered ricochet off the empty stalls.

CHAPTER 7

Kennedy noticed the car as soon as she turned onto her street. It wasn't like it looked out of place or anything. It was a glistening black Chevy Malibu, an older model by the looks of it. The windows were tinted black, obscuring the inside completely. It was parked against the curb leading up to her building.

Kennedy started to wheel her car into her building's lot but quickly thought better of it. Instead, she, too, pulled to the side of the curb and cut off the ignition. She didn't know what she was waiting for. It wasn't like cars parked on the side of the road was uncommon. But she just felt compelled to wait a few moments longer before pulling into her condo. She didn't even know what the hell she was expecting to happen. But something about that blacked-out car brought on a swell of panic. *Was the car there for her?*

As if on cue, the Chevy peeled away from the curb in the opposite direction. Even after the car disappeared down the street, Kennedy's apprehension had her counting an additional ten minutes before she braved pulling into her parking space.

Getting out, she tossed another glance down the empty street to make sure the coast was clear. A sudden breeze tickled her face, and at the same time, an echo of Lisa's words floated in her ear. *I feel like someone is stalking me.* Kennedy shuddered. It was haunting. Was this what Lisa had been feeling?

Kennedy locked her door and broke out in a run to her building. The area was nearly empty with the exception of a few pedestrians walking by on the sidewalk. Somewhere a siren wailed, and the shrill laughter of children danced in the distance. She knew she looked silly as hell trying to run in her red bottoms with a shitload of shopping bags stuffed in her arms.

She fumbled with her door and slammed it closed, leaning up against it to catch her breath. Then, as an afterthought, Kennedy turned and flipped the locks into place. That was when she heard a noise. She held her breath, craning her neck to listen. She couldn't be 100 percent certain, but that sounded like footsteps muffled against carpet.

Kennedy's eyes scanned the living room, the neat placement of her expensive sectional and big screen with abstract art pieces adorning her walls. The ceiling fan whirred overhead, setting a slight chill to the air. Other than that, silence.

She stepped out of her heels and placed her bags on the hardwood floor of her foyer before taking a peek into the galley kitchen. Nothing seemed out of place. Except the cup on the granite countertop. Had she left that there this morning?

Then, she heard it, clear as day. A sniff. Fear gripped her throat as she reached for the knife in the drainboard. A butter knife, but it was better than nothing.

Kennedy took her time, walking carefully toward her master bedroom so she didn't make a noise. Her chest was tight as she struggled to level her breathing. Again, she thought of Lisa and prayed like hell she wouldn't end up like her. Had someone been after Lisa? Then saw her leaving and followed her home to finish the job?

She stood at the door of her bedroom, afraid to go in, all

the while her eyes darting around the mess she had made earlier. Clothes lay strewn across her king sleigh bed from where she had been quickly searching for something to wear to go shopping while absently chatting on the phone. A pile of shoes trailed from her closet. Still, everything was exactly as she'd left it.

Kennedy took a step in the direction of the bathroom. Her heart was beating so hard it felt like it would jump out of her chest and lie throbbing at her toes. She lifted her knife, gripping it like a lifeline as she inched closer to the en-suite.

The figure entered the doorway, and Kennedy's scream broke the air. Without thinking, she wielded the knife, her eyes squeezed shut as she swung senselessly at the thick air.

"Kennedy, what the hell are you doing?"

Kennedy opened her eyes and stood face-to-face with her sister, Deven. Deven was clutching her chest, her mouth rounded in shock. Her eyes were zeroed in on the knife Kennedy still clutched in her sweaty palm.

As if she just realized she was still holding the weapon, Kennedy loosened her grip and let the metal slip from her grasp to clank loudly on the bathroom linoleum. Her breath came out in a heavy *whoosh* that nearly stung her lungs.

"Deven, what the hell?" She didn't mean to shout, but adrenaline had her voice elevated.

"What the hell are you doing with a knife, Kennedy? Damn!" Deven lowered her gaze to the knife before lifting stunned eyes back to her sister in a questioning stare.

"How the hell did you get in here?"

"My key!"

"Shit!" Kennedy hissed and took a staggering breath to calm herself down. "I'm sorry. I thought someone had broken in, so I was trying to—"

"Butter them to death?" Deven reached down to pick up the knife and shook her head.

If the situation hadn't scared her shitless, Kennedy would have laughed. She was tempted to hug her sister, but for what? *I'm so glad you weren't Lisa's killer trying to finish me off?*

Kennedy touched her forehead and felt the beads of sweat pearling on her brow. She let out another grateful sigh as she turned and led the way back into the kitchen. She needed a damn drink. "What are you doing here?" she asked.

"You said I could stay a few days while my carpet was being replaced, remember?" Deven tossed the knife into the sink. "But damn, I didn't know I was going to have to die for it."

Kennedy shook her head as she brought two glasses down from the cabinet. "I'm sorry. I forgot all about that." She reached in the refrigerator for the Sangria she kept in the door and poured some into each cup. She turned then, handing her sister one, and she giggled when she took it gratefully.

Deven was only older by about fourteen months. With the same mother and different fathers, they had inherited a few similar characteristics but more differences than anything. Deven was taller with hair she kept shaved close to her head and dyed a gorgeous blond. They both were the same complexion, but Deven had the natural beauty and body Kennedy had had to get surgically enhanced. Rarely did Deven even wear makeup. Kennedy, on the other hand, kept herself glamorous with a strict beauty regimen from foundation to lashes and every other cosmetic aesthetic in between. Before all of Kennedy's procedures, the two women might have passed for sisters. Now they didn't even look related.

"So, what's going on, Kill Bill?" Deven teased after she took a healthy swig of her alcohol. "You want to tell me what's got you so shook up?"

Kennedy ran her fingers through her hair, allowing the drink to take effect. Thankfully, she had completely relaxed. "It's nothing," she reiterated. "I've been watching way too much ID Channel. Just has me a little on edge."

"Right." Sarcasm laced the solitary word. "You sure it's not anything else? Anything you need to tell me?"

Kennedy lifted an eyebrow but kept her face neutral. "What do you mean?"

Deven shrugged and turned to cross into the living room. She tossed herself on the chaise, tucking her socked feet underneath her. "I'm just checking with you, that's all," she commented absently. "Especially after the cop came by earlier."

Kennedy had been heading toward the foyer to get her bags and purse, but Deven's statement had her pausing in her tracks. She pivoted then, once again facing her sister.

"What do you mean, *came by*?" It was a stupid question meant to stall for a few additional seconds as her mind kicked into fight-or-flight mode.

Deven was pulling a laptop from the floor, and she glanced up with a deep-set frown. "The hell you mean? Came by, like *came by*. Walked up to the door, rang the doorbell, and asked if I knew where you were."

Kennedy's eyes slid to the door as if he would still be standing there on the porch, even though she had just passed the entryway. Her mind flipped back to the black Malibu waiting outside when she pulled up. "What did you tell him?"

"I told him I didn't know where you were because I didn't. What was I supposed to tell him? What was he here for? Are you in some kind of trouble?"

"No," she lied. "Did he say anything else?"

Deven sighed. "He asked if I knew a Lisa Brown."

"What did you say?" Kennedy crossed to her sister and stood right in front of the couch at her continued silence. "Deven, please," she pressed. "It's important."

"Are you going to tell me what's going on?"

"I'll tell you."

Deven's look was weary. She tossed up her hand in surrender. "I told him no, I didn't know a Lisa Brown. He said okay and to tell you he would come by again."

"Come by again when?"

"He didn't say. Now, what's up, sis? Did you do something?"

Kennedy lowered herself to the couch, and Deven scooted over to make room. Thoughts and excuses tumbled on top of each other as Kennedy rested her head in her hands, not surprised when she felt a comforting hand rubbing her back.

"Have you been watching the news?" she asked, but she already knew the answer was no. Deven never cared for the news. Said it was too depressing. Instead of waiting for an answer, Kennedy went on. "One of my coworkers died a few weeks ago." It wasn't exactly a lie, nor was it the truth. But it would do.

She heard the sharp intake of Deven's gasp at the information. "Damn, for real? What happened?"

"They're not sure." Last report Kennedy saw on the Internet, they had concluded it was asphyxiation, but she decided to gloss over that detail.

"I'm so sorry, sis. How are you holding up?"

Truth? Barely. But Kennedy nodded to mask her discomfort. "It's just put us all a little on edge," she admitted.

"Why are the cops questioning you? Well, a detective," she corrected. "Is it some kind of investigation?"

Kennedy didn't know, but that piece of information was news to her, so she went with it. "Yeah, I think they're questioning all of us. You know, her coworkers. Just trying to see if there is anything we can do to help the case." She risked a sideways glance at Deven and felt relief when she saw her face was bent in sheer worry. *Good, she bought it.*

Kennedy rose, pulling out her cell phone. In any other circumstances like this, she would have called Benji. He would know what to do. But she remembered she still wasn't talking to his sneaky ass after the news of his engagement was dumped into her lap. So, she scrolled past his name in her contact list.

"You can stay here at the condo until your place is finished," Kennedy offered. "I'm probably going to stay over at Washington's for a while."

"Speaking of which, what did you decide to do?"

Kennedy frowned. "About what?" At her sister's narrowed eyes, she thought more and then had to chuckle at her lack of focus. "Oh, the proposal. Yeah, we decided against that," she lied. After a thought, she added, "We are going to just take our time, you know. Don't want to rush into things."

Deven smiled in relief. "I'm glad. You deserve to be happy, but I really think that's for the best."

Kennedy nodded as she dialed Washington's number and placed the phone to her ear. Damn right, she deserved to be happy. The lie was to keep her sister out of the loop so she could turn her focus to the task at hand. Because after hearing the police were on her ass, she needed to wrap this shit up with Washington, get his money, and get the hell out of Dodge.

CHAPTER 8

Benji rolled over to sneak a peek at the glaring red numbers on the digital clock on the nightstand: 1:37 a.m. He wasn't surprised. He had planned to at least try to get a few hours of sleep before he needed to be up at two, but that clearly wasn't going to happen now. Lately, with everything going on, it seemed as if he hadn't slept in weeks. The stress lines creasing his forehead seemed so ingrained in his skin that it caused him frequent headaches.

A movement had Benji glancing at his new fiancée. Sure enough, she was shifting to snuggle against his naked chest, the darkened room doing nothing to hide the curvaceous silhouette under the drape of the sheets. Slowly, he eased from underneath her body, and snatching his phone from the nightstand, he padded toward the closet. He would get dressed in there so as not to wake her. She wouldn't approve of him handling business so late again, but duty called.

Benji wore nothing but a pair of boxer briefs, so he quickly stepped into some black jeans and a T-shirt, then tossed a sweatshirt over his head. He shoved his feet into some sneakers and checked his phone once more. He was worried. He shouldn't have been, but he was. Not only did he have a situation on his hands that needed to be resolved, but he hadn't bothered to call Kennedy in over a week. There wasn't really a reason for that other than the fact he knew she was pissed he had gotten engaged. But there was a lot she didn't understand, and the move had been a good one. A necessary one. He was trying to take his street hustle to the next level and snagging the kingpin's daughter came with an allegiance that would ensure his protection. And his protection meant Kennedy's protection. It was strictly business.

Of course, Kennedy would know all about taking extreme measures for business purposes. Especially when it was lucrative. She just needed to get the hell out of her feelings about it.

He had just made it out to the car when he felt his phone vibrate with an incoming notification. Benji didn't bother checking it. He knew who it was, and he knew what it would say once he swiped the screen to view the text message. Instead, he slid into the driver's seat of his black Camry, backed out of the parking space, and wheeled the car in the direction of Park Avenue.

His hand reached for the radio dial. Music would help clear his mind. If he thought too long and hard about everything going on, he was sure it would piss him off even further, and he was liable to react out of anger. So instead, he got lost in the song, letting the windows down so the cool night breeze could mix with the soulful bars of Amel Larrieux. He drummed his fingers lightly on the steering wheel, and again, his mind wandered to thoughts of Kennedy.

Damn, he missed her. He had gotten used to their conversations, and over time, their relationship had flourished. She had become his best friend without him even realizing it. He could still remember how pissed she was when Shawn had revealed he was getting married. Benji frowned. No, not pissed. Hurt. He had seen blatant hurt in her eyes and in the stubborn fold of her arms. Benji wasn't an idiot. He had love for her in so many ways, but circumstances prohibited him from entertaining more than a platonic relationship. But that hadn't stopped the tug Kennedy had on his heart. Or the frequent thoughts and desires that crept in when he tried his damnedest to shift his focus elsewhere. Then, during his recent trip back to Jersey, he saw the new face and the new body had catapulted the little, gangly girl he once knew into a grown-up sex goddess. Amazing what a few dollars and some meat in the right places could do. But still, he had closed his heart off a long time ago. A relationship with Kennedy would just complicate an already sticky situation. And another complication was the last thing either of them needed. Benji shook his head to dispel the thoughts. The sudden longing that clenched his heart was beginning to make him furious.

As expected, the corner was littered with prostitutes. Scantily clad women, from the frail to the sloppiest, in various shades and hues, scattered around the sidewalk adorned in matted wigs and booty shorts that left full breasts and ass cheeks on display. Dingy fur crop jackets seemed to be the chosen attire, apparently a satisfactory barrier between their chilled skin and the October air.

As Benji navigated his car near the curb, a few women immediately made their way in his direction. He lifted his hand to wave them off, not bothering to slow down. His eyes scanned the faces, all seemingly sunken in by either malnutrition or drugs, until they landed on the one familiar face that stuck out in the crowd.

It needed to be done. He comforted himself with that knowledge.

The first time he had killed someone, he was sixteen, and though it had been self-defense, he hadn't cared about hitting the teenager repeatedly until the bloody brick cracked the skull open. Now, murder was . . . second nature to him. His heart had hardened with years of experience, so he sure as hell didn't have room for regrets, either. He only had one Achilles' heel. Thankfully, Kennedy would never know it.

The prostitute wore a jet-black wig, but the hair was stringy and standing all over her head. A neon-green halter top hugged her upper half, while she had opted for a dingy denim skirt that came as high as her crotch with tattered fishnet stockings and red patent-leather pumps. Benji brought the car to a stop right in front of the woman and rolled down his window. Recognizing the attention, the woman smiled, displaying a row of stained brown teeth with a few missing. He was glad he had such a photographic memory. Anyone else wouldn't have been able to convince him this crackhead was who she really was.

The woman struggled to put a little twist in her gait as she stumbled toward the Camry. She leaned down onto the passenger door, bringing with her the stench of musk and cigarette smoke. "What you want, sugar?" she slurred and batted her eyes.

Benji's lips spread into a grin. "What can I get for twenty?" he asked.

Her eyes lit up as if the thought of an extra twenty dollars was as tempting as two hundred dollars. "Whatever you want, sugar."

Benji glanced around and popped the lock on the door. Eagerly, the woman opened the door and fell into the passenger seat. "I just want some head," he said, eyeing her out of the side of his eye.

She licked her crusty lips caked with day-old red lipstick. "I can do that. No problem," she said.

Satisfied, Benji drove a little farther up the street and turned onto a dead-end road. He cut the car off and reclined his seat so she could get to work. The prostitute wasted no time, her movements sloppy as she fumbled with the buttons of his jeans.

His movements were quiet as he slid the leather gloves from the pocket of his sweatshirt. He eased them onto his hands, using one to pat her hair in silent encouragement as she buried her head in his lap.

As he wrapped his hands around her neck, she gagged and Benji squeezed tighter. Suddenly aware of his intention, she snatched up, clawing at his gloved hands, her lips still swollen and wet. She gasped for air as her eyes bulged with the tightening of his grip. Benji didn't think. Just continued to squeeze the woman's frail neck until it felt as if it would snap in two.

A few more choked breaths and her eyes closed, her head lolling to the side with the heaviness of death. Benji held on for a few moments longer until he was satisfied every ounce of breath had left her body. Then, he gently laid her head back on the seat and sighed. He took a moment to observe the corpse. He almost felt sorry for her. She had been dealt a bad hand and it was no fault of hers who her brother was. She looked like she could have even been beautiful once upon a time. But her looks had now been tainted by drugs and abuse.

Benji removed the gloves and dropped them in a plastic bag he had brought along with him. He would be sure to discard them later. Right now, he needed to wrap up his business.

The first number he dialed was to his cousin, Shawn. He knew his boy would be awake even though it was the middle of the morning. Sure enough, Shawn picked up on the first ring.

"Yeah?"

"Has Kennedy tried to contact you?" Benji asked.

"Nah. Why?"

"She will. She's in some trouble, and she needs my help even though she's too stubborn to realize it."

Shawn chuckled. "That's your girl."

"Yeah, I know. Hit me *when* she calls you. I'm trying to keep tabs on her, but she's still pissed."

"I got you. You good?"

Benji tossed an absent glance at the dead body next to him. "I'm good," he answered, before hanging up.

Because he knew his uncle Bernard was asleep, Benji shot him a quick text instead. **UNC, I NEED TO TALK TO YOU ABOUT KENNEDY. HIT ME WHEN YOU GET UP.**

Benji dropped his phone in his cup holder and began straightening his pants. He then fished in his pocket for his weed and lit up, letting the flame dance in the moonlight. Maybe one day, Kennedy would realize how much he would do for her.

Even if that meant murder.

CHAPTER 9

Two Months Later

It was a beautiful day for a wedding. The sun hung low in the sky, casting brilliant rays to glitter across the expansive lake. The gazebo had been decorated in eggplant, white, and lavender sashes draped in a canopy and wrapped around the white wooden railing. About fifty fold-out chairs were arranged in semicircles around the gazebo with a white runner up the middle of the manicured lawn.

Kennedy used her index and middle finger to pull the blinds apart so she could peek through. A small backyard wedding was her idea. Something quaint and casual. But she didn't expect more than ten people to come. Primarily his family. Since Kennedy had told Deven they weren't getting married, it kept her from having to invite her. She hadn't even bothered to invite Benji's family, either. She had wanted—no, needed—something short and to the point. Just enough to appease Washington while she went through the motions of becoming his wife. Then she could rob him blind. *Boyfriends are smart. Husbands are stupid.*

Kennedy turned from the window and walked farther into the master bedroom. The silhouette of her trumpet wedding dress curved around her hourglass figure, ruching at the bodice and waistline. Her bronze complexion peeked through the lace material at her shoulders. The rhinestone belt wrapped around her waist, accentuating the dress and complementing the teardrop diamond earrings in her lobes. It was simple, but expensive. Kennedy indulged in both.

It felt different this time. When she married Lewis, she was panicked and fear-stricken with the decision she felt like she was being forced to make. This time, Kennedy was surprisingly calm. It didn't feel like her. It felt like she was on autopilot, staring down at herself while she moved about the bedroom to put the finishing touches on her makeup. She was content with her decision. And even more so now that she knew all the perks.

A business arrangement. That's what Kennedy had convinced herself she was entering as she held up her hand to look at the engagement ring. Washington was beyond excited when she had finally set a date. She had made sure to be around him more, showering him with attention and affection, and she feigned pure joy while looking through bridal books. She cooked him dinner and talked about all of their future plans and babies. Kennedy made sure to lay it on extra thick, and Washington was weak. He had already made reservations for their honeymoon in Dubai, and he mentioned that he had added her to his accounts.

So, Kennedy would milk this cash cow and then disappear. She had done it before; she could do it again. And after seeing Benji and his cousin Shawn talking all hush-hush at the party, Kennedy had a feeling she could get the help she needed. As soon as Lisa Brown was done with Washington, of course.

The muffled instrumentals of Kenny G's "The Wedding Song" wafted up to greet her from the backyard. She knew as soon as she went downstairs, she would need to get back into character. Pretend the plastic smile was genuine, pretend the material of the wedding gown didn't itch like hell, and pretend she actually planned on spending the rest of her life with the man at the end of the aisle instead of just the next few days. But it was these times she could savor that brief moment of inhibition and actually relax.

Her stomach flipped, and she allowed her eyelids to flutter closed, the exhale of a deep sigh sounding like a comforting roar in her ears. It wasn't nerves. Hell, she had done this before. Different venue, different dress, different crowd, and a different husband. She was even using the same marriage vows she had written before.

Kennedy knew why she felt uneasy. No matter how much she tried to ignore it, Lisa's death had been splashed on every news media outlet across Jersey. Benji had insisted it would blow over, but so far, two weeks later, it still hadn't. Her death had frozen her assets, accounts, and credit cards. Even the small business loan had been withdrawn once every business entity received alerts the Social Security number was connected to a deceased individual. But even if that wasn't the case, fear had prompted Kennedy to start using Washington's funds for everything. She had her condo, but she figured they would be able to trace her there, so she had moved in with Washington. In fact, she had abandoned Lisa's identity altogether, with the exception of this marriage. And as soon as they said "I do," she would disappear just as quickly.

The muffled chime of her cell phone rang and Kennedy crossed to the dresser. One look at the screen had her smile blooming. She paused then, deciding whether she wanted to answer. One ring, two rings. She didn't even know what she would say. But she didn't want to risk not answering and miss the opportunity to talk to him. Then again, what in the hell could he possibly want? At the last minute, Kennedy swiped the screen to reject the call, surprised when only a few seconds later it rang again. This time, the number was blocked. She had to laugh out loud. Oh, she sure as hell was going to clown Benji for that move.

She watched it ring in her hand a couple more times before she went ahead and answered it. She didn't know why he was so insistent on speaking with her, but her desire to talk to him outweighed her stubbornness.

"Hey," she answered, intentionally keeping her voice flat and nonchalant. She was met with silence, which had her face crinkling in a frown. "Hello? Benji?" Kennedy pulled the phone from her ear to eye the screen, and saw the clock ticking away the seconds indicating the call was still connected. Well, he hadn't hung up. "Hello?" she tried again.

"Is this Lisa Brown?"

The voice sounded muffled, as if someone was talking into their palm. Kennedy couldn't even tell if the voice was male or female. Her frown deepened.

"Who is this?" She didn't realize she was whispering.

"Is this Lisa?" the caller repeated, followed by a weighted pause.

Kennedy's heart felt like it had been jolted into hyperdrive with bolts of electricity. Something about the call, about the caller, wasn't right. Not knowing what else to do, she hung up, half-expecting another mysterious call to follow. Thankfully, her phone remained silent.

Again, an image of the Malibu sitting outside her condo flashed in her mind. Maybe it had been the cops trying to get in touch with her. But then, why wouldn't they just say something? Had the caller really been looking for the real Lisa? Or Kennedy? She couldn't be sure but at the moment, she couldn't be concerned with that.

A light knock on the door broke through her thoughts, and Kennedy welcomed the distraction.

"Come in," she called.

A well-dressed gentleman in a suit entered the bedroom, gently shutting the door behind him. He looked way too professional for a simple day wedding. He was bald and clean-shaven, and his attire was obviously tailor-made for his frame. Kennedy's eyes fell on the briefcase at his side.

"Ms. Brown," he greeted, holding out his hand. "I'm Malcolm, Mr. Bell's attorney."

Kennedy's movements were labored with confusion as she accepted the hand. "Nice to meet you." Though she didn't anticipate anything nice from the meeting. Why the hell was Washington sending in his lawyer?

"You look amazing," Malcolm complimented with a nod to the wedding dress she wore. "Washington is an extremely lucky man."

Kennedy nodded but still didn't speak. It was clear he was setting up this conversation, and she was already cycling through a Rolodex of reasons for his presence, all of which were prompting a surge of light-headedness.

Sensing her urgency, Malcolm cleared his throat and lifted his briefcase to rest on the bed. "Well, I won't disturb you for too long. I know you still have some things to do before the ceremony." The sharp hiss of the *zip* met her ears as he opened the bag, all the while murmuring more compliments and apologies for his intrusion. Kennedy ignored his words, instead focusing on the manila folder he pulled into view. ". . . in your best interest," he was saying as he flipped it open, revealing a small stack of papers with small print etched from margin to margin. "You may not have time to read all of this, so I'll be happy to summarize it for you before you sign."

As if on autopilot, Kennedy reached for the papers he held out. "Summarize what?" she asked.

"Are you familiar with a prenuptial agreement?"

Her reaction felt like she was moving in slow motion. The papers slipped lifelessly from her limp fingers as the attorney's words seemed to brand in the recesses of her mind. Shock wiped her mind clean, as if someone had put an eraser to a dry-erase board. Then, just as quickly, anger colored her face so strong it burned. Kennedy didn't even wait for anything else from Malcolm. She was already storming from the bedroom to find her sneaky-ass soon-to-be husband.

"Wait, Ms. Brown, one moment please. Let me explain." Malcolm was calling behind her as she flew down the stairs toward the finished basement, where she knew Washington was getting ready.

The décor was even more beautiful up close, with cream bouquets and ribbons looped and tied down the elongated bannister of the grand staircase. Tulle draped from the ceiling in a canopy effect that drew attention to the charming crown molding in Washington's mansion and led the way to the backyard, where the wedding was to take place. An aisle runner covered the length of space from the hallway to the back door, customized with their names. If Kennedy wasn't seeing red, she probably would have stopped to appreciate the setting.

A few of the guests, Washington's family, gasped as she stomped past, the heels of her shoes nearly stabbing holes into the hardwood floor. She paused at the door to the basement. "Is he downstairs?" she demanded of no one in particular.

Someone chanced speaking up. "Yes, but it's bad luck to see—"

Kennedy was already flying down the winding stairs to the lower level. It was showtime.

Sure enough, Washington was sitting on the couch, fully dressed in his groom's tux, crisp, debonair, and just as glossy as the pages of a GQ magazine. Kennedy was well past rational as she marched up to him, reeled back, and let a satisfying slap connect with his cheek. The contact had her palm stinging, but her gratification came as she relished what his face must feel like.

"You son of a bitch," she spat when Washington leapt to his feet. "How *dare* you send your lawyer to my room to make me sign a prenup right before our wedding."

Realization quickly extinguished the small flame of anger

that danced in his eyes. His face fell, and sorrow had him shaking his head. "It's not like that."

"Oh yeah? Well, how is it? Tell me you don't want me to sign a prenup." Washington's silence only heightened her rage. She sure as hell wasn't going to get tied up with contractual strings. Nothing was keeping her from this man's money. At this point, she had earned every single penny. Insult had her turning to pace. Anything to keep from putting hands on him once more. "I can't believe you, Washington," she rattled on. "What about trust? How can you claim you love me and want to marry me, but you don't trust me?"

"I do trust you." Washington was at her side in an instant, his hands resting on her shoulders. "Please, baby, you have to understand. I'm *only* thinking of us."

"How?"

"Because it's protection," he insisted, nearly pleading. "Not just for me, but for you, too. You worked hard for everything you have, right?" *Damn right.* Kennedy swallowed her retort and instead, nodded solemnly. "Then who am I to take any part of that?" Washington lowered his lips to plant a reassuring kiss on her forehead. "Do you know how much I love you?"

Kennedy shook her head. She was going to have to up the theatrics. The man was too damn stubborn to get it. She shut her eyes, concentrating. Her face contorted into a pained expression, and as if on cue, she felt the first few prickles of tears seep from her closed lids. "I don't see how you love me," she murmured, taking a step back to break their contact. "There is no way you can love me if you would do this to me. And on our wedding day." She continued shaking her head fiercely and lifted her hand to stop Washington when he took a step in her direction.

"Baby, please, you have to understand—"

"I do. You don't love me. Not like I love you. It's obvious." Kennedy gripped her engagement ring between her thumb and forefinger and begin to pull it off.

Washington's eyes widened when he saw what she was doing. "Don't do this," he begged, grabbing her hand to stop her movements. "I can't lose you." Kennedy pretended to actually consider his words. She lifted watery eyes to meet his gaze, keeping the hurt plastered on her face like a mask. Washington sighed and nodded his understanding. "Okay," he relented. "Okay, you don't have to sign it. Just say you'll still marry me." He waited, his eyes searching hers for some kind of confirmation.

Kennedy paused, counting the seconds in her head so the silence hung thick between them like a cloak. She could tell he was holding his breath as she kept her lips pursed shut. Then she gave him a nod and let herself be pulled into his grateful embrace. She blinked back the rest of the tears and had to congratulate herself on the award-winning performance. *Damn, that was close.*

CHAPTER 10

The ceremony was like something out of a fairy tale. If Kennedy's heart had been in it, she would've been genuinely touched by the décor, Washington's romantic vows of undying love and being forever together, and even the gentle press of his lips against hers after they were pronounced man and wife. The entire ordeal felt more real than when she had married Lewis. But she was back in character, so she easily pretended to be excited as they strolled, hand in hand, back down the aisle to Pharrell's "Happy."

Kennedy couldn't say she was actually happy, but she *was* content, especially knowing that Washington had put her name on all his accounts just that morning. The idea of getting her hands on all his money was enough to leave her salivating. She didn't know what she was going to do, but she damn sure knew she would be set for quite a while. As far as Lisa Brown went, well, it was fun while it lasted, but now she could easily settle into a new role with her millions. She felt liberated—as if she was wiping her slate clean once more. But this time, she was starting over on top.

Guests began to trickle back into the house for the reception. Washington and his mother had decorated the dining room and sunken living room and laid out a delicious spread of soul food to satisfy every palate. A collection of neosoul instrumentals played through the speakers as everyone began to mingle. Kennedy made herself comfortable on the couch and politely nodded her gratitude as people came around to congratulate her and shower her with compliments.

Washington appeared with a smile so big it was a wonder it didn't split his face. "Excuse me, ladies," he greeted the two women who fawned around Kennedy, gawking at her dress and Pandora jewelry. "But if you don't mind, I would like a few moments with my lovely wife." Obediently, the women, whom Kennedy assumed were cousins, exchanged giggles and dispersed.

"Who were they?" she asked, shifting her dress to make room for Kennedy on the couch beside her.

Washington's pause was slight. "My sisters," he said.

She probably should have known that. "I thought you told me you had a brother."

"I do, Lisa. Two sisters and a brother." Something flickered in Washington's eyes, and Kennedy knew she'd better leave that topic alone. It certainly didn't sound good that a wife didn't know her husband's family.

"Oh." On a shrug, she turned her attention to the plate of food he carried. He had taken care to pile it high with chicken, macaroni, collards, potato salad, corn bread, and gravy that was nearly spilling over the side.

"I figured my wife was hungry," he said, acknowledging the spread. "It must take a lot of energy to be so sexy."

Kennedy's lips thinned into a strained smile. Yeah, he was definitely doing the most.

"Is that for me, too?" she asked instead, gesturing to the wineglass in his hand. Grateful, she accepted the drink when he held it out to her.

"Do you know how much I love you?" he pressed.

Kennedy swallowed a groan as she took a sip of the smooth,

lukewarm liquid. Twenty minutes as husband and wife, and he was already getting on her damn nerves. How had she not noticed how clingy he was before? Her eye caught the wedding ring glittering on her finger. The ring she had found and already had appraised. *Eye on the prize.*

Kennedy lowered the glass and took the opportunity to lick her lips, slowly and seductively, just how he liked it. "How much?" she said, a flirtatious smile toying at the corners of her mouth.

Washington answered her with a kiss, and Kennedy allowed him to slip his tongue in between her lips to drink the last bit of wine flavor. He smelled of Hennessey. Fueled by lust and liquor, he deepened the kiss, and Kennedy had to swallow a startled gasp as the brief assault on her mouth teetered on the edges of pain. She pulled back then, breaking contact and masking the abrupt gesture by taking another sip of wine.

"Let's go somewhere," he whispered.

It took everything in her not to gag. "Later," she whispered back and winked. "After all these people leave. You know I'm probably going to be loud."

Washington groaned and seemed satisfied by the false promise. Rather than push the issue, he scooped some macaroni and cheese onto the fork and held it out in her direction. "You hungry?"

Kennedy opened her mouth to allow him to place the cheesy noodles on her tongue. No, she wasn't hungry, but she knew she needed to stay in character. They didn't leave for their honeymoon until tomorrow afternoon, so if she played her cards right, she could leave out early in the morning once the banks opened, collect her money, and disappear. For now, she didn't need to draw attention to any suspicious behavior. Hell, after her Oscar worthy performance about the prenuptial agreement, she knew she had Washington wide open like a bitch in heat. Now, as long as she kept him there, she was home free. So, she continued to let her new husband feed her, and she even scooted closer to nuzzle his neck a little bit for appearances' sake.

"I love you so much," she murmured before sucking on his earlobe.

"I hope you can show me just how much tonight," he returned with a devilish wink.

"I plan to." It was a brazen lie. She would find some way to weasel out of that task.

Washington opened his mouth to say something, probably even more freaky, but he abruptly shut it again when someone walked into the room. Kennedy glanced to the arched entryway and had to stifle a groan. Washington's mother.

The woman was tiny with a head full of chocolate curls with black and gray roots evidencing the time for it to be redyed. She looked young even though she was over eighty, and she would be pretty if she ever smiled, but her face always seemed to emphasize the wrinkles from her frown. At least when she was in the presence of Kennedy. She had never bothered hiding the fact that she didn't like her son's young bride, and Kennedy didn't bother hiding her apathy about their strained relationship.

"Lisa." Apparently the clipped tone was supposed to be her version of a greeting.

"Hi, Ms. Bell."

"Where is your family?"

"Ma, please don't start." Washington's voice was weary.

His mother ignored the plea, keeping a pointed look at the woman seated next to him. "Lisa," she repeated. "I was asking you a question."

"Ma, I already told you Lisa is not close with her family."

"Excuse me, son. But I think she can speak for herself."

Kennedy exaggerated a roll of her eyes as she rose to her feet. "And here I was, thinking you were about to congratulate us."

Ms. Bell chuckled. "Of course not." She folded her arms across the beaded bust of the champagne mother-of-the-groom dress she wore.

The two were standing only a few feet apart, with tension so thick it was nearly suffocating. Silence stretched between them as the women continued to throw mutual daggers of animosity with their looks.

"I suggest you get your mother, Washington," Kennedy said finally, not taking her eyes off the woman.

"'*Get me*'?" Ms. Bell took a step farther into the room. "Son, did you get her sign the prenup like I suggested? Since we know exactly what this girl is after."

Kennedy was thankful the woman was still a good bit of distance away. Any closer and she would have slapped the fire out of her smug ass. She felt Washington touch her arm, and she snatched away as if he had put a flame to her skin. "I can't believe you," she snapped, whirling her anger around to him. "How dare you listen to her?" She didn't bother waiting for his response. She stormed out of the room to head upstairs, gaining a little satisfaction when Ms. Bell stepped to the side to avoid being shoved out the way.

"Where are you going?" Her voice still carried an icy arrogance that only came from looking down on others.

Kennedy spun on her heel in a blur of tulle. "Excuse me?" she snapped. "I don't owe you an explanation. I need to get away from your ass."

Ms. Bell tossed her a knowing smirk that made Kennedy's stomach curdle like sour milk. "From me?" she said. "Or from the cops?"

Her words sent a wave of shock piercing straight to the bone. Kennedy's eyes narrowed, even as fear crippled her movements. "What cops? What are you talking about?"

Ms. Bell seemed to be gloating as she stepped to the side. "Yes, cops. There is a police officer in the foyer asking for you. Are you in some kind of trouble, *Lisa Brown*?" She made sure to put great emphasis on her name, so Kennedy rolled her eyes.

"Lisa *Bell,* thank you," she snapped. "I don't know what the hell your problem is, but you're just going to have to get over it. Washington is my husband now, so I don't have to tolerate disrespect from his mother in *my* house."

The woman grunted in response and gestured with her head toward the front of the house. "If you say so," she said. "You should go talk to the policeman who is now standing in *your* house. He is asking for you." Kennedy gave her one last look, digging her manicured nails into her palms to diminish the itch to place her hands around the woman's neck. Instead, she fixed her face like she was unconcerned to hide the fear creeping in. First, they showed up at her house where her sister was, now here, at her wedding. How the hell did they find her?

Kennedy hadn't even made it to the foyer when she heard Ms. Bell's feet as she scurried away. No doubt looking for Washington to tell him everything that was going on. *Great.* Kennedy would have to deal with him as soon as she found out what the hell was going on with the cops.

Kennedy held her breath. Part of her wished the old bitch was just saying something to piss her off. All optimism flew out the window when she spotted the man standing in the entryway. He was dressed casually in a button-up shirt, blazer, and some jeans. Kennedy caught sight of the badge he had clipped to the breast pocket of his jacket.

He turned as she entered and gave her a once-over. She figured he was probably expecting to speak to a guest at the wedding, not the bride herself. Kennedy took a deep breath and plastered on a confident smile.

"Hello, sir," she greeted him. "How may I help you?"

The man glanced from her to behind her at the few guests who had gathered not so subtly in the hallway to eavesdrop. "Are you Lisa Brown?" he asked, just to be sure.

"Well, Lisa Bell now," Kennedy teased and fluffed her wedding gown for emphasis. "But yes, I was Lisa Brown a few hours ago. What seems to be the problem?"

"I'm Detective Jamie Warren," the man said and held out his hand for a shake. "I apologize, I didn't know you were in the middle of such a momentous celebration. Congratulations, by the way."

Kennedy's smile grew. "Thank you. Thank you so much, Detective."

"If you would prefer, I can come back another time."

Kennedy shook her head. "No, I have a few moments. Will this take long?"

"Not at all."

Kennedy nodded and gestured toward the formal living room adjacent to the foyer. "Why don't we go in here for a little bit of privacy," she suggested, and not bothering to wait for a response, she turned and led the way into the formal living room, partitioned by a set of French double doors.

This was one of those rooms she knew Washington never used. Occasionally the maid would come in to clean and dust, but the gray upholstery, pillow-top armrests, and black and red throw pillows were as new as when the furniture had first arrived from the store. Kennedy perched on the couch while Detective Warren took a seat on the matching love seat.

"I won't keep you," the detective began as he pulled out a notepad. "This is in relation to a murder investigation for Lisa Brown." He paused, as if waiting for a response.

Kennedy felt like she was being strangled, but she didn't dare alter her facial expressions. She nodded, prompting him to continue, even as her heart picked up speed.

"Do you know another Lisa Brown?" he went on.

"Other than me?" Kennedy shook her head. "No. How would you figure I know someone else named Lisa Brown?"

A slight pause before Detective Warren spoke up again. "Well, there seem to be a few, uh, *similarities* between the two identities," he said. "That of you and the Lisa Brown in our homicide investigation."

Kennedy concentrated on not looking suspicious as she lifted her shoulder in an absent shrug. She fixed her face to relay confusion. "Lisa Brown is quite a common name. I'm still confused as to why you are here."

"Well, in particular, a credit card that was recently used to purchase some jewelry . . ." He paused and glanced down at his notes. "From Shane Co."

Kennedy nodded, keeping her face neutral. "What about it?"

"It appears to have belonged to Lisa Brown."

"That's because I *am* Lisa Brown." Kennedy exaggerated a sigh and rose to her feet. "I'm sorry, Detective. I don't see how I can be of any assistance here. Is there anything else because I need to get back to my wedding."

"Tell me why you both have the same Social Security number." Detective Warren stood, as well. His tone was now more accusatory. "And the same driver's license. Do those seem like just 'mere coincidences' to you?"

It wasn't shocking news. Kennedy was already prepared for that information, so it was easy for her face to reflect the exasperation she felt. "I have no idea," she said, tossing up her hands. "My Social Security number was issued to me at birth just like yours, I'm sure, Detective Warren. The same number is going to be given to me again when I have my name changed. My driver's license was also issued to me, since I am Lisa Brown."

She pretended to fish for more rationales, easily remembering when Lisa, the real Lisa, had opened an investigation for identity theft. "I did have an issue with identity theft and fraud on my number a few months ago," Kennedy added, struggling to keep a triumphant tone out of her voice. "Feel free to check it out with the credit bureaus where I put blocks on all my stuff. I even filed a police report, so you should have that, too. Thank you, Detective."

As if on cue, Washington entered the room and immediately crossed to circle a protective arm around his wife's waist. Kennedy froze. Part of her was grateful for his subtle support, because maybe then it would prompt the man to leave. Part of her was afraid he wouldn't take the hint and fire more questions that she wasn't prepared to answer in front of Washington.

Thankfully, the detective chose the former and nodded while flipping his notepad closed and shoving it in his back pocket.

"What seems to be the problem here?" Washington asked, and Kennedy silently begged him to shut the hell up before he made the situation even worse.

"And you are?" Detective Warren asked.

"I'm Lisa's husband," he answered.

"Well, I just had a few questions for your wife, but I think we're done for now." Detective Warren held out a business card in Kennedy's direction. "If you think of anything else, please give me a call."

Kennedy nodded and took the business card, then watched him walk away.

He paused at the door and glanced back over his shoulder. "Congratulations," he said, the simple word coming out snarky. "I will be in touch soon." And with that, he left.

Kennedy waited until she heard the front door shut before she let out the breath she had been holding. It was as if the stress of his presence had also brought on a migraine, because a dull ache was throbbing between her temples.

"What was all that about?" Washington said, his face carrying his concern.

Kennedy waved her hand. "It's nothing," she said. "He thought I was someone else, so he was trying to question me about something that I know nothing about." He made another move to speak, and Kennedy quickly laid a hand on his arm. "Sweetie, can you get me an aspirin?" she asked with a smile. "My head is suddenly killing me. I think I may have had one glass of wine too many."

Washington hesitated before nodding and walking off in the direction of the kitchen.

Kennedy collapsed back on the sofa, clutching her head in her hands. Damn, now what was she supposed to do? She could call Benji for help, but she didn't know how likely it was he would bail her out, considering how she had acted at his party. Plus, he had already warned her about getting in over her head.

Maybe his cousin Shawn could help her out. She was waist-deep in some shit. Now with the police on her ass, she surely couldn't keep Lisa Brown's identity. She needed to get her hands on Washington's money and get the hell out of here and under the radar. Fast. Before it was too late.

CHAPTER 11

"I'm sorry, Mrs. Bell."

On a frown, Kennedy glanced up as the teller slid her driver's license and withdrawal slip back through the bottom hole of the glass separating them. "Sorry for what?" she asked.

"All the funds in this account have been frozen."

Kennedy glanced down at the withdrawal slip, mentally running through the account numbers she had memorized earlier. She had pulled out $4,000 only moments before, but having already reached her withdrawal limit at the ATM with the card she stole from his wallet, she had gone inside to withdraw more. She knew for a fact Washington had about $500,000 in this particular account. The account he claimed to have added her name to.

"May I ask why?" Kennedy asked, confusion quieting her voice. "I mean, I was able to pull some money out of the ATM from this same account with no problem."

The teller pecked at a few keys on the keyboard. "It appears you are considered an *agent* on this account," she explained, her eyes scanning the screen to read whatever confirmation about her reasoning. "So, there is a limit on how much you can withdraw without the account holder's authorization."

"That can't be right," Kennedy said, her frustration rising. "He told me I was a joint account holder."

The teller finally met her gaze, but her eyes seemed to reflect her lack of concern. She shrugged and peeled her lips back in a *nothing more I can do* type of smile. "I apologize for any misunderstanding," she said politely. "But I'm looking at this account, and that is the information I have. Would you like to try to withdraw from another one?"

Kennedy tried to get a handle on her anger. She quickly grabbed another withdrawal slip and began scribbling numbers to another account she and Washington co-owned. The woman keyed in the numbers and again, shook her head in apology. "You are not listed on this account."

"It doesn't make any sense." Kennedy's voice had elevated in panic. "He told me he had added me to these accounts. There should be three accounts that list me as a co-owner."

"Well, like I said, Mrs. Bell"—the woman spoke slowly, as if the explanation was taking every ounce of her patience—"on the first account you were listed as an agent, and the second account does not list you as an account holder at all. I'm not sure what you were told, but I'm looking at the account right here, so I apologize for any misinformation. Would you like to try another account?"

Desperate, Kennedy scribbled the only other account number she knew on a fresh withdrawal slip, only to be told the same thing. She swore under her breath. Washington had been two steps ahead of her. He must have been listening to his bald head–ass mother, and he didn't actually follow through with what he said he was going to do. And now, she was broke. Sure, she had a few thousand to hold her over until her next gig, but she was supposed to be on a plane to some tropical island by now, basking in the fruits of her labor. But after all of that conniving and executing and kissing Washington's ass, she was fucking broke.

Kennedy turned and stormed out of the bank. She was furious. But it wasn't like she could actually call Washington. After their wedding the previous afternoon, Kennedy had managed to feign being sick, so she didn't have to have sex with him. And she slipped an Ambien in some punch to knock him out cold. Then that morning, she had simply left. Despite their 12:30 p.m. flight for their honeymoon, Kennedy had gotten up and snuck out to catch the banks when they first opened right at eight o'clock.

She was sure he was probably suspicious right now. Or confused as hell. But she hadn't thought about any of that. Her only focus had been getting his money. Now she had clearly burnt that bridge, and there was no way she could go back to him. Even if she made up some excuse about her early morning whereabouts, how the hell was she going to inquire about his accounts without revealing her own ulterior motives? How could she have known she wasn't on the bank accounts or was just an "agent" on one account without explaining how she had been trying to withdraw funds? And even if he fell for whatever lie she concocted, it wasn't like she could just jump on that plane with him and continue on to celebrate their honeymoon. Not with the police on her ass. She needed to disappear.

Kennedy pushed through the doors of the bank and stepped out into the chilly October air. The sun was certainly deceiving, because the wind was brisk enough to have her pulling her red double-breasted mid-length jacket tighter.

She crossed the parking lot to her car while at the same time pulling her cell phone from her pocket. Just as she expected, there were several missed calls and text messages from Washington. Ignoring them, she was halfway through punching in Deven's ten-digit number before she stopped herself.

She couldn't call her. What would she say? Deven knew

nothing about Kennedy's activities, and to her, the decision to just up and leave her newlywed husband and empty his bank accounts, only to find that he had prevented her from doing so, wouldn't necessarily warrant a supportive response.

First things first, she needed to pawn her wedding ring set. That would put a few extra coins in her pocket until she could decide what to do.

Kennedy typed *pawn shop* in her cell phone's GPS and let the navigation direct her to a plaza a few lights down. The shop had bars across the windows and door, and huge graffiti letters spray-painted in neon pink and yellow colors obstructed the view inside from the parking lot.

A bell chimed over the door as Kennedy stepped into the musty shop riddled with overused knickknacks and dingy glass casings filled with electronics that looked like they came straight from the 1960s. She passed an electric scooter and a bass guitar resting on top of a jukebox and made her way to the older gentleman perched on a stool behind the counter. He rose to greet her, and Kennedy had to ignore the lust-filled roam of his eyes as they devoured her face, then her body, like he had never seen a woman before. Pathetic.

"How can I help you, Miss Lady?" His Northern accent was thick as he all but salivated at Kennedy's presence.

Without a second thought, Kennedy pulled the wedding set from her finger and rested it on the glass. "How much?" she asked simply.

The man let out a low whistle of appreciation as he used stubby fingers to lift one of the rings in the air. The diamonds caught the light and twinkled in the air. "Pretty fancy bling," he commended. He turned his attention back to Kennedy. "What you trying to get for it?"

Kennedy tossed a glance to the sign overhead, displaying the shop's name: PETE'S PAWN SHOP. She leaned forward, allowing her breasts to spill over the low vee-neckline of her shirt.

"Listen, Pete," she said, lowering her voice to a seductive murmur. "I know you don't know me, but I'm in a little bit of a bind. Do you think you can maybe give me a great deal on this? That's not too much to ask, is it?"

Pete licked his lips, and the gesture made her skin crawl. His smile spread slow, displaying a row of teeth that looked more like dominoes. "Of course, Miss Lady. Let me see what I can do." He disappeared to the back.

Kennedy leaned back from the casing, her eyes suddenly catching the guns neatly arranged by size and color. Boxes of bullets sat on display at the foot of each column. She had never so much as held a gun, never considered owning one. But now, the thought didn't seem like a bad idea.

She leaned closer, scrutinizing each piece, a new thrill suddenly causing her palms to sweat. "Hey, Pete," she called. "How much are the guns?"

CHAPTER 12

Kennedy sat outside the pawn shop, sifting with renewed vigor through the few contacts she had saved. Too bad she had to constantly switch phones; otherwise she probably would have more people to call on in her time of need.

Her eyes paused on Aunt Glo's number. She would probably let her stay with her for a bit if she weaved a believable enough story. But then she would be right under Uncle Bernard's scrutiny, and that sure as hell was the last place she needed to be. It was looking more and more like Deven's place. That would be better than nothing. With minimal money and the police keeping close tabs on "Lisa Brown," she wouldn't be able to get very far. Not yet. She needed a new identity, that much was certain. But if that was the case, she would need some documents. A driver's license at the minimum. Calling Benji was out of the question. But just maybe, she had a connection of her own now.

Kennedy pressed the button to make the call and leaned against her truck while she waited for him to pick up. Part of her was surprised when he did. "Hey, Shawn," she greeted Benji's cousin. "It's Kennedy." She hadn't spoken to him since the party, when he went spilling the business on Benji's engagement. But she knew he and Benji did some hustles together. Which made him her new best friend.

"Hey," he said, sounding just as surprised. "I didn't think you would actually use the number when I gave it to you. You good?"

"No, not really. I need your help. Can we meet?"

"Now?"

"Yes. It's an emergency."

They agreed on the King of Prussia Mall, and Kennedy quickly headed toward Philadelphia. She didn't know how much she was going to reveal to Shawn, if anything. But she needed to see if he could somehow help her.

The mall had just opened, so it wasn't crowded at all. Kennedy found a parking space near the entrance and made her way inside.

Shawn had said he would be near the food court, and sure enough, he was already at the Auntie Annie's stand, handing money over to the cashier. He was dressed completely casual in a gray Nike sweatsuit and some all-white sneakers. Kennedy shoved her hands in her pockets and strolled over to stand by his side. "It's a little early for a pretzel, don't you think?" she teased, watching as the teenager handed his cinnamon-sugar pretzel over the counter wrapped in a paper sleeve.

Shawn didn't waste time digging in. "Not at all," he said, taking a bite. "Just woke up, and I need the energy to hear what you got to talk about."

"You don't even know what it is I have to say," Kennedy said.

"I have a pretty good idea." Shawn led the way to a nearby bench, and they sat down.

Kennedy had to stop herself from asking about Benji. She really needed to stop focusing so much on him and worry about herself. Hell, that was exactly what he was doing. So instead, she waited patiently while Shawn polished off his snack and tossed the trash into a nearby bin. "I need some help," she started after an extended hesitation. "I'm not even sure if you can help me, but I have nowhere else to go."

Shawn tossed his arm over the back of the bench. "Tell me what's up, and let me see what I can do."

Kennedy sighed, taking care to choose her words carefully. "The police think I've done something," she said. That much was entirely true. "It's a long story, and I don't want to pull you into my mess, but I can say I didn't do what they're accusing me of. To be perfectly honest, I'm scared as hell."

Shawn nodded. "Have you talked to Benji about this?"

"I have. He told me there was nothing to worry about, but the police came to my house last night. And it wasn't the first time. So, it seems like there is something I should be worrying about." When Shawn merely nodded but made no move to speak, Kennedy rushed on, her words stumbling over her frustration. "I just need to disappear for a while, Shawn. Do you maybe know some people?"

"Where you headed?"

Kennedy shrugged. "I don't know. Just . . . away from here."

"What do you need? Money?"

Kennedy's eyes fell to her hands in her lap. Apparently, he didn't know anything, and there was no way she could come out and say it without sounding suspicious or bringing awareness to something he didn't need to know about.

She heard Shawn sigh, and he scooted closer to her. When she felt his lips brush her cheek, she snatched back in alarm. "Shawn, this isn't—I'm not—"

"Come here." There was something in the two-word command that had her leaning back in his direction, despite her confusion. This time, he twirled pieces of her hair between his fingers as he lowered his mouth to her ear. "This is just in case someone is watching," he whispered. "So, stop acting so damn afraid, because trust me, I'm going to get what I want from you in due time."

Kennedy's eyes darted around. The mall was nearly empty. Who would be watching? And what the hell did he plan on getting from her?

"Does Uncle Bernard know you're meeting me?"

"Don't worry about him."

Kennedy wanted to roll her eyes. He sounded just like Benji. She was sick of people telling her not to worry, as if her life and freedom wasn't at stake. Sure, it was easy not to worry when it wasn't them being hunted down by the police for fraud and possibly murder.

"I can help you, Kennedy," Shawn was saying. "Yes, I know all about what Benji does for you because I help him. And I'll be happy to give you what you need."

Kennedy's breath quickened. "I don't have much money," she whispered.

This time, Shawn planted a gentle kiss on her cheek. "I don't want your money, sexy."

Sickened, Kennedy snatched away from his embrace and scooted over. The edge of the wooden bench bit into her side, but she didn't even feel the pinch as she glared at Shawn's perverted grin. "Benji wouldn't have asked me for that," she said weakly.

Shawn's shrug was nonchalant. "Well, call Benji then," he said.

Kennedy rose. There had to be another way. She would just find another way. But if she didn't, then what? She remembered the detective the day before. She didn't know what evidence he had against her, or if it was even enough. But he had found her, first at her condo with her sister, then under her pseudo name at Washington's house. The fact that he was going through so much trouble meant only one thing. He had something. And the shit was terrifying. Kennedy could bet Detective Warren would love nothing more than to pin a murder on her just so he could close his precious case.

She shut her eyes and sighed. "Can I let you know later?" she asked. She didn't turn but she heard him rise to his feet.

"You know where to find me, *Lisa Brown*." She noticed how he made absolutely sure to emphasize her false identity. "Oh, and check your pocket," he added. Then he smiled before walking away.

Kennedy took the opportunity to let out a shaky breath. She should just call Benji. She knew she needed to. But still, something prevented her from pulling out her phone and making the call. Instead, she dipped her hands in her jacket pockets to see what Shawn had been talking about.

Her fingers brushed a money clip and what felt like a stack of bills. She blinked, surprised. She hadn't even felt him make the drop. Kennedy glanced around before pulling back her pocket enough to see inside, and sure enough, a small stack of hundred-dollar bills was folded neatly in a gold money clip, along with what looked to be a business card. Leaving the money in place, she pulled out the business card and saw it was to a townhome property manager's office in Baltimore, Maryland. A little spark of hope had a smile tugging at the side of her lips. Well, that most certainly solved a few of her problems. But there still was the matter of her identity.

Kennedy didn't know how long she sat there, but she watched as more and more mall shoppers began to appear. Again, she had that eerie feeling, like eyes were focused on her. She glanced around, half-expecting to see Detective Warren, or worse, Uncle Bernard, with eyes locked on her through the crowd. But people carried on around her as if she wasn't even there. No one even seemed to notice her.

A woman strutted by the window in heels and a skirt extremely too tight. A teenager swaddled in tattoos, with earphones in his ears, nearly broke his neck to turn and look at her. A man in a business suit with a cell phone fastened to his ear didn't even break stride when he bumped into a brunette with a pregnant belly bulging from a floral dress that kissed her ankles. A group of teenage girls with voices elevated in excitement hopped off the escalator, clearly ditching school.

For some reason, Kennedy's eyes fell on one woman in particular who seemed to be idly browsing the windows. They were about the same complexion, but in stark contrast to Kennedy's burgundy bob, this woman had her hair in a jet-black pixie cut that stood in a sexy spike at the top and tapered against the back of her neck. She looked slightly out of place. Perhaps it was the glittering Rolex on her petite wrist. Perhaps because the woman was distractingly overdressed in a tailored blazer and slacks with a Michael Kors purse draped over her forearm.

Whatever the case was, Kennedy's eyes stayed glued to the woman as she moseyed casually from store window to store window, appearing as if she was just wasting time as opposed to taking an actual interest in the displays. Kennedy rose to her feet and glanced around nervously. She knew no one was watching, but the sudden thought that sprang to her mind had her paranoid, as if she had uttered the words aloud. She took a breath and made her way toward the woman.

Kennedy tried to make the gesture appear as casual as possible as she walked first behind the woman, and then eased her way up beside her. Without giving it a second thought, she stuck her foot in the woman's walking path and sure enough, she stumbled and fell, face forward, on the linoleum mall floor. Kennedy's eyes zeroed in on the purse and the contents that spilled out.

"Are you okay, ma'am?" Kennedy feigned concern as she knelt to help the woman to her feet. She strategically placed herself over the Michael Kors purse.

"Damn, I don't know what happened," the woman was muttering to herself as she tried to pick herself up. Kennedy bent by her side, one of her hands on the woman's arm while she used her other hand to pull out the black wallet peeking from inside the woman's purse. Her heart was pounding as her fingers closed around the leather, and she kept her eyes trained on the woman as she dropped the wallet into her jacket pocket. She said a silent prayer that no one had seen the gesture.

"Must have been a crack or something on the floor," Kennedy said, now using both hands to help the woman to her feet.

The woman dusted off her clothes, her eyes darting backward to the floor as if she could actually see the source of her fall. She finally brought her eyes to Kennedy, and her confusion was replaced with a grateful smile. "It was my fault," she said. "I wasn't paying attention."

Kennedy nodded as she scooped down to pick up the purse, keys, receipts, and a tube of lipstick. She handed it over.

"Thanks . . ." the woman trailed off as if expecting Kennedy to fill in the silence with her name. She didn't.

"It's no problem," she said. "Have a great day, and please be careful." Not wanting to prolong the awkward interaction, Kennedy turned and tried to walk off as calmly as possible. Just for good measure, she shoved her hands in her pockets and sighed in relief when she once again felt the leather of the wallet. It was a stupid plan, and not well thought out at all. But hell, it had worked. That was all that mattered. Now, hopefully the woman was actually worth some money and not just looking the part.

Kennedy didn't slow her strides until she had made it into the privacy of her own car. She was anxious to see what the wallet contained, but more than that, she was scared as hell someone had seen the theft and was after her. So, she pulled out of the mall parking lot and drove until she reached a gas station. She needed to fill up anyway.

Finally pulling the wallet out, Kennedy flipped open the flap and eyed the driver's license and numerous credit cards shoved into the pockets. Not wanting to waste any time,

Kennedy whipped out the first credit card and stepped out to try it at the pump. A few buttons pushed and she was lifting the nozzle and sticking it into her gas tank. Kennedy smiled as the numbers began to click forward, signaling the gas was coming through the hose and the charges were racking up on the woman's card. Kennedy eased down on the front seat and pulled the license out next, eyeing the picture. Regina Saunders. Sure enough, the woman from the mall was grinning back at her. Kennedy absently fingered her hair. She had always wanted to try a short haircut.

CHAPTER 13

Somebody was blowing up her phone.

Kennedy groaned as she continued to shampoo her hair, her nails raking suds through the fresh haircut. Her phone stopped ringing before starting back up immediately. It was probably Washington. He had called a number of times since she had left him the day after their wedding. That had been almost a week ago. And it was almost a week ago since she became Regina Saunders.

She sighed and drowned out the annoying ringtone. She was going to get that phone cut off eventually and buy a new one. To be honest, the only reason she hadn't yet was because of Benji. He would have no way of contacting her. She could've cursed herself for acting like that man still gave a shit about her. But she just couldn't bring herself to completely sever the ties. Not yet, anyway.

The water had gone nearly cold by the time Kennedy finished the tedious task of washing and rewashing the dye out of her hair. The hotel shower stall was now splattered with the jet-black dye, and the water had even been stained black as it circled to pool at the drain. Kennedy cut off the water and stepped out, grateful she was now engulfed in silence. Water trickled down her wet body and trailed along the linoleum floor as she grabbed one of the cream monogrammed hotel towels from the drying rack.

She definitely wouldn't have chosen black for herself, but after rubbing the excess water from her hair and observing the results in the mirror, she would have to say she did like the look. The water had begun to coil her strands into cute little ringlets. The black was a bold contrast that seemed to bring out the dark color in her eyes. Earlier she had found a stylist to cut her mane to a couple inches and taper the back. No, she didn't look exactly like the woman's picture, but she could definitely pass. She would make a point to stock a few wigs for the next time. Kennedy shuddered at the thought. She wanted to say *if* there was a next time, but she honestly couldn't be sure. The uncertainty was scaring her. But for now, what choice did she have?

Kennedy dropped the stained towel on the floor, and grabbing a fresh one, wrapped it around her body before crossing into the large hotel suite. Her suitcase lay open on the king-sized bed. Brand-new clothes with tags still hanging from the hems and sleeves spilled onto the plush white comforter. The new laptop she had purchased—*Regina* had purchased—was resting on the desk near the floor-to-ceiling window, opened up to expose the glistening water of the Baltimore Harbor.

It felt nice to take a little break. Kennedy felt as if she had been glued to the keys for three days trying to work some magic. Turns out, she was a damn good investigator herself. Because once she found Regina's public profile on social media, Kennedy had been able to obtain enough information to attempt a few hacks into the woman's bank account. It had taken a phone call to the bank with a "forgotten password" allegation, and then some creativity with answering the woman's identifying questions based on the information Kennedy could find on her, but she was finally given access. Ms. Regina Saunders didn't have a whole lot of money in this particular account. It appeared it was just a simple checking account she pinched from here and there, be it for a pair of shades or a caramel macchiato at Starbucks. But to Kennedy, twenty-five thousand was enough for now. To cover her tracks, she set up a dummy account under another alias she had used before, transferred the money, and withdrew every red cent. Kennedy was afraid to use the two credit cards already in the woman's wallet, so instead, she applied for a new one, had it rush-delivered, and indulged in a little shopping spree.

And as much as she loved her vehicle, she needed to get out from under it. So, she listed it on Facebook Marketplace for a super low price, and someone came to pick it up within the hour. Kennedy turned around and purchased a little used Nissan Murano from a Buy-Here-Pay-Here dealership. It had a ton of miles, but it was cheap and reliable, and that was what she needed for now. She would worry about getting her dream car again when she had another fish on the hook. So, she dropped three grand on the SUV, packed it up with everything that would fit, and hit the road.

It wasn't until four hours later, when she was passing the WELCOME TO MARYLAND sign, that Kennedy realized she didn't have any kind of plan. A car full of clothes, a duffel bag of money, a new car, and a stolen wallet wasn't going to cut it. Sure, Shawn had given her another thousand dollars and a business card for a townhome property, but then what? What she needed was a strategy. What she needed was a new idiot to scam. So, she checked into a hotel on the Baltimore Harbor and paid in advance for three nights. That way, she could have time to get her situation straight.

First came the fear. Kennedy wasn't under the protective umbrella of Benji anymore. She didn't know shit about being an identity thief on her own. She had always had Benji to back her up, make sure her shit checked out, and cover her ass if she needed a bailout. She didn't want to be a criminal having to constantly look over her shoulder or hold her damn breath whenever a cashier swiped her stolen credit cards.

Then came the anger. All that hard work with Washington had fallen through, and damn it if she wasn't pissed that as strategically as she'd tried to put her plan into place, he was one step ahead of her. And she was 1000 percent positive it was because of his meddling-ass mama. The bitch.

Finally, came the realization. She had done it before, but Washington was by far the biggest cash-out. So, if she could hook one with millions before, she could easily do it again. All she needed was a new, unsuspecting victim. And this time, she would make sure she didn't leave until she cleaned him out and the money was actually in hand. Then and only then could she retire to her life of luxury. She sure as hell deserved it.

The phone rang again, and Kennedy finally snatched it up from the bed. Surprise, surprise. It was Washington. She swiped the screen to reject the call and then scrolled through the log to see the other twenty-seven missed calls. She frowned when she saw the majority of them weren't from Washington. There were a few from Deven, but most of them were from an unknown number.

Kennedy rolled her eyes and turned to find some clothes to throw on. Probably Washington trying to contact her by any means necessary. Just like him to call from various blocked numbers to see if she would pick up and trick her out of hiding. Damn shame, too. Washington was so desperate, and he didn't seem to be getting the picture. She hadn't meant to hurt him. Well, not too bad anyway. Especially because he was older, so sweet, and so naïve. But instead of pining away over her—or Lisa Brown, rather—he should just let it go. He was just lucky she got out empty-handed. He still had his damn money. What more did he want?

The hotel phone's shrill ring echoed in the quiet room and had Kennedy frowning. Who the hell could be calling her at the hotel? Who knew she was even there?

She sat naked on the edge of the bed. The mattress sank under her weight as she tentatively lifted the phone to her ear.

"Hello?"

"Hi, Ms. Saunders?"

The man's voice was crisp and professional. Kennedy hesitated. Of course, she had given the new woman's name when she checked into the hotel. She *was* Regina Saunders for the time being. But was this some sort of trick?

"Yes," she answered.

"I apologize for disturbing you," the man said. "This is the front desk. Just letting you know that you have a visitor."

Kennedy's heart skipped a beat. "I don't know who the visitor is," she stammered. "But I'm not expecting anyone."

"Would you like me to ask his name?"

His?

Kennedy shifted uneasily. "Please just tell him I'm not accepting visitors. Thank you." She quickly hung up the phone. She would need to cut her little trip short. She wasn't sure who was waiting downstairs, but the chances of them actually looking for Regina Saunders—or Lisa Brown, for that matter—were slim. Which meant they were looking for Kennedy. She didn't know how or why, considering she was now in Maryland as opposed to New Jersey. None of that mattered, though. What mattered was that she got the hell up out of there.

She threw on a new Victoria's Secret panties and bra set, some jeans, and a Polo sweater before stuffing the rest of her clothes in the bag. Her movements stopped abruptly when a fearful thought crossed her mind. What if it was the police? What if Shawn had told Uncle Bernard what she was up to, and somehow they had tracked her down?

Shit. She cursed under her breath, then quickly grabbed her purse and the duffel bag with her money inside. To hell with the clothes. The front desk had rung her room, so if it was the police, they knew exactly where she was. She needed to leave. Now.

Kennedy was only on the third floor, so she opted to take the stairs down to the lobby instead of the elevator. The stairwell was off to one side, so it would give a clear view of the front desk in case her "visitor" was still waiting. Plus, she could exit without being seen.

The lobby was definitely just as elegant as the rest of the hotel, which could account for the high sticker price and the two-night minimum requirement. The floor was tiled in diagonal marble sheets of rich cream and burgundy. An elaborate chandelier embellished with Venetian crystal and black diamonds dominated the domed ceiling, casting an array of glittering twinkles on the numerous patrons below. People were either scattered on the embroidered silk sofas, wheeling luggage through the revolving doors, or clustered against the amber-colored wooden front desk with the etched clear-glass waterfall display cascading behind the attendants.

Kennedy pushed out of the stairwell and stood briefly against the wall, taking in the scene. Though she wasn't sure whom she should be looking for, she scanned the crowd for Detective Warren, Uncle Bernard, or anyone in a police uniform. Satisfied when she saw no one, Kennedy tried to appear as casual as possible as she started toward the front door. If she could just get to her car, she would see what she needed to do. She would probably have to break down and call Benji before she got herself into some deeper shit she wouldn't be able to get out of.

"Ms. Saunders." Kennedy heard the voice but pretended she didn't. She kept her head down and quickened her pace.

Adjoining the hotel was a restaurant and Kennedy breezed past the line of people as if she were searching for someone. She stood between the hostess sign and a sign on an easel welcoming what looked to be the hotel's executive board. "Miss," the hostess said with an apologetic smile. "You're going to have to wait in line. We have reserved seating for dinner this evening."

"Where is your restroom?" Kennedy asked, her eyes darting around the crowded restaurant.

"I apologize, ma'am, but the restroom is only for guests."

"I'm with a party," Kennedy lied and nodded her head toward the sign.

The woman's face wrinkled in doubt, but apparently, the words "executive board" had her bridling her tongue. Her lips turned up in a phony smile. "I'll have someone inform Mr. Walker that you're here. What is your name?"

Kennedy hesitated for just a moment. "Ms. Saunders."

The woman nodded before lowering her voice to speak into the bite-sized microphone attached to a cord at her shoulder. She then began speaking to the couple patiently waiting at the hostess stand.

Kennedy shifted the duffel bag on her shoulder. What was she doing? On a sigh, she turned and strolled back out toward the hotel lobby, praying the front desk clerk had ceased his efforts in trying to locate her. Relenting, she pulled out her phone and began scrolling through her contacts. She would just call Benji and drive down to Atlanta. She needed to get even farther away from Jersey.

"Ms. Saunders."

Kennedy groaned inwardly and didn't bother responding until she felt the light tap on her shoulder. She rolled her eyes. "What is it?" she snapped, whirling around. She gasped when she saw it wasn't the front desk attendant again, but a man in a suit and tie. He was a couple inches shorter than her with a goatee against his caramel complexion. He was studying her now with intense hazel eyes that looked as if they could be contacts. He was definitely attractive, and by the aura that permeated from around him, he knew it, too.

"Sorry," he said with a grin. "The hostess told me you were looking for me."

Kennedy frowned and glanced to the hostess. "Not sure why she would say that. I don't even know who you are."

"My mistake." He was still smiling, as if he knew a secret joke. "Chris Walker. I'm the owner of the Winchester Suites."

Kennedy's eyebrow rose in mild interest. "Impressive," she said. "Nice to meet you, Mr. Walker."

Chris laughed, obviously sensing her lack of interest in his introduction. "Interesting. Most people would fall to my feet at that sort of revelation."

"I'm not most people," Kennedy said, the flirtation subtle. In reality, she felt the inside of her thighs getting moist at the delicious thought. The man smelt like money. Her mind was already churning with the possibilities.

Chris remained quiet, as if he was pondering something, just as a man walked up and touched him lightly on the arm. The man wore an equally expensive-looking suit and tie, and Kennedy guessed he was another member of the executive board. The man leaned in and whispered something in Chris's ear, and Chris nodded his understanding.

"I have to get to a meeting," he said. "Are you staying here in the hotel?"

Kennedy opened her mouth to admit she was about to check out and then thought better of it. "I'm in room three-one-one-seven," she said. "You should come see me when you're done."

The bold statement seemed to catch Chris off guard, but his smile returned. "I'll do that."

As he turned to walk away, Kennedy watched him with a smirk. Yeah, he would do just fine.

If she had been paying attention, she would have seen the person watching her, an equally devilish smirk in place.

CHAPTER 14

She should've known something was wrong. It was entirely too dark and too quiet. Kennedy sat up in the bed, her eyes struggling to make out the silhouettes of the furniture in the bedroom. The ceiling fan hummed and caused a light breeze to tickle her arms and the back of her neck. On a sigh, Kennedy ran her hand through her short crop of spiked hair. The sheets pooled at her waist did nothing to warm her skin, which was exposed by the tank top and cheerleader shorts of her pajamas. Her eyes landed on the bathroom door of the master en-suite. It was dark, but she could see the glint of the mirror from the crack. Kennedy frowned. Why was the door cracked? Hadn't she closed it the night before?

Kennedy tossed a hesitant leg over the side of the bed and rose to her feet, all the while keeping her eyes trained on the door. Her quiet steps were muffled against the carpet as she made her way toward the bathroom. She hesitated at the door, her hand on the knob, before giving it a slight nudge.

The door swung open, revealing the darkened bathroom: the double vanity sinks, the jetted tub, the half-enclosed walk-in shower with brown marble–tiled wall . . . nothing seemed out of place. Her peripheral caught a shadow of a movement, and Kennedy's head whipped around to the mirror. Her own reflection stood frozen in place, her chest heaving with the first few prickles of fear. She didn't know what she was expecting, but Kennedy's hand gravitated toward the light switch.

A flick of her wrist and light from the four fluorescent bulbs hanging over the mirror spilled out. She blinked, waiting for her eyes to adjust to the brightness.

"I always did like the lights on."

Kennedy heard the voice, and her eyes ballooned as she met his in the mirror. The faceless figure stood directly behind her, his large frame so close that she could feel the hot breath stinging the back of her neck. He was dressed in black, and what looked like blood was streaming from under a baseball cap and down his cheek. His lips peeled back into a sinister grin as he lifted his hand into view. Kennedy's breath caught in her throat as she felt the barrel of the gun crush her skull.

"Your turn, sweetheart," he said, and his finger snapped back to pull the trigger.

Kennedy's scream erupted and snatched her from the nightmare. She yanked her body up from the sofa, tumbling onto the carpet with the force of her abrupt movements. Pain immediately seared her arms as she hit the ground. But at least she was alive. At least it wasn't real. Kennedy lifted her hand to her head. It was as if she still felt the barrel of the gun. Still felt the explosion of the bullet as it shattered her skull. Still felt the hole in her head and the warm blood as it mixed to stain her hair. But there was nothing. She sighed, either in relief or with the remnants of fear, and climbed to her feet.

She didn't even realize she had been sleepwalking again. She had gone to sleep snuggled in the hotel bed but had somehow made it over to the sofa of the suite. A strong feeling of uneasiness had settled on her, and it was taking all of her energy just to deal with the insomnia. Then, when she finally did go to sleep, her patterns were sporadic, and now the nightmares and sleepwalking had become more and more frequent. And the fact that she was dreaming about Lisa's killer all of a sudden was chilling.

Kennedy padded back over to the bed and let out a gasp when she heard the light snore coming from the figure tangled in her sheets. She had completely forgotten about Chris. Damn, she knew she was out of sorts because she barely remembered him coming to her room last night.

She was surprised he had come knocking on her door, but part of her, the lonely part, was thrilled because the entire ordeal had been weighing on her extra heavy. And just like some knight-in-shining-armor shit, Chris showed up to her rescue with flowers and to-go containers of fresh seafood from the hotel restaurant.

As she was nibbling on her wood-grilled salmon, she had to admit that his company was refreshing. A distraction of sorts. Between his light skin, hazel eyes, and healthy bank account from owning a chain of exclusive hotels, Chris was a little on the arrogant side. And the fact that he loved to talk about himself made it much easier for Kennedy, or *Regina*, as she was now, to keep her lies to herself.

Kennedy nudged the man's shoulder, and he groaned in response. "Hey," she said. "I have some running around to do today, so I'm about to leave."

Chris turned over, squinting his eyes against the harsh morning sun. "Good morning, beautiful lady," he greeted with a smile. "How did you sleep?"

Did they even have sex? Kennedy had to giggle to herself. If so, it must not have been too good. She flashed him a smile in return. "So good," she lied and leaned down to peck him on the lips. "I hope we can continue this, maybe another time."

"You're leaving?" Chris pretended to pout. He poked his bottom lip out as far as it would go and wrinkled his forehead in a frown.

"I have to go check out some properties," Kennedy said. "Remember I mentioned I just moved to the area." *Which he would have known had he been listening.*

Chris nodded and sat up, exposing his lean, clean-shaven chest. "Right. Well, if you need someone to show you around the area, I would love to."

Kennedy grinned. "I'm going to take you up on that." They shared another kiss before she rose to cross into the en-suite bathroom, wondering how it would feel to own a few hotel chains as the new Mrs. Regina Walker.

CHAPTER 15

Kennedy pulled into the driveway of her new townhome, and turning off the car, she sat back on a sigh. The sky had turned blue with impending nightfall, and the first sprinkles of rain slapped the windshield.

"You just have me worried, sis," Deven was saying on the phone Kennedy clutched to her face. "You just up and disappear, don't call, don't text, don't let me know if you're okay. Who the hell does that?"

"I know, I know. I'm sorry." Kennedy rubbed her eyes wearily. "I just need to get my shit together, to be honest with you."

"Where are you now?"

"Baltimore."

"What?"

Kennedy had to chuckle. She could picture her sister shaking her head at the revelation. "I know," she said. "But I'm just taking the time for me right now. Everything has been so crazy with Lisa's death. I just needed a change of scenery, honestly." *And to lie low for now until I'm no longer a murder suspect.*

She heard Deven release an exasperated breath. "Yeah, I

understand. Well, do you know when you will be headed back this way?"

"I'm not entirely sure, but I promise to let you know when I do." Kennedy tossed an absent glance at the black Malibu that drove by. The rain was starting to come down a little harder. Thunder cracked somewhere in the distance. "Deven, let me call you later. I just got back home, so let me get in the house before it starts storming."

Deven seemed satisfied for now. "Okay, I love you."

"I love you, too."

They hung up, and Kennedy got out, rounding the back of the Murano to lift the trunk. The rainfall was a steady stream that dampened her clothes and hair, so she hurriedly slipped her tote over her shoulder with her purse and pulled out her groceries. To her disappointment, she hadn't left a porch light on or anything, so it was pitch black walking up to her entryway.

Turns out, the property manager business card Shawn had given her was a godsend. Shawn owned the property with Benji, and since it was vacant and completely furnished, she was able to move right on in rent-free instead of wasting money at the hotel. She was debating on staying there for a few months, at least until everything blew over. Especially now that she was working on Chris. Kennedy was proud of herself. *And Benji thought she couldn't handle it.* She couldn't wait to gloat in his face and tell him "I told you so."

Kennedy carried everything to the front door, and fumbling with the keys for a moment, she finally managed to get it open and stumble into the living room, knocking the door closed behind her with her foot. Her arm reached out to brace against the wall while she searched for the light switch. Her hand swiped a picture frame and sent it shattering to the floor. Too sleepy to care for either the picture or the switch, Kennedy walked forward, wincing at the crack of glass under her sneaker.

Kennedy peeled the slick shirt from her body. Soaked. She left the couple of bags full of canned goods and nonperishables by the door. She would worry about putting everything up tomorrow. For now, she needed a bath and maybe some hot chocolate or something.

Tossing her wet clothes in the laundry room as she passed, Kennedy crossed to the bathroom to take a quick shower. She found some shorts and a T-shirt and attempted to towel-dry her hair as best she could. By the time she was done, the rain was coming down in sheets. Slightly unnerved by the silence, she flicked on the TV, allowing the noise to fill the room.

She headed to the kitchen and pulled the hot chocolate from the pantry. Boxes were still scattered around the house, and whether it was from hope or lack of care, she hadn't bothered to unpack them yet.

A sudden noise had Kennedy spilling a little of the water out of the pot as she carried it to the stove. Uncertainty creased her brows as she dried her hands on the dish towel. She crossed back into the living room, the televised laughter echoing off the walls. Uncertain, her hand reached for the porch light as she angled her face to peer through the peephole. Nothing but rain pelting the darkness. Kennedy felt for the lock, surprised when it clicked into place. Hadn't she locked it when she arrived home?

Still uneasy, Kennedy took a step back from the door, her breath catching tight in her chest.

"Told you I would find you."

The voice had Kennedy sucking in a fearful breath as she whirled around. Her eyes ballooned as she observed the figure illuminated by the light in a shadowy glow from her kitchen.

Her mouth fell open as surprise, then fearful recognition, settled. "What are you—" Kennedy froze when the man lifted the gun, the barrel staring her right in the face.

CHAPTER 16

He stood in the middle of the kitchen dressed in a black sweatsuit. He looked rough, and the moon spilled through the sheer drapes, illuminating an eerie glow across his face.

Kennedy let out a staggering breath as her heart picked up speed.

Lewis, her first husband.

Her first abusive and controlling husband, whom she met online and married only to make Benji jealous.

The marriage she annulled and got away from even quicker than she married him.

"I'm sorry to scare you," he said, moving around the counter. His steps were slow. Calculated. Deliberate. All the while, he kept the gun trained on Kennedy's head. Her mind flashed to the gun she kept under her mattress. How fast could she get to it? Shit, had she even loaded it?

"What are you doing here?" she whispered. "How did you find me?"

"Oh, I have folks watching you," he said, a triumphant smile splitting his face. "Now, get in your room, bitch." Lewis's menacing voice was ripe with hatred.

Kennedy lifted her hands and stepped back, nearly tripping

over the bags she had set down just minutes earlier. He didn't displace his eyes or the gun as he moved closer.

Kennedy heard the squeak of his sneakers against the hardwood floor, and her heart stopped. She felt fear suck the color from her cheeks. Kennedy could hear her breath roaring so loud it was a wonder Lewis didn't hear it himself. She swallowed and concentrated on steadying herself.

"Lewis—"

"Your room," he repeated, his voice rising as he motioned with the gun. "Don't fucking talk to me. Don't open your fucking mouth. Get your ass into your room before I kill you right here."

Fear had Kennedy inching backward. She couldn't take her eyes from the gun, as if she could see the bullet in the chamber when it was released. She backed into her room and moved near the bed as instructed. With one hand, his eyes still on Kennedy, Lewis removed the bookbag from his back and tossed it on the bed.

"Open it," he said, his voice deadly calm.

Kennedy moved in slow motion, fumbling for the zipper to unzip the bag.

"Rope," Lewis instructed.

Kennedy swallowed, nearly tasting her heart as it pounded so quickly, it didn't feel like it was beating at all. She hated having to take her eyes off him, but the way Lewis stared, his finger unwavering on the trigger, she knew she'd better oblige. So, she snatched her eyes from the gun and ignored the rising panic as she felt around the bag for the rope.

The blade of a knife nicked her knuckle, and she felt the dribble of blood warm her finger. Horror from the contents must have been evident on her face, because to her surprise, Lewis smirked.

"I wasn't sure what I wanted to do with you," Lewis said, as if the explanation would help. "So, I just came prepared."

Kennedy shut her eyes, knocked aside some pill bottles

and handcuffs, felt the coarse braid of the rope, and pulled it out. "Put it around your ankles," Lewis barked.

With each order, Kennedy felt like she was spiraling even further down in this madness, and she wasn't sure if she would make it out alive. Panic had her mind racing. She needed to find a way out. She eased down to the bed, leaned over to do as she was told, and wrapped the rope around her ankles.

The butt of the gun rammed into her shoulder and Kennedy toppled over, the stinging pain shooting up her neck and down the length of her arm like a bolt of electricity. Kennedy shut her eyes against the ache in her shoulder and grimaced when she heard the subsequent chuckle.

"That felt good." Lewis sighed. "You certainly have been a tough woman to find, Mrs. Kennedy Ward."

He had used her married name from when she was with him. *Mrs. Kennedy Ward.* The man was truly psychotic, the reason for her hasty escape. But of course, she wasn't going to voice that out loud. Not right now, when he was towering over her with a madman's scowl and a gun clenched in his hand so tight it was nearly quivering. More piercing pain shot through her body, so raw that Kennedy couldn't help the tears that stung her eyes.

"Lewis, you don't have to do this," she managed to utter between gritted teeth.

Lewis's stare was unwavering as he leaned over to push the gun against Kennedy's temple. "Yeah, I kinda do." His voice was ragged, the alcohol on his breath prevalent as he hunched an inch away from her ear. "I never signed any fucking divorce papers. So that means, technically, you're still mine, Kennedy."

Kennedy remembered Benji falsifying the signature to finalize the annulment. He was right. She had left like a thief in the night and hadn't looked back. "Please." She was nearly whispering as she sat there, clenched. Time seemed to stand still.

"Oh, don't worry, baby. You'll have plenty of time to beg." Lewis used the force of the gun to push Kennedy's head against the floor. It felt like he was trying to push the barrel through her skull. "I guess all that bullshit you said at our wedding was a lie. Apparently, your snake ass done made a living off lies. How much did you steal?"

"I swear I didn't take anything from you," Kennedy said, desperate. "But I can give you money if that's what—"

"Shut the fuck up!" The force of Lewis's words had spittle flying and slapping Kennedy in the face. He lifted the barrel and punched the butt of the gun against her temple. Kennedy gasped at the impact as the pain seared like a dagger from one side of her head to another. Obediently, she pressed her trembling lips together and blinked to clear her blurry vision.

She heard Lewis move away, heard him rummaging through the bag. Silence. Then the click and whir of a tape recorder, and Kennedy squeezed her eyes shut as the sound of gasps filled the air.

"*Please* . . ." The woman's voice was hoarse as it caught in her throat, and Kennedy's heart broke as she recognized it. *Lisa.* The sick bastard had recorded himself killing Lisa.

Lewis's jagged breathing followed. Then the shatter of glass and muffled movement.

Lewis clicked off the recorder. "There's more, but you get the idea," he said with a careless shrug.

Kennedy shook her head. "Why?" she whispered. "Lisa had nothing to do with this."

"Lisa was an accident, damn. I thought she was you. I thought the bitch was just begging for her life and saying anything because she knew she was about to die."

"Me?" Kennedy shook her head, trying to make sense of his insanity.

"Didn't you change your name to Lisa Brown to avoid me?" Lewis bit off each word like it pained him to admit the truth. "Didn't you change your name, your face, your body, your fucking *identity*, so I wouldn't be able to find you?" Again, he jammed the barrel of the gun against the side of Kennedy's head for effect. "You can't outrun me, bitch. I'm in here. I'm part of you. Whether you like that shit or not, you have no fucking choice. You. Are. Mine."

Kennedy couldn't even wonder how he knew about all of that. A stalker. Lisa had said it, and Kennedy had seen it with her own eyes. "Lewis—"

A combination of disgust and anger had him heaving the recorder at the wall. Kennedy jumped when she heard it crack the plaster right above her head, the ragged device crumpling to the floor beside her.

"Do you know how much I love you?" Lewis asked, his tone softer. Monotone.

Kennedy ignored the headache and managed to open her eyes. Lewis was pacing, nearly stomping his feet with each stride, the barrel of the gun tapping the side of his leg in methodical, calculated gestures. "And here I was thinking you loved me. But your snake ass was trying to use people. Steal. Then disappear like it never happened. Is that what it was? You just wanted to steal from me, too?" Lewis waited as if he really expected a response.

Kennedy struggled to sit up against the wall. Her movements were slow, but she had to get away from this psychopath.

Lewis sighed and collapsed on the bed, holding the gun between both hands. Kennedy saw his jaw clenched and his lips moving, though no sound came out. She started to panic once more. It was obvious this man had some sort of mental issues in addition to his controlling and abusive personality, which made him even more unstable. And dangerous.

"There were only two women in this world I loved more than myself," Lewis murmured. "First you left me. So, all I had left was my sister. Then, when I found out she had been killed . . ."

When he trailed off, Kennedy thought fast. *Keep him talking, keep him talking.* "Your sister? Oh my God, I'm so sorry, Lewis. What happened?"

Lewis shook his head, frowning as the memories pierced his heart. "She was a prostitute. She had been dealt a shitty hand, so a fucking john strangled her. My sister ain't never did nothing to nobody, but some muthafucka thought this world was better off without her. And I couldn't protect her. I couldn't fucking protect her because I was so worried about you!" Lewis hit the side of his head with his fist and began to dry-heave like he was losing his breath. Or his sanity. Or both. Kennedy froze, watching his every move.

"Just come back to me, Kennedy," Lewis's voice lowered with his flooded emotions. "I just want you. Can't you just come back to me and we can work it out? I'll go to counseling if you want."

Lewis's eyes were downcast, so Kennedy glanced around the room for a weapon, a phone. *Something.*

"I know we just went to the courthouse, but I can give you the big wedding of your dreams. Like I know you like." He paused, and his eyes were accusatory as he looked to Kennedy. The insinuation was clear. He knew about her other weddings, and however fake, to him they were very real.

"Lewis." Kennedy held up her hands again, her words slow so maybe he would believe her. "It was all a lie. I never loved anyone like I loved you, okay? Why do you think I married you with my real identity? Because you had all of me. The only true Kennedy." When he didn't respond, Kennedy pressed on, praying her words sounded genuine. "I guess I was just . . . I don't know . . . scared. Scared of not loving you like you deserved. Like I knew you loved me. But I was a coward. It was stupid, so—So I ran, thinking I was doing what's best for you. I know now that . . . we need to be together. I want us to be together." Kennedy's vision wavered. Her shoulder and her head were pulsing in agonizing pain, but she tried her best to focus.

Lewis's face cracked ever so slightly, but her words seemed to penetrate. He looked at the gun before setting it on the dresser nearby. Kennedy released a grateful sigh and couldn't stop the smile that spread.

"Come here," he said, pain lacing his voice. He reached down to gingerly grab Kennedy by the arm to help her to her feet. Kennedy struggled to rise. Her legs were weak as she pulled up, and Lewis dissolved in her arms, the weight of his body heavy on her shoulder. Not knowing what else to do, Kennedy rubbed his back, her eyes settling on the gun he had laid on the dresser. It wasn't exactly close enough to grab. Maybe if she shimmied in that direction . . .

"I love you," she soothed in his ear. "I love you so much, Lewis. I'm right here for you. I'm not going anywhere, I promise."

"I know." Lewis sighed.

Kennedy felt his arms tighten around her body, and she gasped, bracing her hand on his shoulder. "Baby," she whispered, giving him a slight nudge. "Baby, you're hurting me." She felt him squeeze harder, those toned arms of his damn near biting into her flesh as she struggled to pull air into her contracting lungs.

"I loved you," he was whispering. "I really thought we could be something. Never in a million years did I think you would take everything from me and my family." His hand eased up to circle her neck.

Kennedy shook her head, fighting back the wave of dizziness as his fingers burned into her throat.

"You're lying," he went on, his tone dark and sinister. "I know you—the real you. Not Lisa, not Regina, but Kennedy. And you're a lying, conniving, manipulative bitch. There was another woman who hurt me like this a long time ago. I swore to myself it would never happen again."

Kennedy sputtered as she tried to cling to pieces of oxygen. Or maybe she was just weak. Her hands came up to grab Lewis's wrist, struggling to detach the vise-like grip. Her head was heavy, and the edges of her vision began to fade. Tears spewed from Kennedy's eyes as she struggled to suck in snatches of air, but Lewis held on tight. Her mind screamed that it wasn't true, and she moved her lips to voice it. But all that came out was inaudible gurgling sounds as her spit clogged her throat. Her eyes bulged as the life started to seep from her body.

In a last-ditch effort, Kennedy collected as much energy as she could muster and lifted her knee, connecting with his package. "Shit," Lewis hissed in pain. Instinct forced his hands to let go as he doubled over in pain. Kennedy sucked in a greedy gulp of air and coughed as the oxygen burned her throat.

Again, her eyes landed on the gun, but his body was blocking her path. Her mind quickly flipped to the gun she had hidden, and praying like hell it was loaded, she dove on the bed and scrambled across to get to the opposite side.

"You fucking bitch."

The move was swift. Lewis snatched the gun from the dresser, angled it at Kennedy, and pulled the trigger, sending the bullet piercing the tender flesh in her leg. Kennedy's scream erupted as the sting reverberated through her thigh. Blood seeped from the wound, dribbling like warm honey down her leg and pooling on the sheets. Kennedy sucked in a greedy breath as she collapsed on the floor, gritting her teeth to bear the fiery sensation that coursed through her leg.

For a brief second, she could only lie there, feeling each fiber of carpet as it grated against the side of her face. She felt the dead weight of her leg. The rich smell of blood was so suffocating, she could almost taste it. Kennedy's vision wavered once more, but through the haze of tears and blurred vision, she saw Lewis's brooding smirk. As she watched his finger stroke the trigger, she let her heavy lids flutter.

When Kennedy opened her eyes, she saw Lewis's face, but slowly, as if she were watching a movie, the face transposed until it was her own, staring back with that malicious grin and pointed gun. Kennedy watched the lips move, her lips, even though it was Lewis's voice that came out.

"Do you know how much I love you?" he said.

Kennedy didn't bother thinking. Only reacting. With a burst of renewed energy, she grabbed the remote at her side and hurled it at Lewis. As Lewis dodged the device, Kennedy took the opportunity to grab the bedside lamp and heave it in his direction. It shattered across Lewis's arm, and the impact had his finger slipping on the trigger. The shot rang out and penetrated the mattress, sending a burst of padding from the hole.

And there it was. Her gun. It was wedged between the mattress and the box spring. Thank God for Pete's Pawn Shop. Kennedy grabbed the gun, rolled to her back, aimed, and pulled the trigger with so much force and vigor it sent a rippling sensation up her arm. The first shot grazed his shoulder. Kennedy pulled the trigger again, and again, riddling his chest with bullets that had blood pouring from the holes in his opened flesh. His eyes rounded like saucers, and when he opened his mouth, another red waterfall dribbled from his lips. He coughed and sputtered as he grasped at the last few seconds of life.

Lewis's arm lifted, brandishing his gun once more, now aimed in her direction. Kennedy's clip was empty, and she screamed, squeezing her eyes shut. A gunshot popped like a firecracker, the hollow explosion echoing off the blood-splattered walls.

A *thump* sounded as a body fell, and quivering, Kennedy chanced opening her eyes. Uncle Bernard stood in the doorway, smoke billowing up from the barrel of the gun clasped in his hands. His breathing was heavy as he used the toe of his shoe to nudge Lewis's limp body stretched out on the floor.

Sighing, Kennedy let the gun fall from her hand and felt the first few tears of relief dampen her cheeks. "Did Benji send you?" she asked.

Uncle Bernard nodded, putting his gun back in the waistband of his pants.

"Was he mad at me?"

"Yeah," Uncle Bernard said on a chuckle. "He said to tell you he told you so."

CHAPTER 17

"Thank you so much, Dr. Bell," the woman said with a huge grin. She stood up to get a better look at herself in the mirror, a crop top tucked underneath her breasts to show off the defined structure of the liposuction. It had been a few months, and Washington had to admit, she was recovering nicely.

He nodded his approval as he struggled to stay in work mode. But honestly, plastic surgery was the last thing on his mind. He was waiting for a phone call.

The bubbly woman chattered on and on about how pleased she was with the results of the surgery, and all the while, Washington kept glancing from his cell phone to the wall clock ticking away seconds of the day. Thankfully, Sarah here was the last patient on his shift so he could focus on other things. Namely a place he had to be as soon as he got the green light.

At 4:32 p.m., his phone lit up with the incoming call. Washington sighed and took a breath to prepare himself.

"Thanks again for coming in," he spoke up as Sarah collected her belongings. "My receptionist will get you rescheduled for your third follow-up visit."

Sarah nodded and quickly scurried from the room while Washington swiped to answer the call.

"We're here," the caller said. "Feel free to come on down."

"I'm on my way," he said and hung up. Washington gathered his jacket and briefcase and took one last look out of the window of his twenty-third-story office. He noted the beautiful purple sky signaling the transition to night, a sign that the fall back of Daylight Savings Time had already taken effect. Then he flicked off the light and shut his office door.

His receptionist glanced up as he entered the lobby, a young, eager woman who sometimes reminded him of Lisa. "Gone already, sir?" she said with a smile.

"Yes, I have to take care of some business. Call me if you need me, but we shouldn't have any more patients scheduled."

"No, sir. I'll be wrapping up here soon, and I'll be sure to lock up."

Washington gave the woman a pleasant wink. "That's why you need a raise."

"Please tell my boss," she teased.

Washington pushed through the glass doors of his office practice and headed for the elevator stall. He pressed the DOWN arrow and waited as the floors highlighted above his head, signaling the elevator's approach.

His cell vibrated in his pocket, and he quickly pulled it into view to study the caller ID on the screen. That he was surprised was an understatement. He let it ring two more times before answering. "Wow, long time, no hear."

"I know." Kennedy's sigh was heavy. "Um, so sorry about that, Washington."

Washington's jaw clenched in restrained anger. He bridled his tongue, because Lord knew he wanted to call this girl every slur and curse word he could think of, which would probably make his mama proud. "For what, exactly?" he asked instead.

"For everything." A pause. "Washington, there is no excuse for anything I did. I'm so sorry, because you absolutely didn't deserve it."

"Damn right. Shit was foul, Lisa."

Her voice had lowered in shame. "Actually, it's Kennedy."

Washington scoffed. "Damn. Even worse. Well, nice to finally meet my fucking wife."

The bell chimed, signaling the elevator's arrival. "Listen, I'm about to get on the elevator, so this call is going to drop."

"Okay, listen, I want to explain," she rushed on. "And after that, you can never talk to me again and I would understand. I just feel I owe you that much."

The doors slid open to reveal the empty elevator car. Washington lifted his hand to keep the doors propped open. "What's a number you'll answer, then?"

"This one," she assured him. "Just . . . call me whenever you're ready, and I promise to answer."

"Yeah." He hung up as he stepped on the elevator. Time hadn't extinguished his anger, nor did he expect it to. He glanced at the number she'd dialed from, cross-referenced with the GPS tracker he had placed in her phone when he'd purchased it. She sure as hell owed him an explanation. More than that, actually. And now it was his turn to *cash in.*

Instead of pressing the button for the garage where he'd parked, Washington pressed FOUR and patiently rode the elevator down past the various hospital floors.

The doors slid open, and immediately, the ripe smell of death assaulted his nostrils. He had never had a reason to journey to the morgue. Until now, at least. Now, as much as he regretted the trip, he knew it needed to be done.

He met Detective Jamie Warren and his partner, Bernard,

in the hall as they stood near a huge glass window. "Gentlemen." He greeted each with a solemn handshake.

"Dr. Bell," Jamie said. "Thank you for meeting us on such short notice. We sincerely apologize it's under these circumstances."

Washington nodded but didn't respond. Instead, he followed them into the room where a draped sheet covered a body on a stretcher. Without hesitation, Jamie pulled back the sheet to reveal the face of the victim.

Washington sighed as he took in the facial features, now sunken with death. Again, he nodded his affirmation, since he knew that was what the detectives were waiting for.

Jamie started to pull the sheet back up to cover the face when Washington held up a hand to pause his movements. "May I?" he asked, not taking his eyes from the body. Both men nodded their understanding and left him alone in the room.

Washington didn't move immediately, instead taking in the moment. It felt like someone had taken a knife to his heart and snatched it out to bleed on the table. Never did he think it would come to this. Slowly, he felt his anger reigniting once again as his mind flashed to the call he'd received only moments before.

"Don't worry, my son." He lifted a hand to touch Lewis's cold forehead. "I tried to help you get her back, and it failed. Your old man will handle your situation for you now."

About the Author

Briana Cole began writing short stories and poetry at a young age—then used her poems to start a greeting card business in high school. After graduating cum laude with a bachelor's degree from Georgia Southern University, she independently published three novels. Briana is an Atlanta native and a proud mother of two. Her motto and ultimate drive toward success is a famous quote from Mae West: "You only live once, but if you do it right, once is enough." Connect with Briana online at BrianaCole.com, and on Facebook, Goodreads, Instagram, and Twitter @bcoleauthor.

We hope you enjoyed *Justified*!
Keep reading for sneak peeks at
the first in the Parker Crime series,
CONSPIRACY,
by De'nesha Diamond,
and the latest from
Briana Cole,
THE MARRIAGE PASS,
available now
wherever books are sold

CHAPTER 1

Washington, D.C
Winter

A scared and hungry fourteen-year-old Abrianna Parker stepped out of Union Station and into the dead of night. The exhilaration she'd felt a mere hour ago evaporated the second D.C.'s blistering wind sliced through her thin leather jacket and settled somewhere in her bones' marrow. A new reality slammed into her with the force of a ton of bricks—and left her reeling.

"Where is he?" she whispered as she scanned the growing crowd. Abrianna was more than an hour late to meet Shawn, but it couldn't have been helped. Leaving her home had proved to be much harder than she'd originally realized. After several close calls, she'd managed to escape the house of horrors with a steel determination to never look back. Nothing could ever make her return.

Now it appeared that she'd missed her chance to link up with her best friend from school, or rather they used to go to the same high school, before Shawn's father discovered that he was gay, beat the hell out of him, and then threw him out of the house. Miraculously, Shawn had said that it was the best thing to have ever happened to him. Over the past year, he'd found other teenagers like him living out on the streets of D.C. His eclectic group of friends was better than any blood family, he'd boasted often during their frequent text messages.

In fact, Shawn's emancipation from his parent had planted the seeds in Abrianna's head that she could do the same thing. Gathering the courage, however, was a different story. The prospect of punishment, if she was caught, had paralyzed her on her first two attempts and had left Shawn waiting for her arrival in vain. Maybe he thought she'd lost her nerve tonight as well. Had she thought to charge her battery before leaving the house, she would be able to text him now to find out where he was.

Abrianna's gaze skimmed through the hustle and bustle of the crowd, the taxis and cars. Everyone, it seemed, was in a hurry. Likely, they wanted to meet up with family and friends. It was an hour before midnight. There was a certain kind of excitement that only New Year's Eve could bring: the tangible *hope* that, at the stroke of midnight, everyone *magically* changed into better people and entered into better circumstances than the previous year.

Tonight, Abrianna was no different.

With no sight of Shawn, tears splashed over Abrianna's lashes but froze on her cheeks. Despite a leather coat lined with faux fur, a wool cap, and leather gloves, Abrianna may as well have been butt-ass naked for all the protection it provided. "Goddamn it," she hissed, creating thick frost clouds in front of her face. "Now what?"

The question looped in her head a few times, but the voice that had compelled her to climb out her bedroom window had no answer. She was on her own.

Someone slammed into her from behind—hard.

"Hey," she shouted, tumbling forward. After righting herself on frozen legs, she spun around to curse at the rude asshole—but the assailant was gone. She was stuck looking around, mean-mugging people until they looked at her suspect.

A sudden gust of wind plunged the temperature lower and numbed her face. She pulled her coat collar up, but it didn't help.

The crowd ebbed and flowed, but she stood in one spot like she'd grown roots, still not knowing what to do. And after another twenty minutes, she felt stupid—and cold. Mostly cold.

Go back into the station—thaw out and think. However, when she looked at the large and imposing station, she couldn't get herself to put one foot in front of the other. She had the overwhelming sense that her returning inside would be a sign of defeat, because, once she was inside, it wouldn't be too hard to convince herself to get back on the train, go home and let *him* win . . . again.

Icy tears skipped down her face. *I can't go back.* Forcing her head down, she walked. She passed commuters yelling for cabs, huddled friends laughing—some singing, with no destination in mind. East of the station was bathed in complete darkness. She could barely make out anything in front of her. The only way she could deal with her growing fear was to ignore it. Ignore how its large, skeletal fingers wrapped around her throat. Ignore how it twisted her stomach into knots. Ignore how it scraped her spine raw.

Just keep walking.

"Help me," a feeble voice called out. "Help!"

Abrianna glanced around, not sure from which direction the voice had come. *Am I losing my mind now?*

"Help. I'm not drunk!"

It came from her right, in the middle of the road, where cars and taxis crept.

"I'm not drunk!" the voice yelled.

Finally, she made out a body lying next to a concrete divider—the kind work crews used to block off construction areas.

"Help. Please!"

Again, Abrianna looked around the crowds of people streaming past. Didn't anyone else hear this guy? Even though that side of the building was dark, it was still heavily populated. Why was no one else responding to this guy's cry for help?

"Help. I'm not drunk!"

Timidly, she stepped off the sidewalk and skulked into the street. As vehicles headed toward her, she held up her hand to stop some and weaved in between others. Finally, Abrianna stood above a crumpled old man, in the middle of the road, and was at a loss as to what to do.

"I'm not drunk. I'm a diabetic. Can you help me up?" the man asked.

"Uh, sure." She knelt, despite fear, and asked herself, *What if it's a trap?*

It *could* be a trap, Abrianna reasoned even as she wrapped one of the guy's arms around her neck. Then, using all of her strength, she tried to help him to his feet, but couldn't. A Good Samaritan materialized out of nowhere to help her out.

"Whoa, man. Are you okay?" the stranger asked.

Abrianna caught a glimpse of the Good Samaritan's shoulder-length stringy blond hair as a passing cab's headlights rolled by. He was ghost white with ugly pockmarks.

"Yes. Yes," the fallen guy assured. "It's my blood sugar. If you could just help me back over to the sidewalk that would be great."

"Sure. No problem," the blond stranger said.

Together, they helped the old black man back across the street.

"Thank you. I really appreciate this."

"No problem," the white guy said, his teeth briefly illuminated by another passing car as a smoker's yellow.

Once back on the sidewalk, he released the old man. "You two have a happy New Year!" As quick as the blond savior had appeared, he disappeared back into the moving crowd.

The old guy, huffing and puffing thick frost clouds, wrapped his hand around a NO PARKING sign and leaned against it.

"Are you sure you're all right?" Abrianna asked. It seemed wrong to leave him like this.

He nodded. "I'm a little dizzy, but it will pass. Thank you now."

That should be that. She had done what she could for the man. It was best that she was on her way. But she didn't move—probably because he didn't *look* okay.

As she suspected, he started sliding down the pole, his legs giving out. Abrianna wrapped his arm back around her neck to hold him up. "I got you," she said. But the question was: for how long?

"Thank you, child. Thank you."

Again, she didn't know what to do next. Maybe she should take him up to the station. At least, inside, she could get him to a bench or chair to sit down. "Can you walk?"

"Yes. I—I think so."

"No. No. Not back there," he said, refusing to move in the direction of the station. "They done already kicked me out tonight and threatened to lock me up if I return."

His words hit her strange. "What do you mean?"

He sighed. "Let's just go the other way."

With little choice, she did as he asked. It took a while, but the man's stench finally drifted under her nose. It was a strange, sour body odor that fucked with her gag reflexes. "Where do you want me to take you?" she asked, growing tired as he placed more and more of his weight on her shoulders.

When the old man didn't answer, she assumed he hadn't heard her. "Where are you trying to go?"

"Well . . . to be honest. Nowhere in particular," he said. "Just somewhere I can rest this old body and stay warm tonight. I read in one of the papers that it's supposed to dip down to nine degrees."

It hit her. "You don't have anywhere to sleep?"

"Well—of course I do. These here streets are my home. I got a big open sky as my roof, some good, hard concrete or soft grass as my floor. The rest usually takes care of itself." He chuckled—a mistake, judging by the way it set off the most godawful cough she'd ever heard.

They stopped when the coughing continued. Abrianna swore something rattled inside of his chest.

"Are you all right?" she asked. "Do you need a doctor?"

More coughing. *Are his lungs trying to come up?*

After what seemed like forever, he stopped, wheezed for air, and then wiped his face. "Sorry about that," he said, sounding embarrassed.

"It's okay," she said, resuming their walk.

"I really appreciate you for helping me out like this. I know I must be keeping you from wherever it is you're trying to get to. It's New Year's Eve and all."

"No. It's all right. I don't mind."

He twisted his head toward her and, despite the growing dark, she could make out his eyes scrutinizing her. "You're awfully *young* to be out here by yourself."

Abrianna ignored the comment and kept walking.

"How old are you?" he asked.

"Why?" she snapped, ready to drop him right there on the sidewalk and take off.

"Because you look like my grandbaby the last time I saw her. 'Bout sixteen, I'd say she was."

Abrianna jutted up her chin.

"She had a beautiful heart, too." He smiled. "Never could see any person or animal hurting."

The unexpected praise made her smile.

"Ah, yeah. A beautiful smile to boot."

They crossed the street to Second Avenue. She'd gotten used to his weight already, appreciated the extra body heat—but the *stench* still made her eyes water. *Did he say that it was going to get down to nine degrees tonight?* Abrianna had stolen cash from her house before she'd left, but hadn't had time to count all of it. Maybe she could get a hotel room—just for the night. After that, she would have to be careful about her finances. Once the money was gone—it was gone. She had no idea on how she and Shawn were going to get more.

Still walking, Abrianna pulled herself out of her troubled thoughts to realize that she and the old man had entered a park—a dark park—away from the streaming holiday crowd.

"Where are we going?" she asked, trying not to sound alarmed.

"Oh, just over there on that bench is fine." The old man pointed a shaky finger to their right. When they reached it, he dropped onto the iron bench like a sack of bricks and panted out more frosted air. "Whew," he exclaimed.

"That walk is getting harder and harder every day."

"You come here often?" Abrianna glanced around, catching a few figures, strolling. "Is it safe?"

"That depends," he said, patting the empty space next to him.

She took the hint and plopped down. "Depends on what?"

"On your definition of safe," he chuckled and set off another series of hard-to-listen-to coughs.

Abrianna wished that he'd stop trying to be a jokester. His lungs couldn't handle it. She watched him go through another painful episode.

At the end, he swore, "Goddamn it." Then he was contrite. "Oh. Sorry about that, sweetheart."

Smiling, she clued him in, "I've heard worse."

He nodded. "I reckon you have. Kids nowadays have heard

and seen it all long *before* puberty hits. That's the problem: The world don't got no innocence anymore."

"Doesn't have any," she corrected him.

He chuckled. "Beauty and brains. You're a hell of a combination, kid."

Abrianna warmed toward the old man.

"Trouble at home?" he asked, his black gaze steady on her.

"No," she lied without really selling it. Why should she care if he believed her? In a few minutes, she'd probably never see him again.

"Nah. I didn't think so," he played along. "You don't look like the type who would needlessly worry her parents."

Abrianna sprung to her feet. "Looks like you're cool here. I gotta get going and find my friend."

"So the parents are off limits, huh?" He nodded. "Got it."

She stared at him, figuring out whether he was working an angle. Probably. Older people always did.

"It's tough out here, kid." His eyes turned sad before he added, "Dangerous too."

"I'm not looking for a speech."

"Fair enough." He pulled in a deep breath. "It's hypothermia season. Do you know what this is?"

"Yeah," Abrianna lied again.

"It means that folks can freeze to death out here—and often do. If you got somewhere safe to go, then I suggest you go there tonight. I'd hate to see someone as pretty as you wind up down at the morgue."

"I can take care of myself."

"Yeah? Have you ever done it before?"

"You sure do ask a lot of questions," she said.

"Believe it or not, you're not the first person to tell me that—bad habit, I suppose. But I've gotten too old to change now."

"What about you?" Abrianna challenged. "Aren't you afraid of freezing to death?"

He laughed, this time managing not to choke over his lungs. "Oh, I *wish*—but the devil don't want nothing to do with me these days. I keep expecting to see him, but he never comes."

"You talk like you want to die."

"It's not about what I want, little girl. It's just time, that's all," he said quietly.

Abrianna didn't know what to say to that—but she did know that she could no longer feel her face. "Well, I gotta go."

He nodded. "I understand. You take care of yourself—and if you decide to stay out here—trust *no one.*"

She nodded and backpedaled away. It still felt wrong to leave the old guy there—especially if that whole freezing-to-death stuff was true. At that moment, it felt true.

The hotels were packed—or wanted nearly three hundred dollars for *one* night. That was more than half of Abrianna's money, she found out. At the last hotel, she agreed to the figure, but then they wanted to see some sort of ID. The front desk woman suggested she try a *motel* in another district—or a shelter.

An hour later, Abrianna was lost. Walking and crying through a row of creepy-looking houses, she had no idea where she was or where she was going.

Suddenly, gunshots were fired.

Abrianna ran and ducked down a dark alley.

Tires squealed.

Seconds later, a car roared past her.

More gunshots fired.

The back window of the fleeing muscle car exploded. The driver swerved and flew up onto a curb, and rammed headlong into a utility pole.

Bam!

The ground shook and the entire row of streetlights went out.

No way the driver survived that shit. Extending her neck

around the corner of a house, Abrianna attempted to get a better look at what was going on, but at the sound of rushing feet pounding the concrete, she ducked back so that she could peep the scene. She counted seven guys running up to the car. When they reached the driver's side, a rumble of angry voices filled the night before they released another round of gunfire.

Holy shit. Abrianna backed away, spun around, and ran smack into a solid body.

The pockmarked Good Samaritan materialized out of the shadow. "Hey there, little girl. Remember me?"

Abrianna screamed. . . .

Excerpt from THE MARRIAGE PASS

CHAPTER 1

Today seemed like the perfect day to go to jail.

It was cold, too damn cold for an April morning in Atlanta. The low temperature, combined with the rain pelting the Jeep Cherokee in sheets so thick it was nearly blinding, seemed to heighten Shantae's anxiety, and thus her urgency to get to the Southside Women's Correctional Facility. If the weather had been anything other than uncooperative, she would have reneged on her promise altogether. The last thing she wanted to do was spend her Saturday going through the routine security checks and sitting in that musty visiting room while the guards showed entirely too much interest in her modest attire. So honestly, the terrible weather had forced her to make the trip, because like her mother had reminded her only a few hours prior, what else did she have planned? Besides, she needed to get a few things off her chest.

Shantae steered her car up the slick roadway, flashing her ID briefly at the entrance before letting the guard direct her to the visitors' parking lot.

By the time she had fumbled with her umbrella and made a

mad dash for the front door, Shantae's sweat suit was completely soaked through and hung on her petite frame. Though she couldn't see herself, she knew she probably looked a mess between her paled mahogany complexion and sloppy ponytail. But that was honestly the least of her concerns. And apparently from the appreciative stare of the guard at the first checkpoint, her hasty appearance didn't even matter.

"How you doing?" The guard's snaggletooth winked at Shantae as he smiled in her direction. She tried not to be disgusted.

"Fine," she murmured, obediently setting her purse on the conveyer belt.

"What's your name?" he pressed.

"Shaunie." It was a nickname she hated, one she never would have answered to, but it was better than divulging her real name to yuck mouth.

"You too pretty to be frowning up like that."

It took everything in her not to roll her eyes. Shantae spared the guard an absent glance, long enough to catch his name and badge number just in case he didn't stay in his place. She almost laughed out loud. *No, his name is not Denzel. His mama must have a sense of humor.*

"You must got a man or something," Denzel went on.

"I do." Shantae stepped through the metal detector and lifted her purse from the bucket.

"The nigga probably in jail, huh? You seem like you used to this."

Shantae didn't bother responding as she headed down the familiar corridor. The idiot had one thing right. She was used to this.

Shantae followed a small group of people into a visiting room with tables, chairs, and cement floors. The air felt like it was on full blast, which chilled her damp clothes and was enough to sting her skin. She had a seat on one of the benches and waited. Pretty soon, the idle chatter ceased, the door swung open, and a line of female inmates in orange jumpsuits with handcuffs binding their wrists trudged into the room. Shantae's eyes swept over the faces before she settled on one in particular.

Not even incarceration could mask the woman's sex appeal. She was short, like Shantae, with the same rich mahogany complexion and slanted eyes. She had put her braids up in a messy bun, and though her jumper was a few sizes too big, her curves were still just as prominent. Plus, Shantae knew her sister because despite the circumstances, only Reagan had a sway like she was strutting on a catwalk, and a slight smirk that was so subtle, Shantae only knew it was there from the little sexy dimple winking at her cheek.

Shantae could only shake her head as Reagan headed toward her. It was clear she wasn't taking this latest arrest any more seriously than the first six. The girl was young, reckless, and in more ways than their five-year age difference could justify.

"I didn't know you were coming," Reagan said, sliding in the chair across the table.

"Of course you did. I told you I would."

Reagan shrugged absently, as if those words meant nothing. "Still," she said. "Figured you would change your mind."

"Well, do you want me to leave?"

Another shrug, this time accompanied with a slight eye roll. Funny how she was the one that got herself in the situation, and yet she had the nerve to be frustrated.

"I don't know why you got an attitude with me," Shantae said, nodding toward the handcuffs binding her sister's wrists. "This is nobody's fault but your own."

"Oh, so now you're trying to lecture somebody? I thought you had my back?"

"I'm here, ain't I?"

Reagan pursed her lips, unable to argue with that comment. She sighed and lowered her eyes. "Yeah," she murmured.

Brief silence stretched between them, and for a moment, all that could be heard were the hushed voices of surrounding inmates and their visitors. Another chill had Shantae shivering in her damp attire.

"So what happened this time?" Shantae asked when her sister made no move to speak.

"Just'... stupid shit."

Shantae could only stare in disbelief. She wondered if it was "stupid shit" when Reagan had written all those bad checks before, or "stupid shit" when she'd been booked on credit card fraud after opening up a ton of them in their mama's name. Or maybe she considered the time she forged their dad's signature to refinance the house "stupid shit." It was all minor to her, and her spending a few weeks or a few months in jail was only a temporary inconvenience.

"So what you been up to, sis?" Reagan's lips lifted into a mischievous smirk.

"Nothing. Just work."

"Oh yeah? What do you do now?"

Shantae lifted a brow, partially because she knew Reagan was really trying to get an idea of how much money she was making. Baby sis couldn't care less if she was selling drugs, hair, or life insurance. As long as the funds were flowing.

"Banking," she answered.

"Ah shit now, I see you." Reagan's eyes lit up like a kid on Christmas. "My sister doing big things now. Y'all hiring?"

"Girl, whatever. I know you're not serious about a job."

"Shit, I might be. I know you probably work with some fine-ass educated brothers." Reagan licked her lips dramatically. "Probably can convince me to get a legit job so I can get my *head* together."

Shantae chuckled at the sexual innuendo. "Please, it's not even like that."

"Oh yeah, I forgot. You still with ol' boy, then, huh?"

"Something like that." Shantae pictured the three carat, princess-cut diamond engagement ring nestled in the side pocket of her purse, right next to her compact and hand sanitizer. Slight embarrassment had forced her to take it off any time she wasn't around her fiancé. As much as she hated not wearing it, it was much easier than facing the inquisition.

"Something like that?" Reagan echoed, narrowing her eyes in a questioning glare. "What the hell does that mean? You still with him or not? Which is it?"

"Yes," Shantae said, simply.

"Oh yeah? I'm surprised you still hanging in there. He must have that good ass comatose sex." Her eyes seemed to glint in obvious delight.

Leave it to Reagan. Sex and money. That was all that mattered.

"We are not even about to go there," Shantae said.

Reagan shrugged. "I'm just saying, it must be a reason he's still around. You and I both know he ain't the loyal type. Shit, he's probably worse than me honestly."

Shantae felt the sting of Reagan's accuracy and had to swallow a swell of annoyance at her sister's candor. A damn shame what love would make someone do.

"We need to change the subject."

"Don't be salty, sis. I'm trying to look out for you."

"Well you need to worry less about me and my man and more about getting your life together."

Reagan rolled her eyes. "Here you go with that shit. My life is together."

Shantae glanced around the jail before throwing her sister a pointed look, proving her point. "When do you get out?"

"Two more weeks."

"And then?"

"I don't know. I'll figure something out." A smirk touched her lips. "Maybe I'll do like you and snag me a doctor to take care of me."

A voice blared through the intercom, carrying an agitating wave of static, signaling visiting hours were almost over. "You'll put something on my books?" Reagan asked. "The food here is trash, so I'm trying to get some stuff out of the commissary."

"Yeah, I got you." The words were simple, but a familiar reminder of their unspoken and often one-sided pact. It never failed, and no matter how she hated herself for it, she always had her sister's back. Maybe one day, Reagan would push her selfish tendencies aside and realize that, as sisters, they needed to look out for each other.